W9-AVF-360

The Dream Bucket

Ten-year-old Trudy loves Papa more than anyone else until she hears him slap Zoe, her mother. Trudy is so angry at him she wishes he'd die. When he accidentally sets fire to the family mansion and dies in the fire, she is not prepared for the shock.

William has cautioned Zoe not to pry into his financial arrangements. She wants to know where he keeps his money in case his life should end. How will she survive as a widow?

The family has nowhere to call home except a sharecropper's shack.

The Covington Chronicles

1907--*Secret Promise* . . . romance threatened in a climate of racial tension and domestic abuse.

1908—*The Courtship of Miss Loretta Larson* . . . a search for happiness and love.

1909—*The Dream Bucket* . . . two families, many dreams.

1910—*Manuela Blayne* . . . haunting outrage over secrets unfolded.

Award

The Dream Bucket received an award from the Texas Writers Conference of International Writers Alive.

Abi of Cyrene

Set in the time of Christ, Mary Lou Cheatham's novel, *Abi of Cyrene,* is a fictional story about the wife of Simon of Cyrene. The Apostle Paul sends her a greeting in the last chapter of Romans. He doesn't call her by name, but he says she was like a mother to him. Who was she?

Audible samples: Amazon.com and Audible.com

The Dream Bucket © 2015, Mary Gregg Cheatham

ISBN-13: 978-1517095369
ISBN-10: 1517095360

Published by Okohay

Cover Design by John Cooke
Cover Photograph ©11-01-07, Desja, I-Stock

Biblical quotations are from the King James Version.
John Prine's 1980 recording of "Paradise" served as an inspiration. "His Eye Is on the Sparrow" is in the public domain.

With the exception of short segments quoted for review purposes, no part of this book may be reproduced, scanned, or distributed in any electronic or printed form without permission.

The Dream Bucket is a work of fiction. Names, characters, businesses, places, events, and incidents are either the product of the author's imagination or used in a fictitious manner. This historical novel is not to be taken as a factual account. Any resemblance to actual persons or actual events is coincidental.

Dedicated to

Ruth Ishee

The Dream Bucket

Mary Lou Cheatham

Part of the Covington Chronicles

~Chapter One~

Spring 1909

Trudy Cameron climbed the stairs behind Papa. "Two more days."

"You excited?" He raised the upstairs windows to let in the fresh air from the piney woods.

"I'll miss school, but we'll have fun."

Trudy's room was in front of her parents' on the west side of the house, and Billy slept across the balcony from Trudy.

Heaped like fresh butter pressed from a mold on a saucer, the moon sat on the muntin bar of Trudy's east window that opened onto the balcony, which was an upstairs porch enclosed on three sides.

The world was sweet, and it would be a good night to sleep. Nestled in her four-poster bed, Trudy closed her eyes and said her prayers. She planned to rest well so she'd enjoy the next-to-the-last day of school.

Deep in the night a word fight awakened her.

"Of all the men in the world, you are the most stubborn." The vinegar in Mama's voice spilled through Trudy's open window. "It's stupid to refuse to tell me this one thing."

"They're at it again," Trudy whispered to Marcie, her stuffed monkey doll.

How could Trudy stand up to Mama on his behalf? Papa deserved better treatment, but she had to honor both of them.

"You don't trust me, William."

"Zoe." Papa's voice had a don't-mess-with-me sound.

Mama said something else Trudy didn't catch.

Whack!

Trudy's hands went to her mouth. What was that? The noise couldn't have been a slap. No, Papa wouldn't hit Mama. Or would he?

Detecting the faint sound of weeping, Trudy strained her ears. With a fight raging between Mama and Papa, she had nobody to hold onto except Marcie. Trudy's stomach hurt.

Mama, why do you have to be so hard to get along with? I need my sleep.

Oh, to have heard Papa's strong snoring and the funny whistling noise Mama made through her nose. Instead, an argument about money assaulted the peace of the night. *Assault*—that was a spelling word. It described what went on in her parents' bedroom when nobody was supposed to hear.

It seemed odd to fight about money when they had plenty. Except for the Benton twins, who lived nearby, none of her other schoolmates at Gravel Hill Elementary owned as many fancy things as the Camerons did.

"Let not the sun go down upon your wrath." In last Sunday's sermon, Reverend Black quoted that Bible verse. The dropping of the sun behind the woodpile was a signal for squabbles to end.

In the midst of harsh words and what sounded like objects hurling through the next room, Trudy took Marcie to the window seat, where the calmness of the night offered slight comfort.

As the hush fell, Trudy lingered by her window. "Marcie, it's late."

In the faint light of the night, the doll's eyes accused her. Somehow the fight was Trudy's fault. Maybe Mama found out Trudy didn't always hang up her dresses. Was she too friendly to Papa and not enough to Mama? What was it?

The moon buried its face behind the roof of the carriage house beside her room.

The grandfather clock bonged three times. She couldn't leave her window seat because they'd hear her.

When the moon sank lower, its golden light shone through the windows of the carriage house to the west of the big house. "It's so late it isn't the wee hours anymore."

She couldn't breathe out loud, they'd think she was listening, but she wasn't snooping—it was impossible to sleep.

She squeezed Marcie. Somewhere an owl whooed not far from her window. Maybe what they fought about was so important they didn't care who heard them. They didn't love her and Brother as much as she thought—or hoped they did.

She needed to do something. It was up to her to make things right, even though she was just a kid. But what could she do? When they started talking again, they spoke in a softer tone.

"You've got all you need. Few women in these parts live in such nice houses," Papa said.

Oh, Marcie. She twisted the doll's eyes until they were loose.

Trudy waited in the silence.

"True." Mama almost whispered.

Maybe she said, "Trudy."

"You want information a wife doesn't need concern herself about. Don't I provide for you?"

Trudy stayed in the window seat. With a few more twists, Marcie's eyes popped off. Smoothing her tea rose gown over her legs, she looked through the window. When she was small, Papa had put bars over her window so she couldn't fall out.

The wind fluttered through the white Priscilla curtains. On the hardwood floor in her room was a big round Oriental rug with an intricate rose design. It had been her grandmother's favorite. On her writing desk sat a pink lamp with crystals hanging from it. Most of her best things Papa had ordered for her from the Spiegel catalog.

"Here's something for my princess," he would say. She'd tear into the box that came in the mail.

"Why do you make me slap you? You have no right to know what I do with my money. I give you and the children everything you need. Nothing ever satisfies you."

A long pause followed. Mama didn't say anything.

"That's it. You want all I've got." When Papa spoke again, he raised his voice.

Marcie, nothing more than a pile of yarn and stuffing, now had no eyes. She lay limp in Trudy's hand, but Trudy wished her monkey doll could say something, anything to help.

"I can't take much more of this," Trudy whispered. "This is a secret. If I didn't have bars on my windows, I'd jump out about now and go be with Jesus."

Would they ever move about again? When the coiled mattress springs squawked in their bedroom, she crept back to her bed. They couldn't hear the floor creak while their bed was noisy.

~

Trudy felt jolted from a dark, peaceful place to the brightness of her bedroom with Papa shaking her shoulder. "Time to get ready for school, Trudy. Wake up, sleepy girl."

As soon as she stood by her bed, he left her room.

She flung the doors of her armoire open. Underwear. Then a dress. She didn't care which. The lavender one hung near the front. Pulling it over her head, she put it on backwards. When she snatched the dress off, she tore it.

The morning after a fight wasn't a good time to tell Mama about the dress. Instead, Trudy rolled it into a ball and tucked it underneath a folded blanket stored below the other dresses. She yanked the next dress from its hanger.

At the breakfast table downstairs, Trudy stared at the flapjacks and sausage Papa put on her plate.

"You getting sick, Trude?" Mama asked.

"No'm, I'm fine."

"Better eat." Papa buttered the cakes, poured thick cane molasses on them, and cut a few pieces. "You seem tired this morning. You need your breakfast."

Trudy forced a few bites.

"Drink your milk." Why was Mama grouchy?

Most days Trudy beat Brother out the door, but today he walked ahead of her. On the way to school, he asked, "What's got your mind wadded up?"

"Oh, nothing." No need to tell Billy. Even though he was her older brother, he didn't understand such things as fights. Besides, he wouldn't believe her. Boys didn't have as much sense as girls about heart matters.

The neighbors, six-year-old Buddy and Bailey Benton, waited for Trudy and Billy at the edge of the Bentons' yard. Mr. Sam said, "Better move along. Y'all are late this morning."

When they reached the schoolhouse, she slammed her lunch tin on the shelf in the cloakroom with a clang that brought Miss Eleanor Anne out of the classroom.

"What is this about, Trudy?"

"Good morning, Ma'am." Trudy pushed her lips into a fake smile. "I just tripped and set my lunch down too hard. Everything's fine."

"It ain't," Billy said. "Sister's in a fume today."

Spelling drill. Math drill. Conjugations. What she'd loved all school year irritated Trudy.

Story period when Teacher read from a book to the pupils was Trudy's favorite time.

"Today I'll read the last **chapter** of *The Little Lame Prince*."

Trudy rested her head on her desk. She didn't know when she fell asleep, but she awakened to hear her schoolmates snicker.

Jeremy Smitherlin, the awful boy behind Trudy, poked her and caused her to jump. "Now, you'll never know what happened at the end. I ain't telling you neither."

Teacher and all the Bentons were coming to her house for supper. Trudy pulled herself together and behaved so Miss Eleanor Anne would feel welcome. The day dragged on until it was time for the last bell. After gathering her lunch tin, books, and the Bailey twins, she walked fast so she could get away from Jeremy. Besides, Mama would need her help at home.

"What you going to wear tonight?" Bailey Benton asked Trudy on the way home.

"My best white blouse with my taffeta skirt."

"And Mary Janes." Bailey had excitement in her voice. "I'll wear my outfit like yours."

The Bentons' house was up and down a steep hill. The four of them pranced along fast. "We'll see you all at supper," Billy told the twins. "We's got to rush on home. Lots to do."

"See you tonight, Mr. Sam." Trudy jogged home behind Billy. They had chores.

In the kitchen Mama, brushing flour off the work table, handed Trudy a soft cloth. "Wipe the silverware."

She didn't ask Mama why her face was bruised. Without a word, Trudy went to work.

Mama arranged wild pink honeysuckles in a rose-colored vase. It was the fancy one with "Nippon" written on the bottom of it. "We'll put them on the sideboard."

The going-away supper for Miss Eleanor Anne was important. Trudy helped Mama make everything pretty. "Go get dressed now."

"How about the milking?"

"Your papa milked early."

Upstairs, Trudy changed clothes. On her wrists she daubed rosewater.

Walking down the curved stairs, she spotted her father in his new white shirt and pinstriped pants. She caught her breath. "Papa."

"Hi, Trudy Beth. Come give your papa a hug."

She stood on the third step from the bottom and put her hand on his neck. On his cheek, she planted a noisy kiss.

He secured his strong but gentle hands around her waist and gave her a whirl.

She held onto him until he stood her on the floor.

"You look good. Mmm. You smell nice."

Mama had dusted on more powder than usual. Her rouge was too bright. In her new white lingerie dress with frothy gathered fabric lavished with lace, Mama floated from one place to another until Papa stopped her and held her in his arms.

Soon Miss Eleanor Anne would arrive for supper. She had moved to Hot Coffee from the Mississippi delta, where people acted sophisticated. Everything had to be perfect.

"Here they are," Billy called from the front window. "Teacher's hat looks stupid." He laughed as he pointed.

"Stop it, Brother."

Papa flung open the door. "Welcome."

"Mr. Sam, did you comb your beard?" Trudy whispered while Miss Eleanor Anne was busy removing her enormous straw hat. On the brim it had pheasant feathers coming from a bird's nest. She left it in the foyer.

"Yes, Trude." Mr. Sam leaned over to speak into Trudy's ear. "The skin underneath my beard is paining me something fierce."

Trudy giggled. "I see you slicked your hair down with pomade."

He patted his shaggy blond mop. "Does my hair look all right?"

"It looks neat." A new barber had opened a shop in Taylorsburg, but reminding Mr. Sam would have been rude.

Without the floppy hat, Teacher didn't look funny as she had when she first walked in holding onto Mr. Sam. Her white blouse with tucks all over it and her big gray trumpet skirt made her seem almost as pretty as Mama.

Trudy made polite conversation. "School has been good all year, Miss Eleanor Anne."

"I believe learning should be fun." Teacher smoothed her skirt.

Mama reached a stiff hand out to the teacher but didn't look at her or say anything.

Teacher smiled into Mama's stern face. "Thank you for having me come to supper."

Trudy pulled Bailey's arm, and the girls went to the kitchen. "My mother doesn't think Miss Eleanor Anne is good enough for Mr. Sam."

"But everybody has them matched up for a couple," Bailey said.

"Come on, girls." Mama sounded grouchy. "Be seated."

Papa sat at the head of the table, and Mama sat at the other end. A whirl of conversation, laughter, and compliments to the cook kept the party moving along. Life was good again until Papa said, "Zoe, why are you wearing a house dress?"

Mama ran from the table.

Miss Eleanor Anne looked at Papa through fluttering eyelids.

The conversation fell into a flat silence. Trudy wanted to tell the folks that it wasn't a house dress. She'd seen pictures of women wearing lingerie dresses in a journal Mama had received in the mail. The article underneath the pictures said these sweet-looking dresses were the latest fashion for parties. She didn't say anything though because Mama forbade her to read grown-up women's journals. Besides, she wanted to play nice in front of Teacher.

The tinkling of crystal goblets, knives laid on the plates, and forks scraping the food were the only sounds. Smoothing a fresh plain blue dress, Mama returned to her chair.

"Mama." Brother started to say something.

Mama cut her eyes at him as if to say, "Don't you dare speak now."

With trembling hands, Trudy reached for her water goblet. It was impossible to avoid spilling it. When tension became the dominant emotion at the table, she always spilled her drink.

"Trudy, pay attention to what you are doing." Mama rushed to dry the water with her napkin. Billy and Trudy contributed their napkins to the effort.

Thirsty, Trudy dared not ask to be excused to go to the kitchen and walk away in her wet clothing. Choking down spit, she felt her throat knock against her neck.

Will everyone please go home?

After the party Trudy told Billy, "No clowning while we wash the dishes."

"I know. You think I ain't got good sense, but I'm a whole lot smarter than you."

Papa returned through the back door from taking out the garbage. "I'll sweep."

Mama scurried around. The fragrance of gardenias and wild honeysuckle blending with the smell of fried chicken lingered throughout the house.

"Son, take these scraps to King." Papa handed Billy a pan of food.

While Billy was outside, Mama hissed at Papa. "Just because she flirted with you, you didn't have to flirt back."

Trudy didn't hear him say anything. Teacher flirting with Papa— when?

Billy came back to help with the dishes.

"By now Mr. Sam and them have delivered Teacher at Widow Morrison's house. Romantic," Trudy told Billy.

"I bet Mr. Sam kissed Miss Eleanor Anne goodnight," Billy said.

"Not in front of the twins, stupid Brother."

Billy smacked his lips. "I think he's sweet on her. She's going away for three months."

"They can kiss when he takes her to the train Saturday. She's trying to shove him into matrimony. Girls know about such things."

"Speaking of kissing, psst." Billy yanked one of Trudy's red braids.

In the dining room, Mama and Papa stood hugging as they shared a prolonged kiss.

"I think Mama and Papa made a baby," Trudy said.

"Kissing don't make babies, stupid girl."

Trudy let it go. "Brother, what's flirting?"

"What you and Jeremy do."

"I hate him."

"No, you're sweet on him," Brother said. "You want him to kiss you."

"Not ever."

Billy might know.

She decided to ask him. "How do grownups flirt?"

"That's a silly question. When we grow up, we'll know. Why do you ask?"

~Chapter Two~

It was the last day of the 1908-09 school year. Billy took a biscuit upstairs, while Trudy sat with Mama and Papa over breakfast.

Papa cleared his throat. "We received a big blessing when Eleanor Anne Broderick came all the way here from Greenville to teach."

Mama rolled her eyes.

"When she was growing up, her parents provided tutors for her and her brothers in Latin, penmanship, and elocution." He buttered a biscuit. "On top of all that she knows French."

Mama lowered her eyes as she blotted her mouth with her napkin.

"She sets a good example to our girls as to what a woman should be," he said.

"And their mothers don't?" Mama used her vinegar voice on Papa.

"She came from old delta money, but she answered the ad in the *Clarion Ledger*."

"Maybe she wanted to see how it felt to live away from home." Mama wasn't in the mood to agree with anything Papa had to say. "I bet she decided she liked it here once she met Samuel. She's thrown herself at him all year."

Papa laughed.

"And any other man who looks her way. She is a brazen—"

"Time to go, Trudy Beth." Papa extended his hand.

Trudy wore her favorite dress—floral print blue and yellow. Her sunbonnet, tied to her neck, dangled on her shoulders. She held her books in a satchel in her right hand. In her left hand was her molasses tin containing a big biscuit stuffed with sausage. "Do I look okay, Papa?"

"You look better than okay. Remember, you are my lovely little princess."

"Bailey's going to wear her dress like mine."

Papa bent down and kissed Trudy's forehead.

He placed his face in front of hers, and she popped a tiny kiss on his cheek.

"You know your mama can sew anything. You should be proud of her."

"I am. Maybe this summer she'll have enough time to teach me more sewing."

"Good idea."

"Come on, Brother. We're going to be late. Bye."

Mama was already cleaning the kitchen.

Trudy and Billy walked the twins to school. The morning flew by faster than a hawk chasing a chicken until Papa called happiness to a halt.

All the pupils were busy writing farewell letters to Miss Eleanor Anne.

"Boys and girls, give me your best effort. I'll read these every day this summer, and I'll show them to my friends back home so they can see what smart students I've taught."

A faint knock sounded.

"Teacher, someone's at the door," Billy said.

"Shh." Teacher pushed away from her desk. Visitors at the schoolhouse were rare. When she opened the door, her face turned bright red.

Everyone strained to see who was there.

Papa stood in the doorway in his new overalls with his hat in his left hand and the teacher's big hat in his right.

Trudy's face felt hot.

"I need to see you a moment, Miss E. Sorry to interrupt."

Miss Eleanor Anne closed the door behind her. No one made a sound, not even so much as an eraser rubbing across a tablet. Trudy heard what could have been a pat on a shoulder. Silence. A smack like lips touching a cheek . . . or a mouth.

It all happened in an instant. Teacher went to the cloakroom to put the ridiculous hat out of sight, snickering broke out, and all the pupils except Billy and Trudy shuffled in their desks.

The Camerons turned to stone.

The afternoon dragged in misery. Trudy didn't let her eyes meet anyone else's. On the way home she pulled the bill of her bonnet forward.

Billy jerked the string under her chin. "You hiding under there?"

"No, I'm protecting my face."

"You have enough freckles for two or three girls."

"Hateful." She needed to slap her brother.

She'd spend some time talking with Papa, just the two of them. He would explain to her about the noises she'd heard. She wouldn't ask him, but he'd tell her. Papa was a good man.

The empty lunch pails clanged against the heavy loads of books and school materials the children lugged. Billy poked the girls to make them chase him.

"Stop, Brother. I don't feel like putting up with any of your foolishness." Trudy's face lit with fresh heat. "I'll tell Papa."

"I'll tell Papa you hit Jeremy and had to stay in during afternoon recess," Billy said.

"Yes, he'll tell." Buddy jumped up and down like a jack-in-the-box.

"That's not fair. Jeremy Smitherlin dipped my pigtails in ink. Teacher wouldn't let me go outside to the pump and wash it off. She said I'd ruin my dress. I'll tell Mama you don't keep your cap on your head when you're out in the sun."

"Jeremy wanted to kiss you behind the schoolhouse."

"He'll never catch me. If his mouth touches mine, slime will come from his lips."

"Huh?" Buddy curled his upper lip.

Trudy pointed her finger at the twins. "Don't forget to give your report cards to Mr. Sam. Teacher always writes on the backs of our cards. She tells if we've been promoted to the next grade. If you want to be in the second grade, you'll need them. Miss Eleanor Anne could forget to leave her grade book with whoever's supposed to keep up with it or that person might lose it. She ain't coming back."

Billy pulled her bonnet off her head. "You don't know what you're talking about."

"Stop it, Brother."

The two pointer bird dogs inside the fence yapped until Buddy opened the gate.

"Get back," Buddy ordered. "That's enough, Zeke. Spot, don't jump."

Trudy tried not to grin when the six-year-old pitched his voice deep and gruff.

Mr. Sam was not standing in the yard or sitting on the porch. The house was too quiet.

"Papa forgot to wait for us today." Disappointment darkened Buddy's voice.

"Come back. Come back. Chi, chi, chi, chi." The guineas inside the fence shrieked. Chickens joined the chorus with cackles.

"Papa," Buddy called.

They listened.

Nothing resulted. Whatever took Mr. Sam away from home when the twins were supposed to return from school must have been terrible.

The twins didn't need to know she was afraid.

"Where are you, Papa?" Buddy called.

"He's not in the garage, but the Model T's parked in it," Bailey said. "He may be out somewhere on the place, dead."

Billy walked over to the automobile and touched it. "Engine's cold."

Trudy and the twins went inside. Buddy said, "The house feels too still."

Buddy and Bailey laid their school supplies and report cards on the big table in the dining room. As Buddy paced back and forth, he clenched his fists, released them, and flailed his arms.

Billy walked inside from the back porch. "Mr. Sam ain't here."

"If you don't stop saying 'ain't' Miss Eleanor Anne's going to retain you. I'll tell our papa. She can change your report card and her grade book tonight."

"'Tell Papa.' I'm sick of hearing it. Go ahead and tell him," Billy said.

As they waited, they listened. They walked through the barn. "Papa," the twins called. Nothing but the wind blowing through the sycamore tree answered them. He was nowhere.

"We can't leave you here." Trudy gave Bailey a light hug. "Come on home with us."

"Something's wrong. He's always here when we come home from school." On his tiptoes, Buddy moaned as he resumed pacing and slinging his arms.

Trudy caught up with Buddy and placed her hand on his shoulder. "Maybe he had to leave a minute. He knows I'll take care of you. Walk flatfooted so you won't trip."

"It's bad, awfully bad," Buddy said.

Trudy wrapped her arms around him. "Slow down, Buddy."

"Oh, no. He must be dead like Mama." Bailey flailed her hands.

"I hope he didn't forget about us." Pulling away from Trudy, Buddy started to cry.

"He's just had to do something else," Trudy said as they returned to the road.

"You think you are some kind of grown up. No wonder our papa calls you the little boss." Billy sneered at Trudy while he latched the back gate.

So Papa made fun of her to Billy. He'd never called her a sarcastic name to her face. She needed to talk to him about too many issues. Within a short time, Papa was slipping away. She'd always loved him more than anybody else, but now she hated him. How could he be two-faced?

The dogs slinked along a few feet behind them. "Oops, we forgot to close the front gate. Go home," Buddy ordered.

The dogs turned around, tucked their tails, and sulked back home.

"Maybe our papa is showing your papa the corn crop," Billy said. "Let's go down the field trail and look for him." They walked along the dirt road east of the house.

Instead of walking through the barnyard as they did most days, they ended up near the front side of the Camerons' house, where a thicket of tall cedar trees blocked the view.

"What's that smell?" Raising her hand, Bailey halted them and sniffed. "Smells like bacon. You must be having breakfast for supper."

"Pine tar smoke," Billy shouted as they all sped up.

"Papa must be burning trash. Look at all the smoke," Trudy said.

"The woods is on fire," Buddy yelled.

King, limping and whimpering, approached them as they closed the gap. "Come here, King." Billy reached down to pet him. "What's wrong, boy? What happened to your feet?"

Trudy fell to the ground and dissolved into a screaming heap. Collapsed beside her, Bailey and Buddy helped her wail. King licked their faces, but Billy ran ahead.

"What happened, Papa?" Smoke drifted up from the glowing embers. The night before when they had stood in the kitchen to wash and dry the best china, what was a dream? Then or now? Trudy's brain spun until she was going to be sick. Hugging Bailey on her left and Buddy on her right, she took deliberate steps toward the place where her house was supposed to be. The three of them locked steps.

She detested the smell of the layer of ashes behind the four massive stone columns and the metal steps. Dancing wind stirred the gray piles. Her eyes tried to fill in the details of the imposing two-story structure to make it what it was that morning. With all her power, she willed it not to happen, but she had no control over the situation. Her house had disappeared in smoke.

"Your great grandfather built the Cameron home in 1856." Papa had recited over dinner many nights.

"Where are you?" She asked the question to the house. It was her safe place, her castle, her mansion. The majestic old home defined her. Disconnected chimneys on three sides, the coils of beds and couches, the stove knocked down by heavy beams falling from the second story, the shattered sinks, wagon parts in the carriage house—pieces that wouldn't burn— remained in defiance. Maybe Papa could save a few parts of what used to be. The strings of her piano would never resonate with the minuets she'd practiced with perfect light rhythm. It was a silly thought: perhaps Papa could take them and build her a new piano.

The iron cookware lay unbroken and scattered about the place where the kitchen was when she left for school. Impersonal twirls lingered here and there refusing to die. The few remaining chunks of red pulsating boards fell into the mass of the dead house. She gazed into the ruins without knowing what to do about the way the things that mattered to her vanished.

"Papa." The word came out of her mouth with soft expectation. The sand dirt trail along the west side of the house was the road to the barnyard. The barn, unlike the ones in picture books, consisted of several storage cribs and small structures linked together in a courtyard arrangement.

Papa must have gone down there to do some chore he couldn't postpone. He'd pop into view in a moment. She kept an eye aimed toward the little road.

Or since they almost always took the path through the barnyard to walk home from school, he went there to wait so he could prepare her and Brother for the shock. No doubt, he stood at the bottom of the hill below the barnyard looking for both of them. Brother shouldn't have suggested they walk home a different way that day.

"Mama." Trudy found Mama sitting dazed on the ground. Soot streaked her little mother's face and long curly auburn hair. Zoe's deeply set dark blue eyes looked vacant.

"Do I know you?" Mama asked.

Horror overcame Trudy. For a moment, her thirty-one-year-old mother was Zoe Whitten, a child. Trudy would never have her house again and wouldn't have her mother.

"Up by the chimney next to the living room there's a wasp nest as big as a dinner plate. Trudy's room is nearby. Her window is above the wasp nest. William didn't want no wasps.

Zoe Whitten Cameron sat swaying on the ground with her glazed eyes looking into the air as she recited an explanation.

No one but Trudy listened. Why wouldn't the people listen to her mother?

"William tried to swinge the wasp nest. He's done it many a time. He wanted to take off the top of the nest so the new wasps and grubs." Mama heaved. "The sumac pole was floppy. Just as he got the fire up there, a big wind come in from the west and slapped the flames into Trudy's curtains. The house caught on fire like lightard kindling. "

As soon as Mama completed the story, she started it again in the dialect she had learned as a little girl. Mama never talked that way except to play. No one, not even Trudy, listened, but friends wrapped their arms around Trudy's mixed-up mother.

"Papa," Trudy called while she looked for him. She was his girl. When she could find him, she'd lean on him and cry. Until then she had to hold back around the grown-ups. He should have stayed with her mother. In just a few days, he had fouled up in unbelievable ways. Leaving Mama upset the way she was, he'd done something else Trudy would need to talk to him about.

~Chapter Three~

Samuel Benton stood a few feet behind Mama. Bailey and Buddy jumped into his outstretched arms. His clothes were black with smut, his shirttail torn, and he had smudges of soot and ashes in his shaggy blond hair and beard.

"Oh, Papa." The twins hugged him.

"Where's our papa?" Trudy asked.

Folks milled over the yard. Kind hands enveloped her and Brother. She was too dazed to know who held them.

They broke loose and ran toward a long narrow wagon on the side of the yard. Two strangers secured a black blanket over a row of lumps.

"Sir, is that William Cameron?" Trudy asked.

The gentlemen turned and bent down. Mama, jerking back into the present world, jumped up from the ground. Tripping on her torn dress and apron, she stumbled barefoot toward them.

"Stop. No, Billy and Trudy. Stay away from that wagon."

As Mama fell to the ground, women rushed toward her.

"Don't go over there." Mama managed to stand so she could stagger toward them.

Mr. Sam gathered the Camerons into his arms along with his children, but Billy and Trudy pulled away.

"Papa, Papa, Papa."

"Yes, it's him," some man said as he held her and her brother with a firm but kind grip.

The driver of the wagon untied the horses.

25

Another man climbed onto the seat. They tipped their hats to Mama. "Mrs. Cameron," one of them said in departure.

Mama spoke in a scratchy voice. "William ran into the fire to get the pictures and the family Bible." On the front pages of the Bible, the names of four generations of Camerons provided a record of the family tree. Papa had left blank lines to list the husband Trudy would marry in the distant future and her children she'd have, also Billy's future wife and children. Mama trembled. "He—he."

"Go on." Billy crowded Mama.

"He didn't survive."

Billy stood over his mother. Grabbing her shoulder, he dug his fingers deep enough to leave bruises.

"You're hurting Mama." Trudy wedged between them.

"You should have stopped him." Tears were popping out of Billy's eyes.

"I tried." Mama spoke in a soft monotone. "King tried to save him too." The dog approached her upon hearing his name, and she stroked his fur. Water streamed down her dirty face.

As the driver clucked to the horses, a man holding the team released his grip and stepped aside. Trudy ran behind the men taking away Papa's body. Brother came along beside her. At the end of the cedar-lined lane, they stopped.

Neighbors walked away in family clumps.

"We need to stay here and make sure the fire dies down," Billy said.

"Yes, we do." Trudy wasn't human. She was a wooden girl puppet like Pinocchio, but she and Billy would have to take charge.

"I showed him the wasp nest," Mama said. "It was on the northwest side of the chimney in the corner. It was all my fault. He didn't want . . ."

Trudy didn't listen.

Four men with shovels turned up dirt along the edges of the house to keep the fire from spreading. Leaning over like an elderly man, Billy spoke in a deep tone meant for only Trudy's ears.

"Them digging reminds me of something me and you need to talk about."

With Trudy following him, he walked away from the scattered onlookers. "Come over here, Sister. I heard them men say they'd go ahead and dig Papa's grave under the live oak tree." He shook his head with emphasis. "I'm not sure that's a good idea. What do you think?"

"I think I agree with you," Trudy said. "Can't think why they'd do that."

"Me neither. Mama's pretty. Some man'll marry her."

"I can't believe you can even think, much less say, such a thing right now. Papa died today."

He kept on. "Or the new man will build a new house in this same spot behind them columns, and it won't seem right to have Papa's grave so close by."

"You're sick in the head, Billy, but I can see what you're saying. You're loony, but you're still my brother. Smart, I'll give you credit for that." She grabbed him around his waist.

"She might sell the place and move off."

"Nope." Trudy held onto Billy's arm as she fluttered her eyelids and shook her head with deliberation. "Papa taught us to hold onto the land."

He hugged her before letting her go. "I intend to farm and keep this hilltop as long as I can."

"Me too." She nodded.

"Sister, I want you to help me. Promise me you will."

"We'll help take care of the crops. I'll pick corn. We'll milk and feed and help Mama keep up this land. You've got my word." She wondered if they would get a chance to be children again.

Billy placed his hand on his cheek with his pointer finger in front of his ear and thumb on his chin. "But still some man may come along and try to sweet talk her into selling it."

"You're thinking right, Billy, as bad as I hate to imagine it happening."

"I tell you what. Let's hold out for burying Papa in Friendship Cemetery."

"Of course. With Grandma and Grandpa," she said, "and by our baby brother."

"That's the only thing to do."

"I don't know if Mama is all there right now," Trudy said.

"Been talking out of her head."

While Trudy and Billy stood talking, Mr. Sam and the twins held all of the Camerons close, then started to walk away.

"Wait, Mr. Sam," Billy said. "I want you to hear what I got to say to Mama."

"Yes, Son."

Walking back toward Mama, Billy pitched his voice in the direction of the diggers. He tried to talk in grown-man tones like bass notes. "Me and Trudy don't want them neighbors to dig Papa's grave here. We want him buried in Friendship Cemetery with Grandma and Grandpa."

"Bury William?" Zoe's puzzled voice sounded flat.

"He passed away," Mr. Sam reminded her, and then he left with the twins.

Papa, the most important person in Trudy's life, would never come back. The house, where would they live? How could two kids do all the chores and take care of Mama too? Would Mama get her mind back? Billy could be smart for twelve years old when he tried, but still.

"We got to go." Billy walked toward the barnyard.

Looking over her shoulder, Trudy saw Mama approach the fellows who were digging. A few neighbors remained in the yard. They wouldn't get to see how she felt inside, no matter how much they gawked. Even though she was still nine, she'd be tough.

"What about Mama?" She caught up with Billy.

"Them diggers will be here a while. We'll come back and check on her. Me and you have got work to do."

The cows stood lowing, ready to go to their places in the barn. The herd was late most afternoons now that it was spring. The grass must taste delicious. Trudy usually brought them in from the north pasture, but today the cows found their own way home. It was a good thing because she didn't feel like going off and getting them. The skin around her head pulled tight against her with the sorrow of losing Papa.

When Billy opened the cattle gap, each cow bolted to her own stall to wait and give milk in exchange for nubbins of corn. Unaware of the routine she'd followed every evening, Trudy latched the stable doors.

Did it really happened or did she make it up? Maybe a daydream. She'd been upset with Papa. When he hit Mama, when he stood outside the classroom kissing the teacher, when she found out he made fun of her to Billy, she wanted to die. No, she wanted *him* to die. She caused his death.

Billy wasn't close by. It was safe for her to sniffle. Air stuck inside her chest when she tried to blow it out of herself.

Then she saw him. Along with a bucket and a stool, he took a wet rag to wipe udders. They had plenty of corn to feed each cow. Trudy liked to milk, but Billy hated it. For the moment though, he seemed glad to do the chore.

Papa was a good man, and she was his favorite person. Would she ever be able to think about anyone else again but Papa? He always let her choose the cows she milked.

"You can milk One Horn." Billy allowed her to start with her favorite cow.

She pulled the oversized bucket from its hanger. One Horn was the only cow that required the large bucket. She placed a peck bucket of corn in the tray and walked to the side of the cow. "Back, One Horn."

When she touched the cow's hip, the animal pushed its right leg back.

The sound of the milk on the bottom of the bucket was good, something real she could depend on. She played a little game of covering the bottom of the bucket. The cow let down her milk fast. One Horn was smarter than the rest of the herd.

When Trudy finished, the bucket was full. She eased out of the stall so the milk wouldn't slosh. With deliberate steps, she walked across the sand road towards the milk storeroom.

The cats waited in a row along the outside of the building. Blue Cat, the pushiest one of them, came meowing loud. If he got too close, he'd make her spill the milk.

"Scat. I ain't in no mood for cats." She and Papa had always poured milk for them in little bowls, but tonight they would have to wait until she finished with a cow that didn't give so much. It was too hard to manage pouring from a full bucket. Besides, it was dreadful doing something alone she'd enjoyed doing with Papa.

Trudy was a dazed mess. Despite her best efforts she spilled milk on herself. Stripes of salt stung her cheeks. When she stepped into fresh manure, she didn't bother to scrape it off her good shoes. In addition to everything else wrong, the ink made her hair feel hard.

In the adjoining stall, Billy finished milking another cow just as she finished her second one. On the way to pour up the milk, they saw Mama.

"You don't have to help. Me and Trudy have got this job almost done."

Mama didn't answer. Instead, she gathered milking supplies.

About that time, Mr. Sam and the twins walked into the barnyard from the opposite direction. Bailey and Buddy had changed from their school clothes, and Mr. Sam had put on clean overalls. It looked like he had tried to wash some of the soot from his face, but he'd smeared it. His beard had black streaks.

"We want to help," he said. "B. J., show me where to start. Buddy and Bailey, come stand outside the stall and watch for snakes."

As soon as Trudy milked another cow, she called to the twins. "Come on. Let's feed the cats." They poured Jersey-rich milk into the bowls.

"Mr. Sam, we're going to feed the pigs," Trudy said. It was too late to gather eggs because the hens had gone to roost. King lay sprawled in a sandy spot in the barnyard. He didn't seem to be in pain just then. She checked the horses. That night she didn't give them any hay, because they had plenty of fresh grass every day

"Stand outside while I milk another cow." Trudy pointed to a spot where no fresh manure covered the ground.

"Yeah, we'll watch the bats," Buddy said. "I bet there's a hundred of them."

After milking two more cows, she took them to see the one-month-old calves.

"I'm trying to count them, but they keep moving," Buddy said.

"Five," Bailey told him.

They finished the chores in the gray light. Mama stood in the barnyard and blew on her arm. A red spot about four inches long and two inches wide glowed in the dimness. Mama used cooling breaths. The cooked flesh must have stung her.

"It doesn't look like a very deep burn. For now, we'll leave it open to the air." Mr. Sam, inspecting the burn, poured water from the rain barrel over it.

"Thank you, Samuel," She winced as she continued to swing her arm and blow on it.

The chores finished, the three Camerons stood and watched the Bentons walk away.

~Chapter Four~

"Mama, where're we going to sleep tonight?" Trudy asked.

"Stuart and Melva." Mama's eyes lost their blurred look.

"We can camp out," Billy said.

"We don't got no blankets to sleep on. Nothing to eat." Trudy said. Billy could be so smart sometimes and so dumb other times.

"We can get something out of the garden," Billy said. "The sun ain't down yet. Besides we know where stuff is."

"That'll take all night. I'm hungry." Why couldn't her brother hush? "We need some place to sleep."

"Uncle Stuart and Aunt Melva said we could spend the night with them." Mama seemed to have her mind back.

"Yes, Ma'am," Mama might have another confused spell any minute. They drove the cows to the night paddock next to the mules and horses.

Dear God, please send an angel to watch over the animals and the barn. If thieves come near here, Lord, strike them dead, and don't let anybody steal Mama's cooking pots. They're all she's got left.

Climbing Cameron hill, they walked by the house site one more time to inspect it in the twilight. Their home was nothing more than ashes, metal, columns, and chimneys. No coals glowed. It was finished. Trudy's chest squeezed her heart to pieces.

They resumed their brief journey. Billy leaned toward the dog. "Let's go, King. You can sleep in Uncle Stuart's hay crib."

Bobcats meowed, something hissed, whip-poor-wills repeated their bizarre four-syllable phrase, owls swooped past with their slow heavy wings, somewhere in the distance unidentified creatures howled, in front of them a brown animal twice the size of Blue Cat darted from a clump of trees on the right into the garden on their left.

King poked along, acting like he noticed nothing but Billy.

Katydids made shrill strident noises, and crickets joined the chorus.

Trudy walked close to Mama, who repeated what she'd drilled into Trudy's head. "Don't be afraid of the friendly dark."

"Okay, Mama." Trudy's voice was small as she pretended it was real and new.

The whimpering dog fell behind. Billy hovered over King. "Slow down. Just stop."

Trudy walked back and pulled his arm. "Come on. The bobcats are going to get us."

"Can't you see King's a hurting?" He stood up and jerked her shoulder. "The poor dog burned his feet, all right? Or did you forget? Think about somebody besides your spoiled self."

"Mama, make Brother stop."

"All you ever think about is Trudy. Little boss thinks she's a princess. The bobcats are scareder of you than you are of them. You're meaner."

Mama stopped to pet the dog. "Good doggie." Her voice wavered. "Come on. We'll wait for you."

As she stood up, she spoke in a harsh tone. "Both of you, that's enough."

Trudy didn't speak another word. She could have spent the night with Bailey, but she needed to help with the milking and make sure Mama was all right. Plus that ink was in her hair. She had to get it out before the funeral. She had a right to be mad.

They walked along under the indigo sky until they reached her aunt and uncles' house.

What right did the moon have to glow like that?

They went around to the back of the house and walked up the porch steps. Having removed their shoes and washed their hands and faces, Mama, Billy, and Trudy sat on a bench at Uncle Stuart and Aunt Melva's kitchen table. Mama sat between the children.

The smell of scorched turnip greens violated the air.

Ink, what a scary thought. She swallowed a hard lump about the danger. What if she left stains on Aunt Melva's pillowcases? If Billy tattled, Trudy would get even.

Uncle Stuart's blessing insulted the family. He prayed in general terms about the day's events without mentioning the fire or the death of his brother. Scream at him—she chewed her fingers instead.

"Hand me your plate, please." Mama passed Trudy a bossy look.

"Don't give me much. I'm not hungry. No need to waste food."

With the full plate sitting in front of her, Trudy picked at the stuff. Packy fried cornpone, cold peas, and lukewarm turnip greens. Aunt Melva couldn't season greens right. A tiny piece of fried ham. Cool sweet tea. Trudy mouthed, "I don't like leftover turnip greens. I don't like Aunt Melva's tea."

As Trudy curled her lip underneath her scrunched nose, Mama pinched the soft young flesh of her leg so hard she jumped.

"Aunt Melva, this food looks delicious." Trudy flashed a fake smile. "You were so kind to have us come to supper with you."

Mama moved her focus away from Trudy's plate. "Billy, hold your fork correctly."

Trudy drizzled a spoonful of tea over her piece of cornpone and then choked down a chunk of it while the adults discussed the pine box the men of the neighborhood would build. Their talk was a verbal haze.

After supper, Trudy helped Mama scrape the plates.

"Junior, come with me. We'll feed King the scraps and put him up in the hay crib," Uncle Stuart said.

"Please check his feet first," Billy said. "They're burnt."

Trudy giggled because Uncle Stuart called Billy "Junior."

"Sure. When we finish seeing about King, I'll find you some of my underwear to sleep in. You can wash up in the shed behind the house."

Both Billy and Trudy laughed until Mama contributed her sternest look.

Uncle Stuart walked into the night with a lantern. Billy followed.

Trudy and her mother helped with the dishes. "Melva, I burned my arm. Do you have some old white rags I could dress it with for the night? And do you have any salve?"

Melva sorted through the shelves of her chifforobe. Finally, she found something clean and soft. "I don't have any salve," Melva said through pursed lips.

"Could you spare a little butter?" Mama asked.

"I'm almost out, but take what I have." Melva's voice quavered.

Afterwards they bathed with face towels rinsed in a basin in the guest room. Aunt Melva had laid some old shirts on the bed for them to sleep in.

In bed Mama whispered, "Papa used to laugh and say, 'Stuart Cameron still has the first dollar he ever made.'"

"We can't stay here many nights. They don't love us enough." Trudy placed her hand on Mama's shoulder.

~Chapter Five~

In Muhlenberg County, Kentucky, Elvin Trutledge pulled his suspendered gabardine brown pants over his dingy long johns. The temperature inside the cabin was so cold the water in the drinking bucket had a thick layer of ice on top. The cold snap timed itself just right to add to his wife Betty Jean's misery. She breathed hard enough to keep him from sleeping. This baby was coming fast. Elvin pulled a second pair of wool socks on and stuck his feet into his high tops.

"Arnelle, Arnelle," Elvin called. "Wake up, little woman."

"Okay." Arnelle, Betty Jean and Elvin's oldest daughter, dressed without making any noise.

"Go get Mother Magee. This baby ain't wasting no time."

The three Trutledge brothers shared the sleeping loft. Elvin climbed two rungs up the ladder to call his eldest son. "John Bob, get your lazy self out of bed. Saddle up Clover. Make haste."

"Where do you want me to go?" John Bob scrambled to put on his clothes.

"Nowhere, fool. Just saddle up the mule for Arnelle. She's going to fetch the midwife. Put a move on or I'll beat your hide as soon as the sun comes up."

"Micah, you'll have to go help your mother. Do what she says."

"What's happening, Pa?" A wee sleepy voice inquired.

"Did I call your name, Raven? Listen here, all the rest of you. Stay in bed and keep your mouths shut until somebody tells you to do otherwise."

He stuck his head into the girls' sleeping room. Reckoned he'd reconsider his former order. "Mary Margaret, go help Micah."

He took time to trail his fingers over Betty Jean's forehead. Soaking wet. Elvin started a fire in the fireplace. In the kitchen stove, he discovered the coals from the night before had not died. It was easy to build a new fire on the embers. On top of the stove, he placed a big pot of water to heat, and started another one, which he filled with some rags he tore. Twelve times before, he had followed the same procedure. It seemed like all the babies came in cold weather.

In the firelight, he groped for his best shirt, the red and yellow one. When he put it on, he left the tail hanging out. He laid his jacket by the front door.

"Pa, where are you going?" Mary Margaret asked.

"Help your ma."

Betty Jean didn't say anything. He knew she was pushing even though she didn't make loud noises. Her labored breathing and muffled grunts came out fast. Having done his part, he had nothing more to do than to stand around.

Micah caught the baby in her hands the moment Mother Magee walked into the room. Bustling around, the midwife gave orders.

"Micah caught her first baby at twelve," Elvin said. "It ain't no big deal. Mountain women grow up fast. Betty Jean had her first baby at thirteen."

"Come over here and take a look," Mother Magee said.

"Coming to see my new baby boy." He swaggered toward his wife.

"Another beautiful little girl."

"Call her 'Florida.' That's where I'll take off to. I'll make some money picking fruit and come back for y'all."

"What on earth?" Mother Magee grabbed his arm. "You're walking off from your responsibility."

If Elvin had looked back at his wife and thirteen children, he would've never left. Scarcely glancing at the new baby girl named Florida, he jerked away and turned toward the door as he fastened his worn-out coat. When he opened the door, a gust snatched it hard enough to loosen the hinges. Outside he managed to push it closed.

"Why did some idiot call this dead forsaken coal hole Paradise?" Shoulders hunched forward in the biting wind, Elvin trudged along the trail covered with crunchy ice and coals. Around the side of the mountain on the down-winding road, he approached the black dirt around Rogue's Harbor.

"It ain't so hard on Betty Jean. When you've got thirteen children, they take care of one another. Her papa ain't going to let them starve. All I'm good for is number fourteen. I'd best be on my way."

The four layers in the hutch averaged no more than an egg apiece every other day. Too bad the old ribby cow didn't give enough milk to help feed the Trutledge brood. They barely got a sip of milk apiece every day. Dishwater and table scraps were not enough to fatten up the pig. He was sick of looking at starving livestock and listening to pitiful children.

"Pa-in-law, you're going to have your hands full." Elvin muttered what he would have said to Betty Jean's papa if the old geezer had been there. "Yippee, I'm out of here."

Instead of hopping onto one of the few boxcars in a coal train as he'd planned, Elvin walked down to Green River so he could catch a boat out of Paradise. He'd go as a legitimate traveler doing honest work.

He sidled up to a riverboat captain, who looked him over.

"You don't look like no escaped prisoner. Y'ain't wearing black and white stripes. You look like a man who's used to pulling his share of a load." The captain walked around him. "One of them coal miners, huh?'

"You're right. I ain't no prisoner. I just want to get out of town. I've got folks in Florida. I'd be glad to hire on to help with the barges on the way to New Orleans."

"Consider yourself hired." The captain inserted a crusty pipe into his mouth. "Blye's my name."

Captain Blye and his crew followed the Green River until it flowed into the Ohio. The little tugboat, connected to two coal barges, headed toward the Mississippi.

What a relief to float farther and farther from thirteen snotty-nosed children and a weary wife. The openness of the Mississippi invited him. His escape from the mines felt like being turned out of prison. Never again would Elvin Trutledge go back down into the earth.

Night covered the cracked white cakes of snow on the banks. "Icy rain, go ahead and drop from overhead onto my nose. See if I complain."

With the coming of the morning, the sun in a shade of light butter with a hint of a rainbow around it shone from the sky and the water beneath. Light fog rose from the azure waters. All was well except for one problem: the second guy in charge gave him an uneasy feeling.

~Chapter Six~

Trudy awakened to the sound of sniffles, but when she stirred, Mama's crying stopped. While her mother pretended to sleep, Trudy turned to the window to stare into the black of the night where the moon had set but the sun had not risen. Despair loomed over her. Papa wasn't coming back, they had no place to live, the odor and lumpiness of the worn-out cotton mattress annoyed her, and the coarse sheets scratched her face. Trudy's tears lulled her back to dreams of sun-kissed days when her family and her home were whole.

How much time had passed? The window was still a square of blackness when her mother tugged on her shoulder. Mama stood in the same filthy, ripped dress beside the flickering lamp.

"What is it?" Trudy asked.

"Don't make any noise. Get dressed, and we'll spread the bed. I'm go--ing to wake up Brother."

While Mama was out of the room, Trudy had an opportunity to ex-amine the pillowcase. It was as white as it was the night before, and the dried ink remained stiff in her hair.

Whew, Mama didn't know.

She changed from the borrowed shirt to yesterday's school dress, stiff with milk spilled during the last milking. The smell made her stomach sick.

"Don't forget to wash your face and smooth your hair. I'll braid it later." Mama held a glass of water. "Wipe your teeth with your face cloth. Then rinse your mouth."

Trudy hurried.

"Your dress is on wrong-side out," Mama said. "Quick. Fix it."

Trudy changed it while her mother made the bed and turned down the wick to extinguish the coal oil lamp. Something sharp stabbed inside Trudy's chest—she had never gone through an entire day without Papa.

The three of them tiptoed out of the house, left almost as neat as they had found it. Never had the morning smelled sweeter. Except for the bobcats and rattlesnakes, they could have slept on the ground and been happier than in Uncle Stuart and Aunt Melva's house.

Billy unlatched the crib door. Turning his head sideways with a smile on his mouth, King wagged all over but whined when his feet hit the ground.

"We'll come back later to pick the garden and collect the eggs. Right now, we've got other work to do." Mama was keeping her mind. They grabbed tomatoes and ate them for breakfast without slowing their pace.

The columns stood like phantoms in the gray morning as they left the garden and walked past the pile of ashes. Fog loomed over the ruins. *Eerie* was a school word. Now Trudy experienced eerie.

The giant basins in the paddocks contained plenty of water for the livestock. Papa took care of everything the animals needed

"Watch for snakes and pitchforks up there." Mama stood by Papa's hay crib door. Billy climbed into the crib so he could throw down some loose hay for the horses and mules.

"Come on, King. Let's go feed." Trudy rubbed the dog's head. First, she carried hay to the horses and mules. Billy jumped down from the crib and helped her feed. The familiar sound of the animals' crunching comforted her.

"I'm learning the routine." Mama followed Billy J. and Trudy.

Trudy took Mama's hand. "You're doing good. Just tag along and copy us."

"What's the matter with you?" The pigs' accusing eyes staring at Trudy, made her feel guilty. "Don't look at me like that. I'm feeding you as fast as I can."

After they finished the milking chore, fed the cats, and turned the cows into the pasture, Billy poured frothy milk into a Mason jar. He drank the warm liquid with cream clumps so fast he spilled it on his shirt. As he wiped his mouth with his shirtsleeve, he hummed with pleasure.

"You're making me ill." Trudy curled her lips. Disgusting.

On the southern corner of the barn complex, the wagon shed was attached to Papa's locked crib. They backed the big wagon out. Mama's hair fell over her eyes, the blood vessels popped out on her face, and she broke into a sweat. Seeing Mama straining was scary.

"Watch this." Trudy held a nubbin of corn in front of Molasses. "He can't keep away from this bribe." Billy and Trudy caught Bob and Molasses.

"The mules respect me because I lead them to the pond for a cool drink on hot days." She led Molasses with an air of authority. "He don't pull back or jump up when I'm leading him."

"He don't jump up for nobody." Billy laughed. "That's because he's too lazy."

"You're just sassing at me because I know how to help hook up the hames, traces, and doubletree. Lots of girls don't."

"Stop your bickering." Mama's eyes cut into Trudy.

"Billy started it. He always does."

"Enough." Mama started hitching the mules up.

"Mama, you've never done mule work. Billy and I will do this."

"They can tell we don't know how to do this like William." With her hands on her hips, Mama stood watching. Bob Mule frisked his tail and set his ears back. While Bob refused to move, Molasses backed so far he bumped into the wagon.

"I can do it Papa's way." Billy gave Bob a whack on the neck with his fist. "Straighten up."

Both mules adjusted their behavior, but why did Billy take charge—why did he have to hit Bob mule? Mama didn't need to give orders about farm stuff without having an inkling of which jobs they should do first. They needed a leader—Papa.

"It feels like he'll come back any time." Trudy stared down the road. "This all seems like a nightmare."

"Idiot," Billy said.

"Stop it." Mama shook her finger at Billy.

"Can we take some eggs to town?" Trudy asked. They'd need money.

"Not this time. We're in a hurry. We will soon. Also fruit and vegetables." They piled into the wagon, and Mama drove the team down the back trail. It was a surprise that Mama knew how to drive the mules once they were hitched up.

"Can King go with us?" Billy asked.

"I don't see why not."

Trudy tucked her braids under her bonnet. "Where are we going to live, Mama?"

"Here on the place." The wagon wheels groaned along crunching into the sandy roadbed.

"Where can we sleep?"

They passed the falling-in, unpainted cabin. "Here."

"We can't stay in the shack." Trudy sank into the wagon seat. "It's so rotten sharecroppers won't live in it."

"We'll fix it up." Mama's face was stern. Blood dripped from one of her soft white hands.

"What's the matter with your hand, Mama?" Trudy asked.

"Oh, nothing. I cut myself on a nail in the shed."

Trudy, having helped her father with the milking and having practiced her five-finger exercises on the piano, had strong hands, but all the hard chores made new blisters pop up. What did it matter? No time to practice, no piano, no Charles-Louis Hannon book. She'd been, Papa always said, on her way to becoming a virtuoso. No money to pay for lessons with her teacher, Mrs. Bromwell.

King sat in the back of the wagon while Mama, Billy, and Trudy sat on the bench. They rode past the well behind the shack and on down the sandy road on the way to Taylorsburg.

"Model T's gone," Billy said. As they passed the Bentons' house, the bird dogs bawled, and the guineas chattered.

King, sitting up proud, remained silent.

The empty garage sat toward the back of the south side near the road. The Bentons could sleep in the garage if their house ever burned. It was bigger than the log cabin where Trudy's grandparents lived when they first moved to Mississippi. That old cabin, nestled on the southwest side of the Cameron farm, was in worse shape, however, than the sharecroppers' house where Mama wanted to move. "If our carriage house hadn't burned, we could sleep in the surrey."

"Dummy," Brother poked her. "If the carriage house hadn't burned, we'd ride to town in the surrey."

"You were stupid to push me. I'll bump you out of this wagon." Trudy made her strong little hands into fists. She was smaller but she could knock him to the other side of a cornfield.

"Silly girl." He gave Trudy a fake smile.

"Enough," Mama said. "Lord, guard what we have remaining, help me to guide these children, and don't let it rain before we get back home. In the Son's name." Mama kept her hands on the reins and eyes on the road. "And one more thing, blessed be thy name as thou givest and taketh away."

"Amen." Billy slapped Trudy too hard on her back. King growled. Nobody spoke again until they reached the edge of Taylorsburg.

Trudy had never gone to town in the wagon. It was embarrassing. The Camerons wore clean clothes at home, but now all their clothes were filthy. Appearing in public that way disgraced the family name. She wished she could remove her soot-smudged bonnet, but it covered her ink-stained hair. They were doing their best. Once she had been proud to be a Cameron.

At MacGregor's Mercantile, a black bow on the front door announced Mr. Jake's loss of a dear friend. Some man Trudy didn't know took the reins from Mama and tied them to a hitching post. Other men helped them down as if the Camerons had become eggshell fragile.

One of the men milling around left the group and ran around the side of the Mercantile toward the back. The men removed their hats and held them in front of their chests. A man Trudy didn't know said, "Mrs. Cameron, wait out here a minute with your children. We want to honor you. We're a little late, but we wanted y'all to hear it."

From the town's first church, which stood on the street behind the paddock where Jacob MacGregor kept his horses, the giant bell in its belfry rang out the announcement of William's death. Loud, mournful, and in a throbbing rhythm, it resonated forty times.

"Stay, King. Guard the wagon."

The dog, perched in the back, eyed Billy.

Inside the Mercantile, clothes waited on hangers supported by rods along the far right side. Mrs. Bently, who was always in the store as though she belonged nowhere else, helped Mama select some clothes. She went straight to three dresses Mama's size.

"This will fit, I'm sure. No need to try it on." Mama pulled a plain black dress from a rack. "What do you have for the children?"

They found black pants, a white shirt, and a black polka-dot bow tie. "Mama, don't make me try that on." Billy folded his hands. Mama held the clothes up to him.

"Son, you're too dirty to try on clothes. These should fit."

"I'm afraid you're going to have to settle for this navy blue dress." Mrs. Bently placed a hand on Trudy's shoulder.

"Yes, ma'am." Trudy turned to hide her secret joy.

She stayed close as Mama reached into the pocket of her soiled dress and with trembling fingers pulled out Papa's old coin purse.

46

"Let me pay you with this, please, Jake." She held a twenty-dollar gold piece.

"No charge, Zoe." The big store owner with a kind face laid two lacy handkerchiefs and a tailored one on top of the pile.

"I can't let you." Mama stiffened her shoulders.

"Just say 'thank you.' You all are good people. William was my friend. Also, but not that it mattered, he bought a lot of merchandise from me and paid up at the end of every month."

"Thank you." Mama swallowed. "Thank you so much."

"Mrs. Bently, find them some hats to go with these clothes." Mr. Jake had a catch in his throat.

"You have to get some dress-up shoes too." Trudy pulled her mother's unburned arm.

"I can't wear these boots to the funeral." Mama seemed to notice the boots for the first time. "Undergarments . . . now let me pay for my shoes and underwear for the three of us. Oh, I almost forgot. We need combs and a hairbrush."

Mrs. Bently placed the items on the counter as the three Camerons stood nearby.

"Let me see your arm." Mr. Jake took Mama's hand and raised her arm. "Burn?"

"Do you have any salve and something to wrap around it?" Mama asked.

"This jar contains a mixture of petroleum jelly and almond oil. It ought to help." He opened the lid. "Smell it."

Mama sniffed. "A sweet light scent."

He placed it and some cheesecloth a few inches from their clothes.

"Whatever money's left, put it to my credit in your book. I'll be back soon."

"Only if you'll accept this bread Caroline baked for you and some hoop cheese. I want to give you a case of Coca-Colas." He cut six thick slices of bologna, which he wrapped in butcher paper, and added a butcher knife to the supplies.

Walking out the door toward the wagon, Mama held her head high as they passed the men hanging around on the boardwalk. Zoe Cameron knew how to be a lady. Trudy copied her behavior. Billy assisted his mother into the wagon.

Billy put the food up near the front. "King, lie down."

Their big furry black dog lumbered to his place.

A man walked up to Mama's side of the wagon and mumbled about being sorry it happened.

"Thank you very much," Mama, holding the reins, began coaxing Bob and Molasses. "Good day, gentlemen."

Trudy knew she should think sad thoughts all the time, but she had a pretty new dress. The dark blue would show off her red hair.

~Chapter Seven~

Trudy dreaded the funeral.

It didn't matter that Papa's body lay somewhere in a carpenter's shed while the men of the community finished nailing his box together. The family couldn't sit around and mourn. The farm jobs forced them to work. The Camerons couldn't survive if they neglected the garden and the livestock.

Back from town, Billy tied the mules to a fencepost on the north side of the front yard. The family sat on the floor of the porch to eat lunch. Trudy raised her food to her mouth, but before she could bite the bread, the rank odor of dead rats forced her to take her sandwich and soda to the wagon.

Her middle tightened as pain rumbled from side to side. It was no time to be sick. She had to try to eat. Didn't Billy and Mama smell the worst stink in the world too?

"Can we leave the wagon down here with the mules hitched to it while we rest?" Trudy could lie in the wagon away from the smell of rats.

"You know better." Billy untied the mules. "Come help. We have to return the wagon to the shed in front of the locked crib and the mules to the paddock."

"Who says?" Trudy's shoulders sagged.

"I do." Billy spit on the ground like he was a grown up or something.

"Why, Mr. Smarty?"

"Because William Cameron Sr. always did it this way. It's something about the locked crib. We don't need to call attention to the front of it."

"Why?"

"Papa had his reasons."

Trudy didn't roll just her eyes. She rolled her entire head at her stupid brother.

When they finished putting away the wagon and mules, Mama asked, "Do you think you can handle the smell long enough to take a nap on the porch?"

"I want to sleep on the grass in front of the cabin."

"Chiggers, ants, snakes." Brother was saying whatever mean thing he could think of.

"Right now I could sleep anywhere except in the rat smell."

"Go ahead." Mama sprawled out on the north end of the porch.

Billy, lying on the south side, began snoring instantly.

"Lord, please keep them critters away from us." Trudy, curled in a soft spot of sand on the side of the road, fell asleep mumbling.

After naps, the afternoon whirled by like a flying Ginny. They shucked dry ears of corn for Billy to feed into the corn sheller, which was attached to the crib wall next to the wagon shed. After feeding the corn to the chickens and gathering the eggs, they harvested tomatoes and picked butterbeans in the garden next to the ground where the house used to stand.

"We don't have anywhere to store this food." Trudy pointed at the pile of produce.

"I don't know what to do." Mama hesitated a second. "Everything is a big problem. We'll give Aunt Melva the eggs. Let's ask her if we can place the tomatoes and beans on her porch overnight."

"We got to get busy." Billy took off back down the hill. "We can't waste time standing around and grieving about what we ain't got no more."

All three of them went to work cleaning the cabin. Spider webs drooped like lace doilies suspended from the porch ceiling. A part of Trudy wanted to keep them as art objects now that all her lovely belongings had burned up.

When they pushed the door open, it creaked. The rat odor smelled stronger than ever. In the corner of the front room, Papa had stored some old plows, feed sacks, and firewood. Lizards scampered.

"I can't." Trudy inched forward but shrank back. "Don't make me go inside."

"Coward." Assuming the posture of a brave man with shoulders squared, Brother walked over to pick up a piece of firewood.

"We'll stack that outside a little ways from the cabin." Mama pointed to the place.

When something scooted out of the pile, he threw the wood and darted back out the door.

"Ugh." Trudy ran off the porch into the yard.

"Rats. It's okay, kids. We can get rid of them. Come on. Get to work and stop thinking about it."

"It stinks." Trudy's belly turned a fresh somersault.

"We don't need you to tell us." Billy marched back inside. "We have noses."

"We can handle this." Mama picked up some rotted feed sacks. "Come on, Trudy. I need you to help."

"Revolting," Despite her horror, Trudy resolved not to let Billy outwork her. She piled the rotting firewood on her bare arms, and Billy piled a bigger load on his arms

Revolting was another spelling word. The final spelling bee of the year, Trudy and Brother were the last two standing. It went on for twenty minutes. Finally Teacher pulled out some geography words. It wasn't fair. Brother won because she couldn't spell *Mediterranean*. Teacher always took up for the boys.

"Papa stored this junk for later use, even though the time never came." Mama picked up a load of old tools. "None of it served any purpose except a home for vermin."

"Stop daydreaming and get to work." Billy poked Trudy.

After a lengthy work session, Trudy asked, "Ain't it time to go get the cows, Mama?"

"Go ahead. It's early, but it's okay."

Trudy liked the way they fell into their routine. Because they managed to start their barnyard chores early, the spring sun had not set when they finished.

Having milked the cows and turned them into the paddock, they dipped water from the rain barrel and washed themselves with rags and lye soap stored inside the barn.

"Tonight, we'll leave King in the house. I'll close the inside doors so he can concentrate on the front room." Mama led the dog back to the cabin. "He'll get rid of the rats."

"I don't want our dog to stay way down here all night." Billy made a crying face. "With the rats."

"Son, rats are in your uncle's crib. This is no different."

"An evil person might steal him." Trudy wished they had a lock.

"Not King." Billy pushed her shoulder. "He'd scare them off."

"One more time and I'll clobber you."

"Trudy." Mama wouldn't have spoken to her that way if Papa had been alive.

Laden with eggs, tomatoes, and butterbeans, they trudged to Uncle Stuart and Aunt Melva's house to spend a second night.

As soon as they made their arrangements about the food, Mama looked perplexed.

"What is it?" Trudy asked.

"We shouldn't leave our new clothes in the barn." Mama was already walking back. Trudy and Billy followed her on another trip to fetch the stuff they needed to wear to the funeral.

Supper was bread and milk—crumbled cornbread stacked inside Mason jars and covered with buttermilk. It was much tastier than Aunt Melva's vegetables.

Thank you, dear God, nobody remembered it was my birthday. So this is how it feels to be ten.

~Chapter Eight~

When the morning came, the William Cameron family once again dared the rising sun to catch them in their borrowed beds.

"Don't forget your bonnet, Trude. Billy, wear your cap."

"Mama." Trudy suppressed a grin.

"What is it?"

"You look funny. Your hair is all crooked."

"I couldn't see how to comb it." Mama ran her fingers through the tangles.

"It looked bad yesterday, but today it looks worse, and Brother looks a mess." Trudy laughed at them with the hope they wouldn't notice the ink in her braids.

"It's just one more problem I can't solve."

"Remember Papa had a mirror in the milk storage shed." Trudy would need to think for them now that Papa wasn't there to do it.

"Oh, yes. We'll get it down off the wall." Mama reached for a pan of tomatoes. "Trudy, can you carry our dresses? Billy, take your clothes. Finish out your load with tomatoes."

As they loaded up, Mama said, "Don't take more than you can carry all the way back to the barn."

"How about the rest of it?" Billy laid down the heavy sack and picked up a lighter one.

"Trudy and I'll come back while you let the cows into their stalls."

"Can I go get King?"

"Yes you may."

When they placed their loads inside the wagon, Mama reached into her pocket. "Trudy, say grace."

Hoop cheese and bread. Mama'd been secretly toting it in a bag since the day before. They sat in the wagon to eat breakfast.

"Thank you, Lord, for our clothes." Trudy fingered a streak of milk on her dress that looked and felt like spilled starch. "Thank you for hope. Thank you that we are refreshed after sleeping well even though the bed was stinky, the sheets were scratchy, and the mattress was full of lumps. Thank you for Mama. Brother and I want to let you know how glad we are she's making sense and got her mind back. Bless this surprise breakfast that my mama has toted in a sack since yesterday. In Christ's name."

"Amen." Billy hit her shoulders hard.

"If you don't stop it." Trudy pushed him.

"What you going to do about it?"

Mama stood staring with her mouth open. Why didn't Mama stop the fight before one of them got hurt?

Trudy calmed herself so she could enjoy the cheese. She could have said even more out loud to God. She could have asked him to give Mama the ability to carry on with the farm the way Papa did. She could have prayed about the way Billy was, but he was always going to be Billy, no matter how God or any adult human on earth tried to change him.

As soon as Mama and Trudy returned from their trip to get the rest of the butterbeans and tomatoes, Trudy sparkled with new enthusiasm. "Let's play a game."

"We don't got time to play games." Billy shook his head.

"This will make more time. Here is my idea. Let's see whether we can do the chores faster and better than we did last time."

"How will we know if we did or not?" Billy couldn't turn down the chance to play.

"We have to have a judge. Mama, will you be it?"

"Yes, I'll be glad to."

They went to work. When they finished, Mama said, "We did finish sooner today."

Trudy stuck her tongue out at Billy when Mama wasn't looking.

"We may not have gathered all the eggs thoroughly yesterday," Mama said. "Since we can't be sure the eggs are fresh enough to take to the store, we ought to feed them to the pigs."

Despite her oppressive sadness, Trudy busied her brain with ways to make it fun. "Billy, let's throw the eggs into the hog trough so we can watch them splatter."

"No. Them pigs don't need to try to eat the shells."

"You spoil everything." She brought a bucket. "We'll do it your way."

They moved on with their work. None of the eggs were bad, but they had to be sure. If an egg had been rotten—Trudy's eyes fluttered at the possibility of the worst smell she could imagine.

Lye soap, buckets, pans, and rags for bathing found a place in the wagon. Papa had kept all the stuff in the barn his family would need to wash up for his funeral. It was a short trip, but they rode the wagon and stopped in the road near the well behind the cabin, where Billy tied the mules to a tree. Then they drew water to fill the buckets and pans.

"Billy, take a pan of water, a towel, and a washcloth across the road. Come back and get your clothes."

"Yes, ma'am." Billy reached for a pan.

"Clean up good," Mama said. "Scrub yourself and rinse off the soap. Remember you're a Cameron."

After removing her bonnet, Trudy dipped her braids into a pan of cold water. That well always had cold water good for drinking, but using it for bathing would be awful. Caked ink swirled, blackening the water.

Mama shrieked.

"Jeremy Smitherlin dipped my pigtails in ink at school." Trudy pulled at her matted hair.

"Undo your braids." Mama spoke in the frank, flat tone Trudy never liked to hear.

"I can't. My hair is stuck."

"Sorry, this is cool," Mama poured ice-cold well water over Trudy's head.

Trudy screamed. "You're freezing me."

"Sorry." Mama poured more cold water. They worked the lye soap into her braids and rinsed again.

"We can't get all this ink out." Undoing the wet braids, Mama pulled Trudy's hair. "It'll have to wear out. Maybe more ink will come out next time."

Mama braided Trudy's wet hair tight. "Or I'll cut your hair when I have time if it's not out by then."

It was time to change into their new clothes. Mama's face remained hard. "The only choice we have is dressing behind the bushes."

"Yes, ma'am." Trudy felt a quiver coming up through her throat.

"Unless you want to go up to Melva and Stuart's."

"No ma'am." Focusing on her new dress, Trudy didn't cry.

After dressing, they inspected one another.

"Stay, King." Billy secured King inside and untied the mules.

The Camerons loaded into the wagon, Mama taking the reins.

"You're a good driver." Trudy realized too late that she could have hurt Mama's feelings. "I hope King is all right."

"We'll have to trust him." Billy smoothed his hair as they rode. "And trust God."

It was good he had the decency not to mistreat Trudy. Maybe he behaved better because he had good clothes, but she doubted his niceness would last long. Billy was just Billy.

~

When they passed the Bentons' house, people were starting to park nearby already,

58

"We'll go on into Taylorsburg as we planned. I'm in no hurry to stop here." Mama clucked to the mules to keep moving toward town. At the Mercantile, men stood just as they had the day before.

"When do they do their chores?"

"None of your business, bossy girl." Billy pushed Trudy's shoulder.

Stupid boy.

"Mrs. Bently, we need to buy half a dozen rat traps. We brought some tomatoes and butterbeans for you to sell." Mama was sweating through her new dress. "Please put the rest of it on my account. Whenever I owe Jake, I'll stand good for it."

"It's all right." Mrs. Bently grinned with a twisted mouth.

"Thanks. We've never come to the Mercantile so soon after leaving. It's usually once a week. We're disorganized, you see."

Mama didn't need to apologize to Mrs. B. for being at the store.

When they returned to the Bentons' house, wagons, new Model T's, and surreys lined the road. Horses and mules waited where the neighbors tied them along the fence. Sweet-smelling flowers picked from the yards of surrounding farmhouses, blended with the smell of decaying burned flesh and less-than-fresh food.

Trudy placed one foot into the front room. After staying long enough to look around, she backed away and escaped. She didn't want to talk to anybody. Maybe Bailey wouldn't find her.

"Come look at your papa." Bailey pulled Trudy's sleeve.

"Papa went to be with Jesus. The cold stiff body in the pine box isn't Papa. Mama told me."

"But she stays in the room with it—him—and talks to folks," Bailey screwed her nose into a question.

"She's just doing it because she's supposed to. Nobody can make me go inside and look inside the casket."

"It's a pretty box." Bailey twirled one of Trudy's braids.

"I'll wait and see it with the lid sealed shut in the graveyard."

"It's got white shiny satin all puffed like little pillows all over the insides. It's got fancy round nails with metal ball heads holding the cloth in place."

"I don't care," Trudy said. "Mama's going to make them close the lid, but I don't want to see that cloth in there and I don't want to see that body they're calling Papa."

"You won't believe all the food on the sideboard."

"Disgusting." Trudy felt sick.

"And all over the tables."

"Here's something for you, little Miss. I put some fried chicken and mashed potatoes with gravy on this plate and a big yeast roll." Miss Jones, who lived up the road toward Taylorsburg, thrust a dinner plate into Trudy's hands. Her voice resembled tea that had been boiled and ruined with too much sugar. "I brought you some iced tea."

Trudy didn't look up. "Thank you, but I'm not hungry."

Miss Jones took the plate from Trudy's limp hands. "Well, I'll set this beside you here on the floor in case you develop an appetite."

Miss Jones, stinking with her repulsive *eau de toilette,* stood by Trudy an uncomfortable minute.

"Oh, I hear a friend calling me inside." The woman walked away.

~

Trudy was glad Mama asked not to have a wake. Mama was practical about some things.

The funeral procession inched through Taylorsburg and west of town to Friendship Church led by the Camerons, known for their fine surrey and prancing Tennessee Walking Horses. Riding in the mule-drawn farm wagon with mousetraps under the seat, Trudy held her head high because Mama expected her to, Papa would have said she looked pretty in her navy blue dress, and Bob Mule and Molasses moved along with dignity as if they sensed the importance of the occasion.

Mama didn't want an inside funeral. To sit closed in with the stench of the burned body—the thought of it was dreadful. Again Mama used good judgment.

Trudy found herself being jolted from her thoughts as the pallbearers lowered the pine box into the six-foot deep hole. Papa would have loved his box because it was long enough for his tall body. On top was an inlaid square with "WJC" burnt into it like a fancy brand. Nothing was too good for Papa.

Reverend Black said a prayer, read the twenty-third Psalm, and spoke the eulogy. Why was it necessary to announce Gertrude Elizabeth, her given name, to the entire world? People called her Trudy or Trudy Beth.

Jeremy, staring at her and smiling from the other side of the grave, stirred her anger. He'd have something to say now that he heard her official name.

Shiny blades lifted red clay clumps of soil onto the grave. The noises grated on her nerves. Those shovel-blade squeals were unnecessary.

"It's over with," Trudy whispered. What had the minister talked about? Even though she was mad at Papa just before he died, she didn't need the preacher to tell her he was a God-loving man. Everybody knew Papa was a great man. Someday she'd want to remember what Reverend Black said, but today she couldn't listen. The words were forever lost.

The hurt within her chest was so bad she thought her ribs would split, but the pain in her head felt worse. Her greatest misery, her braids, were too tight. On the way to church, Mama had tucked and pinned them into a row across the back of her head because it was impossible to wash out all the ink. The balled up hair made her new hat too small. She didn't know how she could live another second.

Trudy could die and go be with Papa. She'd stop breathing and fall over dead into his grave, and they could shovel dirt on her. She wouldn't need a box.

Trudy stood erect with Mama and Billy, even though she perished inside. Reverend Black stood in front of the family. The funeral must have ended. Billy extended his hand and shook the preacher's like a grown man. When Reverend let go, Billy wiped the tears with the back of his fist.

The preacher patted the top of Trudy's hat like she was a tiny child, but she didn't cry. Nobody could force her. He handed Mama a Bible and walked away. In the graveyard with her arms around Billy and Trudy, Mama turned the whitest shade of pale.

Lord, I decided I need to stay here and take care of Mama. Forget what I suggested because I ain't ready to go.

They rode in the farm wagon back to the cabin, where they hid behind the bushes to change to their other clothes so they could do the chores.

As they walked back to the barn, they heard Mr. Sam's Model T. "I've been so busy helping build the casket, digging the grave, and talking to the preacher plus having every woman in these two counties leave food in my house that I forgot about all this milking you Camerons do. We came to help." He motioned to a pail on the floor board. "I brought some leftovers for King."

Having Mr. Sam help when he made the time was pleasant, but he had his own life. The Camerons were daily dairy keepers. The cows came first. Papa would have wanted his family to take care of his livestock.

Trudy rushed ahead so she could milk One Horn. She needed to talk, and One Horn was a good listener. "Papa would have been ashamed we didn't ride in the family surrey with the Tennessee walking horses to his funeral. Too bad the surrey burned. We could have at least hitched a team of the prancing horses to the wagon, but the mules were easier for Mama to handle. Besides, Papa would have been proud of the way they behaved."

When they finished the chores, Mr. Sam waited on the front porch with the twins, while the Camerons washed themselves and changed behind the bushes back into their new clothes.

"Pile into the Model T and I'll give you a ride." Mr. Sam opened the door for Mama.

"No, thank you." Mama's smile looked forced. "I just want to be with my children a minute. We'll walk over there soon."

~Chapter Nine~

Trudy needed to go up to her room and rest alone on her bed, but she didn't have her bed and she couldn't be alone.

Billy gave King enough water to last several hours. Mama spread plenty of the food scraps Mr. Sam had brought in front of him. Then she locked the dog in the front room. The Camerons walked the short distance back to Mr. Sam's house, where people waited.

On the way, Mama held Billy and Trudy's hands. "Both of you have to eat something."

"I can't go inside. Papa's gone, but the smell is still everywhere." At the edge of the yard, Trudy backed away.

Mama hugged her. "I'll bring you a plate. You can sit on Mr. Sam's porch."

Clusters of kinfolks stood around. Six cousins, close to her age and mostly from places a few miles away, tried to talk to her, but they didn't have the right words. She stopped listening.

"Hi, Gertrude Elizabeth. Oops, I mean Trudy Beth." Jeremy Smitherlin stood over her.

That boy was nothing but sludge. "What do you want?"

"A chance to apologize." Jeremy sat down on the floor beside her. "I'm sorry about what I did. I didn't mean nothing bad when I dipped your pigtails in ink. I held them up to dry so you wouldn't get ink on your pretty dress. And then your dad died. I felt so bad."

"Go away." Trudy turned away from him. A wedge of reddened sunlight glowed past the corner of the house.

As he hopped off the porch and stood in front of her, she glanced at him quicker than it took her to blink. His puppy dog face aroused no sympathy.

"I don't mean to be grouchy. I just don't feel like talking right now." She turned her face toward the wall until he left.

Mama brought deviled eggs, carrot sticks, and chocolate-pecan fudge on a plate. Trudy sat against the front wall of the house with her mother sitting beside her but not close enough. It was necessary to edge over until she could lean her chest against Mama's shoulder. With identical expressions, they stared in silence until the sky changed to solid red and then gray.

Whatever Mama did, Trudy did at the same time—not to copy her. It was deeper. They were close. Half of Trudy was half her mother.

The untouched plate remained on the floor.

When neighbors and kin came near with silent pats in the falling dusk, the two of them plastered on identical smiles.

"Where's Billy, Mama?"

"He's with Samuel."

The blackness of the night air spread over them. Sentences could not contain the thought that William Cameron would never walk this earth again. At a time such as that evening, losing the house didn't matter, except they needed it for a place to go back to. She couldn't stop one thought—where were they going to live? They could spend a few days in that shack, but what next? Horrible misery swept over the porch like a windstorm blowing up sand from the yard.

Billy didn't mean to be ugly. He was as upset as she was. As if he sensed her need, Billy came and sat with them. The three Camerons held hands until Trudy lost her sense of the passing of time.

Mama stood. "We'll go now."

"We got to go by and check on King." Billy jumped off the porch.

"Sure. We'll go around that way." She started the walk from Mr. Sam's house to Aunt Melva and Uncle Stuart's place. "We can spend one more night with them, but we need to move on."

Because of the demands of milking twice a day, they couldn't go home with any of the other relatives. The closest ones lived on Byland road west of Friendship Church. Also, Trudy would have been miserable having to talk to her cousins all the time.

"I heard Aunt Melva tell you she was afraid we were going to take up permanent residence with her and him. That old hen knows how to hurt with her words." Trudy kicked a rock.

"Wait a minute." Mr. Sam stood behind them. "I'll drive you there in my Model T. Let's take a cake to Melva Cameron. That ought to sweeten her up."

"You don't owe us a ride." Mama walked away.

"Load up. Come on, Bailey and Buddy." He blocked the wheel, cranked the car, and removed the block. Soon they were puttering toward the cabin.

When they stopped in Uncle Stuart's driveway, Mr. Sam said, "We'll meet y'all on your porch in the morning at six o'clock. We'll bring you some leftovers for breakfast." Trudy hugged him, Billy shook his hand, and Mama smiled at him.

Her aunt and uncle had left the door locked, but they hung a key on a nail on one of the porch posts. Except for Aunt Melva's snoring, the house was quiet.

Trudy muttered, "I can't wait to get out of here. I don't care where we sleep at night as long as it's somewhere else."

"How will we know when six o'clock comes?" Trudy asked.

"We won't worry about it." Mama dressed for bed. "We're always up before then."

"We going to milk first?" Trudy needed to make sure Mama had a plan.

"No we'll milk after breakfast."

Trudy undid her braids. At some point during the day, her head had become numb, and now it felt good to have her hair hanging loose. Sleep came too fast for her to notice the scratchy pillowcase. The night passed in an instant.

As on the two previous mornings, they slipped outside before the sky lightened. King waited at the front door.

Trudy threw her arms around the dog's neck. "How did you get here?"

~Chapter Ten~

Trudy, Billy, and Mama ran down the hill to the cabin. Why would someone invade their home? No matter how wretched the dirty, unpainted little house looked, no matter how bad the air smelled, it was the only home they had.

"I'll go in first." Billy panted as he ran ahead. "You girls wait outside."

"No." Mama sprinted to catch up. "I'll go first. You children wait till I check things over, but don't go far. Stay alert."

King, prancing with glee, jumped from one to the other.

Trudy tousled the dog's fur. "Doggie thinks we're having fun. Everything must be okay."

"Sh." Billy placed a finger over his mouth.

As soon as Mama unlatched the door, they tiptoed inside. Instead of barking at an invader, King frolicked to the kitchen.

"How did you get the kitchen door open, Pup?" Billy asked.

King jumped onto the ground from the hole in the kitchen floor.

When the Bentons arrived, the Camerons were already cleaning the cabin. Breakfast was a picnic on one of Mr. Sam's blankets spread over the dew-kissed grass, far from the nasty odors of the cabin. Mr. Sam brought them lunch pails full of day-old biscuits with fried sausage, baked ham, fried bacon, and blackberry jam. He furnished fresh drinking water and buttermilk, also a jug of coffee and two mugs for him and Mama. Mr. Sam thought of everything to make people comfortable. No wonder Papa liked him for a best friend.

"You don't have any way to know what time it is." Mr. Sam handed Mama a delicate brass clock. "Here's a little something for the mantel."

"I can't accept this."

"Oh, yes you can." Mr. Sam held it in front of her. "Take it."

"Thank you." Mama extended her open palms.

"That's better," he said. "Now let me see your arm."

While unwrapping the loose cheesecloth, Mama forced a chuckle. "These blisters are bulging out like bodies of engorged ticks."

Every time Trudy saw the sores, the fire's embers glowed in her memory. With tenderness, Mr. Sam placed new ointment on the burn and applied a clean bandage.

After breakfast they hurried through the chores.

"Mr. Sam, you're excellent help." Trudy gave him the appreciation he needed.

With the chores out of the way, they collected supplies for cleaning the cabin. The lye soap supply was on a shelf in the milk shed. Trudy took two bars, two scrub buckets and some rags.

Billy walked with the razor-sharp hoe over his shoulder. Papa knew how to file hoes so they didn't have burrs. He wouldn't let anybody else try. Now who would file them when they got dull?

Mama carried rakes and brushes. Sam found a hammer, some nails, and a hand saw. Bailey took a stick broom; Buddy, a mop. It was good that Papa had kept his tools in the barn.

"Mr. Sam, before we do anything else, please come help me draw some water." With the twins tagging along, Trudy followed him to the well behind the cabin, and he loosened the rope.

"Papa said this well is fifty-five feet deep. The one at our house place is 155 feet."

"Don't ever come down to this well alone. The platform is rotten. It's dangerous."

"Papa was planning to fix it." Trudy stood close as Mr. Sam poured water into the bucket.

After he carried the water up the little hill, he swept the ceiling of the porch. Dirt daubers' homes, spider webs, and a bird's nest fell to the floor. Trudy and the twins brushed the mess off the sides. The three of them made soap bubbles in the scrub bucket. Trudy's attempts to wash the window made a big mess, but her efforts would have to be acceptable for the time being. The children washed at least some of the nastiness off the porch.

"Every time we get it clean, a grown-up brings out more dirty stuff." Trudy's face was the same red as her hair, and the fabric of her dress was moist.

"Let's not unload any junk on the porch." Mama came to her defense.

They scrubbed all the porch except a path from the door to the outer steps. Trudy pushed her chest out as she made an announcement. "Nobody needs to walk over here until the floor dries."

Rest time came and while Trudy, Mama, and the twins lay on the blanket, still spread where they ate breakfast, Buddy looked up into the nearby trees. "See that little green snake?"

"I see him," Bailey said.

"He won't bother us if we leave him alone."

Trudy, picking her teeth with a twig, jutted out her chin, but her hands shook.

Returning to the chores, they carried firewood outside. "We saw a rat yesterday." Trudy held out her hands to show how long it was. "Rattraps are everywhere. Be careful. They're big traps that could hurt us."

"They're up high out of the dog's reach," Mama said.

A neighbor brought a pile of old clothing, bed linens, and broken furniture.

"Please place those items on the porch out of the way of the door." Mama pointed to a clean spot. "We need to clean up before we can move things inside."

"Here we go again." Trudy, standing by the edge of the porch, slammed her fist into the floor.

The hole in the kitchen floor was as wide as Trudy was tall and twice that long. Mr. Sam and some other men patched it with boards he brought from his house.

At noon, he took everyone home with him to eat leftovers.

As soon as they finished lunch, Mr. Sam stared at Mama. "Do me a favor, Zoe."

"I owe you a few," Mama said.

"Would you stay here with the kids long enough for all of you to take a little midday nap? The day started early."

"All right, but so did yours."

"If it gets quiet, I may snooze on the porch at the cabin."

"Aw, Mom." Billy made a token protest, but Mama whispered something into his ear.

A few minutes later Mama Zoe and the four children stood on the Bentons' front porch.

Bailey said, "Me and Trudy'll bring some pillows out."

Trudy was tireder than she realized.

"Don't go in the house," Mama mumbled.

"What did you say?" Trudy asked, but Mama was talking in her sleep.

After naps when they returned to the cabin, a crude old table with benches sat in the kitchen. "Who brought this table?" Trudy asked

"R. J. Hayes," Sam said.

"I'm sorry we missed them." The neighbors north of the Cameron property, Mr. R. J. and Miss Liz, told fascinating stories about living as slaves when they were young.

Billy brought a pile of fresh limbs into the house and piled them in the back of the main room. "Watch me design a tent. This is my bedroom."

Trudy erected her tent closer to the front of the room. "Now, let's fix Mama a bedroom."

Sorting through the clothes, Trudy and the twins found worn-out garments mixed with rags. Trudy took time to change into a funny-looking

70

dress to wear the rest of the day. Mama wouldn't stop working long enough to change clothes. Neither would Billy.

"We've got to keep the rats out." Trudy, with the twins' help, poked rags into the spaces between the boards until her arms felt as though they'd break. "I supposed the rats can eat through the rags, but we'll slow them down."

They brought some old buckets from the barn to turn upside down for furniture. Trudy gathered quilts and placed them on bushes in the front yard. "I hate this stench." Some of them had large spots with yellow borders where liquid had dried. "Ugh. Why would anybody give us these?"

"What are you doing?" Billy asked.

"I'm airing out bedcover."

They found some folded clean sheets. Discarded chicken feather pillows smelling like someone else's old sweat waited for them to rest their heads when bedtime would come.

By four o'clock, the house was clean enough not to terrify them. The gifts of old clothing were migrating into a stack in the back room. Some people brought jars of canned goods.

Soon it was time to milk again.

~

After another meal in Mr. Sam's kitchen, the Bentons walked the Camerons back to their new home in the dark. The night sounds didn't scare Trudy with Samuel Benton walking along beside them.

"Don't try the old wood stove till I can help you check it out," he told them.

"If you insist." Mama released a heavy sigh.

"God bless you, Zoe." He handed her a yellow cake with chocolate fudge frosting. "Breakfast."

"Thank you. Good night."

Sam and the twins walked away.

"Samuel," Mama called.

"Yes."

"You don't have to come back tomorrow. We'll be all right."

"I'll come check the stove."

With King stationed on the porch, the little family faced the dangers of their first night in the shack.

Nothing had ever hurt Trudy the way it did that moment. "I love you, Mama."

"I love you, Mama," Billy echoed.

If only her mother had more sense about what they needed to do, they'd survive.

"We're going to get through this." Mama spoke with force. "I love both of you."

In lantern light, they sorted through the piles. Trudy found something to lay out to wear the next day, a happy yellow dress with a big skirt. She took it to the back room and closed the door behind her so she could try it on.

"How do I look?" Trudy prissed in front of the lantern light.

"Baby girl, you look lovely. Come on, Billy J. Let's find something for you to wear tomorrow."

He held up some work dungarees and a khaki shirt. "I'll try these."

The pants fit, but the shirt, which was oversized, lacked two buttons.

Mama rummaged until she pulled out a dress that needed the hem mended, but she had no needles, thread, or time. Neither did she have any pins.

"You'll look pretty," Trudy said. They'd go back to MacGregor's Mercantile in a day or two to buy essentials for sewing.

"We want to start our life here right." Mama opened the Bible Reverend Black had given her. Flipping the thin pages to the book of Matthew, she said, "We'll read through the New Testament." They gathered near the lamp sitting on the table.

They said things in their prayers they wouldn't share with their eyes open.

They dragged their pallets into their tents before Mama darkened the lantern. She passed by Trudy's pallet on the way to the window to sit on a large inverted bucket.

Trudy watched her mother remain in the light of the window.

Sleep came fast. "Ugheh!" A bloodcurdling scream awakened Trudy. Had the scream come from her?

She awakened patting her mother's pallet. Empty. "Mama. Mama."

No sounds.

Trudy screamed again. "Eoww!"

"I'm right here, Girlie."

"Mommy." She'd quit calling Mama that when she was five.

"It's okay," Mama held her and soothed her by stroking her hair

"It was bad. Papa had fire all over him. He was running away."

"It was a dream."

"It was real."

Billy popped out of his tent. "I can't get no sleep. Trudy Baby woke me up." He dragged his pallet to the kitchen. He slammed his fist onto the tabletop.

"Don't you dare break our table." Trudy spoke in a half voice.

"I can't take it." He pulled a bench from the table so he could arrange his pallet under the table. "This is my new bedroom."

Trudy curled up and forced her eyes to stay closed. She slept in a fitful fashion and awakened startled. Familiar night sounds coming through the window seemed closer than they had in her former home. Goose bumps popped up on her arms. King was no match for large wild critters. Nothing could stop a wild animal from jumping through the windows or walking through the door.

Thoughts of black bears, bobcats, owls, and coyotes disturbed her but not as much as the sound she failed to hear—Papa snoring in an adjoining room. Her father's sonorous sleep had always been a constant part of her life.

A hot breeze blowing in from the window caused the door to the backroom to creak until it slammed.

~

At the first gleam of sunshine, Trudy looked around. The three Camerons had moved out of their tents. Her pallet was lying close to Mama's left side, and Billy's was on the right. "King sounded like something was trying to come in here last night," he explained.

"What was it, Brother?" Mama asked.

He blushed as he looked away.

~Chapter Eleven~

Vicksburg, a magnet for gamblers, sat perched on a high bluff east of the Mississippi River. The captain stopped to indulge in the vices of the town. Blackburn, second in command, took charge.

Elvin Trutledge rested cross-legged staring at the water. It wouldn't be long before they'd reach New Orleans, where Captain Blye would pay him. A free ride on the way to Florida was a huge fringe benefit. Maybe he could get a job on a ship that would take him from New Orleans to the west coast of Florida.

Comforted by pleasantness, he reclined on the deck and drifted where the water took him. The next thing he knew Blackburn loomed over him. "Get up, you lazy swine." Elvin sprang to his feet. "Coal miner, I could push you into the river and no one would miss you."

Elvin collected his thoughts. "Why would you do that?" Fear removed the sleepiness from his voice.

"Because you smell as rotten as homegrown pig manure." Blackburn placed his thumbs in the belt loops of his trousers and spat tobacco juice toward the edge of the boat.

Elvin cowered in front of the massive brute.

"That ain't the main reason though. I know what you're running from. You got tired of taking care of your family," Blackburn's voice boomed. "Stand in front of me like a man."

He jumped up but tried to slink out of Blackburn's reach. "It's my business." Elvin's voice quavered.

"I'm making it mine. You deserve to be keelhauled." Blackburn grabbed Elvin's bearded throat. His hands tightened around the coal miner's scrawny neck.

"You ain't got no cause to hate me." Elvin choked.

"It's what you think." The big man's rank breath blew into Elvin's face. "Me and Betty Jean grew up together. I was planning to marry her one day, but you went and ruined her." Blackburn decreased the size of the circumference made by his hands. "You'd make a buzzard fly straight. It pains me to see my woman living with a varmint like you. Carrying on the Trutledge name."

Oh, Bobby Blackburn. Betty Jean talked about him. She was always dwelling on memories of him. Sometimes she sounded as though she were still in love with the man. He hadn't realized this Blackburn's first name was Bobby.

Elvin was done for.

Large drops of rain mixed with hail pelted them. Elvin weaseled into himself. Lightning cracked the black sky.

"Pay attention, polecat. If you're such a tough man, you ought to be able to take a little weather without jumping around. When we get paid in New Orleans, you'll give me your money. I'll send it to Betty Jean," Blackburn paused to jerk Trutledge again.

"How can I trust you?"

Blackburn loosened his grip to wipe rainwater from his face.

"What makes me think you'll mail it to her?" Elvin asked.

"Your problem. Don't forget. You are to turn your money over to me." The moment Elvin relaxed his neck muscles, Blackburn grabbed his long beard. "If you don't give me your money, I'll pull every flea-infested whisker out of your ugly face."

The big man encircled a hand on one of Elvin's wiry arms. Emitting an insane-sounding laugh, Blackburn said, "I could go ahead and toss you now, but I'd lose money. Why not just wait and have a little fun watching you squirm?"

Elvin ducked his eyes and began planning his escape. He wouldn't finish the trip for his wages. Blackburn could murder him in a New Orleans alley a block or two from the shipyard. No one would defend him.

As soon as Captain Blye returned and the tugboat started moving again, he'd look for an opportune moment to jump into the river. He'd heard of people using shoes as flotation devices, but he had his doubts. Maybe he could use his coat.

The captain stayed out until three a.m. Within a few minutes after three, Blackburn began snoring louder than thunder.

Elvin stuffed his buttoned-down pockets with jerky and filled his belly with bread and ham. Curled like a cat near the edge of the boat in the thunderstorm, he removed his shoes and waited. He hoped Blackburn wouldn't wake up and find him doing strange things.

The storm passed. When the sky produced a glint of gray and the foghorn sounded, he jumped into the river. In his left hand, he carried his shoes, and he held his coat in his right. His body, a long narrow column, went straight down feet first. Needing a free hand, he released the shoes. Against the force of the Mississippi River, he brought his tied-up coat to his chest. When the water soaked through his coat, he let it go.

The murky river water in his mouth nauseated him.

At first, he paddled in panic, but after he adjusted, he took the river into stride. Drowning could be no worse than facing murder in New Orleans. Moving out of the channel and into the shallow water near the sandbars on the east side, Elvin drifted ashore.

~Chapter Twelve~

"When a neighbor I know has a disaster, I hope I do better than this."
Trudy picked through chipped fruit jars, cracked plates, forks with bent tines,
worn-out spoons, and dull knives.

She dragged the stale quilts to the porch. Her nose worked too well for
her to enjoy living. Mama helped her tote them to the bushes to prevent
dragging them through the sand in the road. Next went the pillows.

"Papa had a whetstone in the milk shed, Mama. We should put it in
the kitchen."

Another evening of chores and a night of horrible dreams brought
chocolate cake for breakfast. It felt a little like a party, albeit a gloomy one.

"Mama, we need an icebox." Billy studied the kitchen. "It can go over
here away from the stove."

Within minutes, some men Trudy didn't know brought an icebox to
the cabin. Mama wiped it clean so it would be ready for the iceman's weekly
run. "God's giving us everything we need."

"I liked it when we needed nicer stuff." Trudy wrinkled her nose.

After cleaning the icebox, they picked tomatoes, cucumbers, butter
beans, and squash in their beside-the-burned-house garden spot. They would
have no time to make pickles. Trudy and Billy conducted a contest to see who
could toss overgrown cucumbers farther. He won.

"Let's smash the columns." Trudy gathered all the giant yellow cucumbers she could carry, and Billy filled his arms too.

Wham, splat. She was mad. Throwing cucumbers satisfied her.

Billy threw harder than she did.

Green onions needed to be pulled. In the lettuce bed under the shade of the pecan tree, they found some loose leaf lettuce not yet killed by the heat. Mama cut some roses along the fencerow of the yard for the table. They gathered eggs.

The old curds in the milk room was good for nothing except pig food. They washed the cream separator and resumed its operation.

"We need our churn," Trudy told her mom.

"We'll wash out this jug. All you have to do is shake the sour cream. As soon as we get some from the separator, I'll show you."

Back at the cabin they drew fresh water to wash the vegetables. Billy brought some possum grapes from the vine on the far edge of the field.

"We've never done this, but it's all right to eat squash raw." Mama sliced and chopped vegetables. "As soon as Mr. Sam fixes the stove, we can cook. We have to go to the gristmill. Maybe I can buy a bag of flour and a can of lard. Then we'll be set."

"I didn't know squash could be crisp instead of squishy. I like this raw stuff." Trudy bit and chewed with pleasure.

What scared her in the daytime was that her mother wouldn't know how to do everything to keep the farm going. They needed Papa to organize the chores and care for sick animals, they'd be unable to harvest the big corn crop, Mama was sure to fall behind on the jobs of separating the cream from the milk and making butter. The garden was huge, and in separate fields were peas, corn, beans, and so on.

In the best of times, all the Camerons had worked every day to keep up with Papa's projects, but these were the worst of times. Trudy wanted Mama to sit and talk to her, but coping with a double tragedy left no spare time.

When rest time came, Trudy pulled a novel out of her school supplies—*Little Women*. Lying on the porch in the heat, she read one page before the book slipped out of her hands.

One day ran into the next.

Trudy's turn to milk Slow Cow came. She wiped tears. The cow was skilled at taking forever to let her milk down. On the other hand, Slow Cow had a reputation for her fast tail she used to swat flies. Papa used to tie a string to the cow's tail and anchor it to her right hind leg so he wouldn't have to avoid the fast-flying slapper.

When Trudy was eight years old, she tried his method once. After a horsefly bit Slow Cow, the beast had no choice except to try to remove the attacker by making a quick leg movement. With a solid kick into Trudy's shoulder, the cow knocked her off her stool. She vowed she'd never tie another cow's tail.

Not able to see well through the brown blur of tears, she failed to dodge Slow Cow's fast tail tossed at her face. The slap hurt. "I've had it." Trudy hurled the milk at the cow. "Now see how many flies you get."

At supper they faced a dinner of tomatoes, old bread, cucumbers, raw squash, and cake. Billy's eyes were red-rimmed. When did he have time to sneak off and cry? He pushed his plate aside and stood to leave the table.

"Come back here, young man." Mama didn't look up.

"May I please be excused?"

"Certainly. Fold your napkin."

Sitting at the table alone with Mama, Trudy whispered, "I heard you."

"Heard what?"

"I heard you arguing with Papa."

"You misunderstood."

Trudy knew she didn't misunderstand. Papa had been rich. Why were they poor now?

~

When the Bentons came to help with morning chores, Trudy managed to have a word with Mr. Sam. "Do you ever make pickles?"

"No, I've never tried it."

"We've got cucumbers to throw away. It's important to pick them when they're little and crisp. Mama ain't got time to make pickles, but you do."

"I don't know how." Mr. Sam pulled his beard.

"Here's what you do. Go to the Mercantile and ask Mrs. Bently how to make them. She'll sell you what you need."

"Why do I want to do that?"

"So we can have pickles." She blurted the obvious to him with exasperation.

"I'll do it."

A day later Sam started a smelly stove fire, which he let burn down while he observed. He declared the stove to be in good order.

~

"We have to lay the corn by. I ain't going to lose Papa's crops." Brother hitched Bob Mule to the big middle-buster plow while Trudy held Bob's reins with a dare she'd make the mule pay if he moved. Mama helped him raise the plow to a standing position, but within seconds, Billy and their little mother allowed the plow to fall over.

After the two of them lifted it back in place, they leaned against the handles to keep it upright. Trudy led Bob to the cornfield with Mama holding one side and Billy the other of the big middle buster. It skimmed over their dirt road without digging enough to start a ditch. With Mama and Billy straining until their breathing was hard, they aligned the mule between two rows of corn. Billy took charge of the reins. Mama stood behind him as both of them held onto the handles. Leaning over him, Mama tripped in her effort to keep up.

"Move out of the way, sweetie. I don't want you to get hurt." Mama said. They couldn't get the plow to dig deep into the soil the way Papa did.

The moment they reached the point of giving up, the twins appeared. Buddy announced, "Papa's coming,"

"Whoa, Bob," Mama said. She pushed the hair out of her eyes, straightened her dress, and smiled. "Morning."

"Morning, Zoe. Ladies don't plow." Mr. Sam spoke in a stern tone as he reached for the plow handles. "Children don't do more than their bodies are ready for."

82

"I have no choice unless I want to lose the crops William left us. I plan to carry this corn through to the harvest."

"I'll plow what I can for you with my tractor, but I need to plow this corn with a mule. I'll teach Billy Jack to do all he is able to do."

"Neighbors don't impose on each other." Mama placed her hands on her hips in protest.

"Friends don't insult each other. Let me plow in my friend's cornfield. If you just have to work every minute, take the twins and Trudy to the garden." He patted her back.

"You're very kind." She turned toward him. The frown she offered wouldn't hold. Soon she flashed a big smile.

"Just being a neighbor and honoring my friend. I've never known a finer man than William."

"Thanks," Mama said.

Mr. Sam's face passed within inches of hers.

Mama let him do the plowing, and he taught Billy how to plow. The twins hung around with the Camerons. Trudy, Bailey, and Buddy toted water to them in the field. Mama fed both families dinner and supper every day. Sometimes Mr. Sam brought Mama food to cook because she didn't have some of everything to make complete meals.

"We've got that last field to do. William planted it later than the rest of it," Sam announced.

~Chapter Thirteen~

That summer brought Trudy closeness to her mother that never existed during Papa's life. Challenges filled the days, and scream-producing nightmares took her to Mama for comfort most nights.

Friendship Church surprised them with a pounding. The members stacked all sorts of staples on their kitchen table.

"Thank you." Trudy, Billy, and Mama chanted.

Every day was a trip on a wheel in a cage like the one they used to have for a baby squirrel they caught. They milked the cows, fed the chickens, cared for the horses and mules, collected the eggs, harvested the garden, fed the pigs, shelled beans, rolled out biscuits, and sifted cornmeal. Life moved on. Hope within said they'd soon find more than a routine.

They wrapped the eggs in clean rags and placed containers of butter and sweet cream in a wash pan of cool water. With all the force they had in their developing muscles, they hitched up the wagon and drove to the Mercantile. Always in the summer as long as Trudy could remember, Mama had canned vegetables and fruit, but now they didn't have time. She didn't make jam or jelly either. Grasshoppers died that way.

Had Mama spent all the gold coins she found in Papa's purse? She seemed to have no money. What were they going to do?

On the way to town, Mama let Brother drive the wagon. "We'll charge a few supplies at the Mercantile. Don't let me forget to buy needles and thread. You can each have a little sack of candy."

"How're we going to pay?" Trudy asked.

"Credit." Mama's jaw looked hard.

"What are you getting for yourself, Mama?" Brother asked.

"I'll get a sack of coffee."

After they passed Mr. Sam and the twins' house, Trudy asked, "Mama, do you like beards on men?"

"What made you ask such a strange question?" Mama said.

"I just wondered." Trudy covered her silly grin with her hand.

"The truth is I don't like full beards. Don't tell Bailey since her papa has one. I mean it's okay for a man to have a full beard. I just never thought— never mind."

When they delivered eggs to the Mercantile, Mama stood biting her lip. "Jake, I hate to ask—please charge us a washboard and a washtub."

"Sure. Let me load those into your wagon for you."

~

Another night came, but Trudy didn't welcome sleep. She dreaded what dreams might come. Despite her efforts to stay awake, her mind drifted away. No more than a minute seemed to pass after she closed her eyes and the madness started. She stood by Billy in front of the house. The fire shot up into the sky as far as she could see. Papa wouldn't stop. He ran straight into the fire. "Come back, Papa. Don't go."

Her screams wakened her and the others. "It was real, Mama. I saw Papa heading into the fire."

"But it isn't real now. Look at the cabin. I'm here. Brother is here."

"I saw him." Why would her papa go into a fire to die? She shuddered at the thought that tried to find a place within her.

"I know. I dream too, but I have to keep telling myself it isn't happening."

The sunrise welcomed a dreamless day. After they completed the morning chores, Mama found three pairs of work gloves in the barnyard shed where they stored the cream.

It hurt to go looking around at the old house site, but they searched for any stuff they could use. They excavated the black residue of what was once their kitchen. All of Mama's iron cooking pots remained. Also the flat iron lay on the ground in the rubble.

"Thank God robbers didn't walk off with these." Mama held up her favorite skillet. "The heat didn't hurt—it cured them."

The three-legged cast-iron wash pot stood between the backyard and the chicken yard. They piled all the smaller pots next to it and lugged the three sets of andirons into a pile.

"Maybe we could clean the extra andirons up and sell them," Trudy said.

"Where?" Billy asked.

"To Mr. Jake. It's going to take us days to get these heavy pots and pans to the cabin,"

"I have an idea," Billy said. "Let's haul them."

"Sure. Smart thinking, Son."

"King, you can ride in the wagon." He gave the dog a shove to help him load.

"May." Trudy grinned at him.

"Good English confuses dogs," he said.

They drove down to the shack and picked up some buckets and enough rags to create a protective lining in the wagon. Mama said, "We don't want the smut on the wagon boards."

When they returned, they loaded their iron belongings. "Mama, you'll have us scrub these in the sand. You'll make us think it's fun."

"Sister, stop talking that way to Mama."

Wearing their gloves, the three of them tried to lift the twenty-gallon wash pot. Mama turned white again. "We can't."

"We can ask Mr. Sam to help us," Trudy suggested.

"Botheration." Mama clamped her teeth tight.

They climbed back into the wagon and drove to the Bentons' house. Spot and Zeke sounded a greeting reserved for stray dogs. Samuel, followed by the twins, ran outside.

87

Billy said, "I guess they want to see what's going on."

"I hate to trouble you but I need your help." Mama brought the mules to a halt.

"Why you persist in hitching up that wagon is beyond my understanding, Widow Cameron. Tell me what you need."

"We tried to lift the wash pot into the wagon, but we couldn't budge it." Mama, her color bright red, stood in front of the wagon seat.

"A wash pot weighs sixty-five pounds, ma'am." Sam helped the little Bentons pile into the wagon.

The three youngest children sat cross-legged near the back. Mama handed the reins to Mr. Sam. "You drive,"

"This is fun," Bailey said.

Mama, Mr. Sam, and Billy Jack managed to grab the pot. After they situated it in the wagon, they loaded the three rocks that Papa had set the pot on and loaded the other iron stuff. King, sorting through the ashes, made a mess of himself.

Trudy took Bailey and Buddy with her to collect the eggs from the nests. "We have to do this every day to make sure the eggs are fresh."

Mr. Sam and Mama picked the apples. Was he standing extra close to Mama, and did he brush her hair out of her face?

"Come go with me to dig up some potatoes." Trudy showed them how to use sticks to dig near the cracks in the earth without scratching the peelings.

"Mama, I think the carrots are ready."

"Let's go check."

Papa had left them all sorts of treasures—ripe eggplants, onions ready for thinning out from the row, white pattypan squash.

Mr. Sam placed his hand on Mama's waist to pull her near him. When he kissed her cheek, she turned pink.

"I can't believe he did that," Bailey whispered.

"Mama looks upset."

"We've imposed on our neighbors enough." Mama climbed into the wagon. "Let's go unload the wash pot and take the Bentons home."

With nowhere to sit, King trailed along behind. On the way down the sloping hill, the pots shifted, forcing the back riders to dodge a rolling Dutch oven.

Back at the cabin, they unloaded the big pot midway between the house and the well.

Billy fetched a shovel from the parlor corner.

"Thanks, Bill." Mr. Sam secured the three stones on the ground, dug a shallow pit in the middle of the triangle, positioned the pot, and checked to make sure it wouldn't tumble over.

"Now, we'll take you all home," Mama said.

"We can help you a few more minutes." Mr. Sam raked a blackened hand through his beard. "Do you want to unload all these down by the well so you can use water to clean them or do you want to unload them on the porch so you'll have a work surface even though you'll have to tote water?"

Mama hesitated. "Put them on the porch."

Mr. Sam looked at her, but she didn't look straight at him.

"Please let me share some of these vegetables with you," Mama said.

"Yes, ma'am." Mr. Sam hitched Bob and Molasses to a fence post. "What are you planning to do with this washtub today? Let me guess. Laundry."

"Right." Mama ground her teeth.

He laid wood for a fire under it.

Mama wiped it out with rags until she was sweaty.

"Let me take a turn," Trudy said.

"Get me a couple of buckets so I can draw some water for you," Mr. Sam told Billy. "We need to put water in the pot before we start a fire so we won't crack it."

They piled sheets and dirty clothes on the ground a few feet from the wash pot. As the water heated, they added shavings of lye soap.

Mama filled the pot with bed sheets. "Be careful near the fire," she warned as Trudy went to work poking the boiling clothes with a hoe handle.

"Papa always took me in the surrey to Guinea Ridge to get Miss Bessie to do the laundry." Trudy tried to explain.

Mr. Sam put water in the washtub too and stationed it on the porch so Mama could use her new washboard.

"I suppose you're planning to hang your clothes on the fence."

"I haven't planned yet." Mama looked down at the dirt by the porch.

"Billy Jack, come help me put up a clothesline for your ma."

"Thanks, but that's too much trouble," Mama said.

While the others rode in the wagon to gather supplies for the clothesline, Trudy helped Mama with the laundry. "I can tell what's on your mind." Trudy spoke to Mama, who didn't seem to hear her.

Time dragged as they worked. "What's taking them so long?"

"Who knows?" Mama kept washing the laundry.

They showed up with clothespins and wire from town. Mr. Sam furnished a late lunch of liver loaf, bologna, hoop cheese, crackers, iced cookies, and Coca-Colas—all purchased from the Mercantile.

"We'll hang up the clothes. We all worked too hard getting them clean for you to get blood on them," Trudy said. Mama had no choice but to cooperate. Big red drops fell from Mama's knuckles into the sand.

After the Bentons left, the Camerons rested on the porch.

Trudy asked, "What is it, Mama?"

"I don't know what you mean."

"Are you sad because Papa ain't here to go get Miss Bessie?"

"Of course," Mama snapped, "but I couldn't pay her."

Trudy blinked sleepy eyes at Mama.

Mama took a deep breath. "Okay, that's not the main thing bothering me. What upsets me is having our neighbor poking into our dirty clothes."

"He helped. Mr. Sam was being nice."

"He's into my business every time I turn around. I just asked him to move the wash pot. He didn't have to help me start the laundry."

"And hang a clothesline. Then buy lunch," Trudy added.

"Let's not talk about it anymore."

~

From his mailbox, Sam pulled a letter that smelled like Eleanor Anne, a mixture of lavender and lilac. Its fancy silver border reminded him she lived a cultured life far removed from what he experienced each day with Zoe Cameron. He opened it with his silver letter opener.

Eleanor Anne Broderick, 7 Mossy Lane, Greenville, Mississippi

Dearest Samuel,

Thank you for your kindnesses during this school year. I loved teaching your children. It is apparent to me you will continue to be my dear friend.

With affection . . .

He considered the note no more than an expression of gratitude, and yet he wondered whether it contained an underlying message. He returned the paper to the envelope and placed it in his roll-top desk.

~Chapter Fourteen~

Zoe leaned against the roof of a dilapidated shed not far from her wash pot. Her hair wet from sudden perspiration and her dress clinging to her, she retched. She couldn't control her upset digestive tract. The harder she tried the worse the problem became. She resumed her laundry.

It didn't matter where Samuel was as long as he wasn't at her house. He hadn't shown up that morning.

Did she react to Trudy's complaints about the smell of the quilts or was the stench as bad as her nose told her? She drew water from the well and filled the wash pot. Next she built a fire underneath it and added lye soap. The ache across the middle of her back demanded Zoe to rest a few minutes. After immersing her quilt into the water, she poked the quilt down. When frothy brown streaks came out of it, she succumbed to nausea again.

Someone crunched the grass. Was it Samuel? She didn't look up. "Mama, I want mine washed too." Trudy said.

Thank you, Lord.

"First let me see if this works. It may be too lumpy after we wash it."

It seemed to take hours for the water to boil. The wet quilt was almost too heavy for the three Camerons to lift over into their washtub. Zoe splashed a bucket of water to remove the dog hair off the porch. With the children's help, she spread the quilt on the floor to dry.

Throughout the passing days, all sorts of odors insulted her nose, which conveyed a message of disaster to her throat. Butterbeans cooking with their too-fresh greenness, the smell of sulfur emitting from eggs in the skillet, the laundry, the barnyard manure, even the dog—all the smells caused her to sneak behind bushes and regurgitate. Her stomach never relaxed.

Why couldn't Samuel leave her alone? Go away and let her manage their lives. At a moment she was wishing to be rid of him, he drove his tractor with his trailer attached to it to the cabin. The twins rode standing in the front of the trailer.

His was the only tractor she'd ever seen. It was good he had such a thing to play with, even though it was an expensive toy of little use to him. He could take his tractor somewhere else, but it was always a joy to see the twins.

"What are those?" Zoe, trying to keep her back from swaying, pointed toward three rolls covered in brown paper.

Samuel beamed as he killed the tractor. "Something for you from us."

"You shouldn't." She couldn't stop the frown forming on her face.

"Look." He unwrapped three tufted mattresses, single-bed size.

Zoe threw her hands up. "I'll pay you for these as soon as I can."

"Zoe Cameron, stop it." Sam unloaded the thin cotton mattresses one at a time and took them inside the cabin. "All you need to do is be glad."

"Okay, I'm glad." Arms folded and foot patting in the sand.

~

Most of the time, Zoe managed to serve good meals to Trudy and Billy, but sometimes she ran out of supplies. It was a paltry pantry the night she served boiled eggs, sliced tomatoes, carrots, and buttermilk.

"No bread." Billy sounded disappointed.

"Almost out of salt. No baking soda. Not much flour. Low on meal."

"I like hot water bread." He poked at the carrots on his plate.

"It requires more meal than I have and salt. The lard has been used too many times to fry."

"I'm hungry," Billy said.

"Eat then." Trudy cut her egg white into tiny cubes.

"We'll go to the Mercantile tomorrow." Zoe didn't like the lavender circles underneath her children's eyes. "And we'll go by the gristmill. Try to make a meal out of what we have tonight."

Billy wouldn't understand how she'd love a cup of coffee. Her throat revolted at the smell of the egg on her plate. When the buttermilk crowded her mouth, she rushed to the front door.

It was not the first time. The children followed with a wet face towel.

"I'm okay. Go back to the table. Let me sit here a minute." With the towel on her face and her soul full of blame for the misery she'd caused, Zoe sat on the side of the porch

Something she did must have made William use poor judgment. He tried hard to be perfect for her. If she hadn't pushed him so hard, she would still have him.

Lord, you know how desperately I need support. Please lead me through this dark valley. Give me the strength to embrace the new life within me.

~

The next day they went to the Mercantile as Zoe promised.

"Caroline told me to give you these the next time you came into the Mercantile," Jake MacGregor told Zoe when she brought eggs and butter to trade.

"Oh, wonderful. Thank her for me."

Jake loaded a box of Mason jars filled with canned peach halves, fig preserves, blackberry jam, and strawberry jam. The fruit flavors would taste good. Resisting the temptation to pop the lid off the peaches and drink the fragrant, soothing juice straight from the jar, Zoe lacked the power to keep a tear from sliding down her gaunt face.

"All three of you are losing weight." Zoe heard concern in Jake's voice, but he needed to stop meddling.

"We're fine." She forced a laugh. "Kids just growing up over the summer. Billy's shooting up taller by the day. Active in the warm weather, you know."

"I suppose you have an excuse for yourself," Jake said.

"Grieving." She wiped her tears with a tattered handkerchief.

"You getting enough to eat?"

"We're fine."

"Working too hard?" Jake asked. "Fretting over your bill here? Stop worrying about it. "

"Just give me a little more time." When her face felt that way, she knew it was covered with splotches.

"You know I won't don you." He cut a large wedge of hoop cheese and wrapped it. "No charge for this."

~

On a fresh day, Zoe called the children from their new beds at four o'clock to get a head start on the chores before the heat took over.

Tired by midmorning, they enjoyed a lull. Trudy sat reading, and Billy worked on a scarecrow for the cornfield. Zoe stacked a pile of mending by her chair. Work eased her grief.

Wet in the heat, the Bentons showed up. Holding one another's sweaty hands, Samuel and his twins appeared at the side of the porch. "Hey, y'all. We came to visit," Buddy said.

"Can we, may we, go play?" Trudy placed a scrap of paper she used as a marker in her book before laying it down.

"Yes, Sweetheart. Watch for critters." Zoe pushed her hand sewing aside. "Don't go near the pool below the well. Stay away from the fishing hole. Brother, you ought to go with them."

"I don't have time to play." Billy finished his scarecrow. "I need to take this to the field."

"Trudy, grab your bonnet." Zoe nagged Trudy too much, but apologizing would just cause more resentment.

"Oh, all right." Trudy covered her head.

"It would be best if you don't get out of sight of the front of the cabin." All sorts of dangers threatened the children if they started talking to one another and forgot to pay attention to their surroundings.

The three youngest ran off in a joyful chase. With King at his side and the scarecrow in his hands, Billy walked the opposite direction. Zoe and Samuel sat and watched.

Rushing from one chore to another kept Zoe in a state of tension. Her body relaxed as she stopped, and the relief felt good. Trudy and the twins, barely in view, frolicked in the fallow garden patch on the north side, where they collected wildflowers and rocks. Samuel sat on the edge of the porch with his feet dangling. A caressing breeze whispered through the oaks as birds contributed music refreshing her soul.

The crinkles on the outer edges of Samuel's eyes deepened. He must have smiled. His face may have looked pleasant, but she couldn't see much of it. Soon after his wife died, he grew a long beard of curly strings hanging from his face. He kept a poorly trimmed moustache. She couldn't remember what his chin looked like, and she could catch only glimpses of his mouth.

Always needing a haircut, he had blond curls that puffed out from his head. He reminded her of pictures she'd seen of pioneers living in the mountains, but the looks of her fuzzy neighbor mattered little. For six years he had been William's closest friend and her good friend. Although he was a year older, he seemed as close as a little brother who constantly needed advice and often asked for help.

When his babies were small, he came to her in despair. "What can I do about colic?"

"Walk them. I know it's difficult to walk two crying babies at once, but you're a strong man."

When they were two, he told her, "Their screaming fits and breath holding are enough to drive me insane."

"Try to ignore their negative behavior." She remembered how stubborn Trudy had been at that age.

Throughout the years, he'd asked, "Could you watch after them a few hours? I need to tend to some business."

Never would he have considered sending them to an orphanage. She and William had always made time to assist him. She felt a constant concern for his struggles to care for two little ones without their mother.

Torn clothes waiting for her as she sat a few inches from Samuel on the side of the porch, she dropped her eyes to her tired hands in her lap. At least the calluses were hard. No bleeding. The scar from the burn had faded. She drew pictures in the loose white sand with her bare toes.

"Hear those mockingbirds?" Zoe asked.

"Yep." Samuel appeared to catch her pensive mood.

"Sad." Her shoulders heaved with a sigh.

"Yep."

It reminded her of the mournful old song about a mockingbird singing around a sweetheart's grave. They sat and toed the sand. Zoe let him share her mood.

Sam whistled with the birds. It was difficult for her to determine whether he was copying the birds or whether they were imitating him.

He cleared his throat. "I'm concerned about you and the kids, Zoe."

"No need to be. We're doing fine." She made an effort to brighten her voice. "We just need some time. Thank God, it's summer."

"I've wondered how you get all your supplies."

Where was he headed with this? He knew the answer. He wouldn't try to have her children placed in an orphanage if he thought she neglected them—not Samuel.

"We have eggs and milk." She smiled at him. "You've helped me get everything set up, and I thank you. We're able to do all the chores except for some of the heavy farming you've done. We churn butter. I robbed the honeybees yesterday."

"How did you do that? Use smoke?"

"No, I just climbed up in the tree and took some honey."

Sam shook his head.

"What?" A slow grin spread across her face. "I used to do it when I was a girl, but William wouldn't let me."

"How many times did you get stung?"

"I never have been stung." She shot him a wink. "The bees know I mean them no harm, so they don't bother me."

"Zoe!" He shook his head again.

"The garden feeds us. The roasting ears are delicious. You've brought us supplies numerous times, and I thank you. Remember the church gave us a pounding."

"You must have used up all the food the church gave you by now," he said.

"We go to town and stock up."

"How?"

"Why do you ask? You know the answer. In the wagon. Sometimes we drive right by your house, and sometimes we go the front way."

She caused William's death. Samuel must have thought so too. She annoyed her husband with all her demands until he had an accident while trying to get everything right. Samuel really was planning to take her children. She forced herself to smile instead of looking defensive.

"I don't often see you. Sometimes we're out checking on our place." He paused a moment before taking on a demanding tone. "I told you hitching up the wagon is too hard for you and your children to do. You're a lady."

"We do fine. We go fishing at least one day a week. The berries are delicious this year. We have a good time." She stood and walked to the door of the house. "I'll be right back."

A couple of minutes later she returned with two bowls of blackberry cobbler covered in whipped cream.

"That's beautiful."

99

"I whipped the cream not long before you all showed up."

He pushed the beard away from his mouth and carefully inserted a bite. "Mmm." He hummed with pleasure. He spooned the buttery crust, juicy berries, whipped cream, and soft dumplings into his mouth through his whiskers. "This is the best I've ever tasted."

"Thanks. William—William liked my cobbler." She fell silent as she set her bowl down. Unbidden tears slipped from her eyes.

Samuel placed an arm around her. "Excuse me, Zoe. Your whipped cream is melting. I hate to see it go to waste."

She picked up her bowl and set it down again. She didn't have an appetite for cobbler. A wave of nausea passed over her. "Sorry." As she tried to suppress a burp, tears flowed.

"As I was saying, it's a shame to see good food not eaten." He looked shy. "Would you mind if I—?"

"Sure. Finish it." She handed him her bowl, which he cleaned up as though he were ravenous.

She laughed. "You've got berry juice on your face."

He pulled out a white handkerchief to wipe his mouth. "That get it?"

"Let me help you." She took the handkerchief from him. He leaned forward and she wiped his face through the beard. She stood in front of him. When a rock in the sand caused her to lose her balance, he reached out to steady her.

"Do you have salt, pepper, and stuff like that—chocolate, cinnamon, vanilla, coffee?" Samuel asked.

"I don't have many frills. As long as I've got a box of baking soda for leavening, we can get by. In fact, the funny thing is those two kids of mine keep using all the baking soda to brush their teeth." She looked for the children.

"I want to help you." His hands lingered at her waist.

"I told you when we run out of essentials, we stock up." She dared not tell him how she longed for a cup of coffee.

"Zoe, you're doing a fine job rearing your children. Billy Jack amazes me. He goes about his business in a quiet way. Most of the time he's looking around for something he can do to help others."

"He's trying to survive." She pulled away and returned to the spot where she sat earlier.

"He is the best of you and the best of William."

"Sometimes he's mischievous. He likes to pull innocent pranks on Trudy," she said.

"Typical boy."

A cacophony of shrill feelings stabbed at Zoe. As in "Listen to the Mockingbird" her heart sang sad lyrics to a snappy tune.

~Chapter Fifteen~

"Bailey, I have a secret I'm not supposed to tell," Trudy whispered while Buddy wandered a few feet away to look for rocks.

"I have one too."

"You go first."

"I think my daddy and your mama should be boyfriend and girlfriend."

"They won't."

"Why?" Bailey looked down and frowned.

"My secret is the answer to your question. Mama don't like beards."

"Really?"

"Tiny moustaches are okay." Trudy paused to let the idea sink in. "And sideburns."

"But what about short beards?"

Trudy brought her finger to her chin. "I don't think Mama would mind that."

"Look what I found." Buddy returned with his hands full of rocks.

They picked multicolored daylilies. Bailey pointed across the field. "Why did y'all plant flowers way down here?"

"We didn't. They just come up every year. My Indian grandmother planted them."

Marching home, they sang "Farmer in the Dell."

Billy and King, returning from the cornfield, joined the parade.

Trudy rushed inside the cabin and came back with a fruit jar. "Here's a vase."

Buddy presented irregular rocks and pine knots. "Look at this, Papa." He handed three perfect arrowheads to Samuel.

"Wait a minute." He took one back. "This one is for you, Miss Zoe."

"We'll add these to our collection on the mantel. Where did you find the arrowheads?" Samuel asked.

"Right down yonder." Buddy pointed.

"Let's all go back again soon and look." Samuel told Zoe, "Buddy is my future archaeologist. He amazes me."

As Trudy returned with water in the jar of flowers, Sam said, "Tomorrow I'm going to town. Zoe, could I take you with me?"

She hesitated. "I suppose so."

"The children can stay here. Billy can watch over them."

~

Back home with his twins, Samuel looked at his mail. A letter. The return address was "Eleanor Anne Broderick . . ." The envelope had a lavender border, and the letter smelled like flowers.

My dear friend Samuel,

    The summer is hot here, but it is good to be home. I trust all is well with you and the twins. It's sad about the loss your neighbors suffered, the husband-father and also their house.

    It looks as though the enrollment at Gravel Hill will be diminished next year.

    Since I have been home, I have attended a steady stream of parties each weekend.

    I am not sure which choice I want to make in life. Perhaps I misunderstood you, but I had the impression you were interested in pursuing a future with me. Here a Mr. Worthington Beauchamps, an affluent planter, takes me to all the soirees. Also, I have been offered a teaching position at the community of Wayside, south of Greenville.

You could help me know what I should do by clarifying your feelings.

As ever,

Eleanor Anne

Samuel folded the letter, returned it to its envelope, and placed it in the drawer of his roll- top desk alongside the earlier one.

~Chapter Sixteen~

Elvin Trutledge swam toward the gray glow of early sunrise. He was so exhausted he would have drowned had he needed to swim another stroke. On the shore, he collapsed with raindrops peppering him until the sun overhead met his open eyes. A crystal beach glistened around him.

Blackburn didn't have his money. Neither did Elvin, but he didn't care. Free—nothing else mattered.

He hoisted his body. Trudging back and forth barefoot on foot soles not accustomed to going without shoes, he confirmed that the sandbar was a little island, not a peninsula. Leaning low, he splashed brown river water into his mouth. Hungry. Nothing but soggy jerky. At least it was easy to chew . . . didn't lose another tooth. Damp wet woolen clothing itched his raw skin. Having worked underground most of his life, he needed to be careful about the blazing rays of sun. Parts of him had never experienced daylight. Besides, it might snow again. Was it already summer in Vicksburg?

On the west side of the island, the Mississippi River washed the sparkling sand. He could live on the little silver beach forever—Elvin didn't need anybody's company—but food was essential. The vile jerky wouldn't sustain him. He had to move on, find a way out. The only way to go was through the swamp on the east.

Best to cross over in the brightness of the day while some of the predatory critters rested. He dropped a foot into the paste, but it felt the way a dose of castor oil tasted. He stopped the way he used to turn his head when his mother approached him with a spoon. He'd starve on the island unless he left, and he couldn't dawdle until the setting sun caught him in the swamp that lay ahead. His body, already wet with fear, obeyed his mind's command to slice into the slime.

Elvin, an intruder in a territory not claimed by human beings, slithered deeper into the thick water until he met a serpent face-to-face. A fat green-gray snake on a limb turned to face Elvin. Quick as a blaze, the creature stuck out his needle-thin tongue, retreated it, and opened his white mouth. Fangs aimed for Elvin as the moccasin slapped his jaws shut.

How he dodged the snake he wasn't sure. "Lord! I'm calling out to you . . . like I never have before. Save me. Oh, please save me. Deliver me from this snake. I'll be good to my wife and children. I'll stop cussing and stealing."

The moccasin didn't move again.

"I'll head back home right now, dear God. Just send this snake somewheres else."

It slid off the other side of the tree. More snakes greeted him in the green-gray murk, and tiny creatures—possibly minnows—bit his ankles. Elvin dared not make any splashes. His breath came fast and shallow. Green goo stuck to his upper body. He reformulated his ideas of what hell must be like. The swamp was wider than he had supposed—it seemed endless. He grabbed a tree limb to pull himself out of the mire. Feeling queasy, Elvin tried to take deep breaths, but he vomited up the jerky.

His numb feet rebelled when he tried to walk on the boggy surface. He removed his red and yellow shirt but left the sticky underwear clinging to his frame.

"I can't endure this no more." His voice, loud and pitiful, echoed back to him. As soon as he found firmer earth where he could plant his feet securely, he unbuttoned the top of his long johns, used it to mop away the slime, and then dropped the underwear behind him with the sleeves tied around his small waist. He put on his outer shirt. "Mississippi is too warm for my Kentucky clothes."

Elvin arrived at another slough. Before wading into it, he peeled off the slime-stiffened yellow and red shirt, loosened his belt, and dropped his pants onto the ground. With impatience he skinned the union suit off his hairy body and tied his clothing in a bundle. Naked with the bundle held high above his head, he worked through the mire, then into water, which covered him to his neck before he reached the shallow side again. If the water had been two inches deeper, he would have been forced to swim out. Might have lost all his clothes. How would that have been?

Leeches fastened themselves to his tender skin. He forced his leech-covered feet to carry his lanky frame through a grove of trees. Beyond the rocks and briars, he found a high spot, where flies, wasps, mosquitoes, and yellow jackets pestered him.

God, how can I withstand this torment?

After a walk that felt endless, he arrived at a thicket planted by human beings. He pulled the vines from a sign that said "Grand Gulf." On the other side of two giant magnolia trees, a cemetery spread before him. Spanish moss covered gnarled crepe myrtles. The green eeriness evoked the memories he had of death. It oppressed him as much as the coal mines did but in a different way.

"I hear the sun over Florida is so bright it hurts your eyes. Orlando, I'm on my way." He needed to talk although nobody heard him. "By the time I get there, my skin's going to be tanned like a piece of leather."

"Must be a military cemetery from the Civil War. I wonder if it was built forty-something years ago or if it goes back further." Recent graves lay mixed in with the soldiers from both sides. A monument would do to lean on. Better yet was a grave with a bench beside it. He sat down.

Using his long fingernails to pinch a leech from his groin, he howled at the sight of blood. They were everywhere. Profanity flew from his mouth.

"Betty Jean has been onto me about my fingernails. Thank God, I didn't pay no attention to her."

Leeches covered his groin. One after another, the bloodsuckers succumbed to the challenge offered by his grubby pinchers. Each time he removed one, more blood oozed out until it dripped onto the dirt. Blood exuded from the open lesions. Mosquitoes—he scratched the itchy welts. His mouth was dry, and his brains dashed against the inside of his skull when he turned too fast.

Tiny red bugs he could barely see tortured him. They snuggled close to his coarse hairs. At first they didn't hurt so badly, but his misery increased with each one he removed. They were the source of his worst pain.

"I should have stayed and let Bobby Blackburn choke me or shoot me."

When he tossed the last slimy leech to the ground, he made sure there were no invaders in his pants, pulled them back on, and spread out on the marble bench for a short rest. Black clouds covered the sun, but he didn't care. He didn't know how long he slept.

Awake again, he couldn't suppress his mirth. Across the way a statue of a United States officer stood by a stone horse. Laughing, he hobbled over to it. Elvin Trutledge took the time to dress the Union soldier in his dingy union suit by tying the arms of the shirt onto the statue's neck and the legs around the officer's waist.

He surveyed the nearby graves. A mound of fresh dirt revealed a new burial.

"I need some shoes. Hmm. Let me see what the grave marker says. Seventeen-year-old female. Not here. I bet she died of malaria and they buried her in her socks."

The sun appeared and told him it was about three o'clock. On bleeding bare feet, he walked north. Hunger, an old companion, gnawed at him. He was thirstier than he'd ever been. Berries in the woods and corn in the fields sustained him as he walked, making slow progress. Dodging sharp rocks and sticks, he crunched leaves with his bare feet. Looking back from a rock where he sat to rest, he saw a red trail.

He must have stirred up a bed of skunks. Snakes left curling paths where the dirt was unexposed. A fat rabbit allowed him to get almost close enough to catch it. With no knife and no way to build a fire, he decided to leave the rabbits alone.

In the early evening a farmhouse—enormous and elaborate with impressive columns but in desperate need of repair—appeared ghostlike before him. How long ago did it turn gray with mildew? As he walked across the porch, the boards creaked. He found it necessary to dodge holes in the floor. His polite knock on the door produced an elderly woman in a plain navy dress. On one foot and a peg, she stood tall and prim.

"I ain't never seen a woman with a peg leg."

"Gangrene." The lady of the house spoke in a matter-of-fact voice.

She smoothed her thin mouse-colored hair, parted down a severe line in the middle of her head and pulled back. Over wire-rimmed spectacles she blinked at him. To show respect he tried to wipe some of the green gel from his face. She turned her head away. A tight chignon at the nape of her neck bobbled up and down.

"Ma'am, I need some help. If you have any jobs I can do for you, I'd be willing. I worked on coal barges from west Kentucky to Vicksburg. Another man in the crew decided to kill me if I didn't give him my money; so I jumped off and swam to Grand Gulf. Since the boss hadn't paid me yet, nobody got the money." He lowered his cobalt blue eyes and tried to smile. "I had to wade through the swamp."

He waited for her to say something, anything. She stared.

"You don't have to believe me, but I'm telling you the truth. My brother lives in Florida. I'm trying to go to him so I can get a place to bring my wife and children from Kentucky to. I had to throw away my shoes when I jumped into the water. I've got sore feet."

He paused again. The woman looked at his feet covered with blood-streaked layers of caked mud.

"I'd do any odd jobs for a pair of socks and a decent meal. If you have any shoes I could use, I'd be much obliged."

"I'm Widow Clayton . . . my husband died in the War of Northern Aggression. Wait here." She closed the door.

In a moment she returned with towels and soap. "There's water in the rain barrel by the barn. Dip out of it so you don't dirty it up."

"Much obliged."

"Come on around to the kitchen door after you wash off."

Chicken and dumplings and collard greens with cornbread and hot pepper sauce, sliced fresh onions, fried green tomatoes—Elvin was hallucinating. No, it was real. The flavors exploded inside his mouth, he really was eating.

"Sleep in my barn if you don't mind sharing it with the varmints."

In a crude fashion, he repaired her back porch. She gave him socks and some shoes, two sizes smaller than his feet. While he worked she stood and watched. "It must get lonely out here," he said.

Late the second night he washed his clothes and hung them on bushes. The only thing he borrowed from her was a multipurpose military knife he found in the barn. He cut the toes of the shoes open and placed the knife inside his pocket instead of back on the shelf. He'd return it if he passed that way again.

In the middle of the third night, he walked away without saying farewell. Following the big dipper, he returned to Vicksburg. He wandered through the old town—the battlefields didn't interest him—he was looking for the street where the drunks slept. Passing attractive old homes illuminated by gaslights, he went from street to street.

Tripping in his tight shoes down a sharp hill toward the river, he found the winos late at night. A drunk with feet about Elvin's size lay sprawled against a building. He removed the shoes from the inebriated fool. They were in good shape except for a broken sole on the right foot. "Here, old pal. I'll leave you these. You don't need to walk far nohow."

Elvin hiked to the train depot, where he sneaked into a boxcar facing east. Nobody bothered him, except one talkative man, who insisted Elvin share from a bottle already empty. Elvin Trutledge was a smart guy. Here he sat in a dry place moving on toward Florida, and he did it all by himself.

With a jerk the train continued his happy journey to Florida. In Jackson, he heard a rumor that the train he was riding was going back west. He hopped out.

On the edge of the big Jackson terminal, someone said, "This here freight train's headed to Mobile, Alabama." A minute after he climbed aboard a car full of tramps, the train jerked into motion. The transportation was crowded and smelly, but he was accustomed to bad smells. The ride was a good one because it was free.

The train passed rolling pastures and neat farmhouses visible through the open door. Two or three hours must have passed. "Do you know where we are?" Elvin asked a fellow traveler.

"In Schmidt County. We're about a mile west of Taylorsburg."

"Where in the world is Taylorsburg?" Elvin asked.

"Half a mile or so west of the Hastabucha River."

"I like the looks of that dairy farm." He jumped from the rolling train.

"A place to sleep in the barn and two meals for helping with the milking." The dairyman set his jaw hard.

"I'll take the deal." He'd stay a few days and rest in the bright colorful world of Taylorsburg. He needed a break. Then he'd hop a train to Mobile and head on to Florida.

God, I said I'd do better. I'll pick oranges and scout out a place for my folks to live.

How would Elvin pay for the fifteen of them to move from Kentucky to Florida? He'd think of something. Maybe he could make enough money picking oranges. He could buy a wagon and live in it with the wife and kids as they migrated to Florida. That would take months. No matter what, he wouldn't return to the coal mines.

Lord, you've kept me alive this long. Now take me to Florida. Lead me to my promised land. I keep praying to you, but I doubt you listen to a bum like me.

"I bet they ain't got no locks on the doors in this here community. Heh heh."

No animals crept near Elvin Trutledge. He mashed a spot in the hay and scrunched some of it for a pillow in the barn loft. After the morning milking, he laundered his clothes in the rain barrel with a generous amount of the dairy's lye soap supply, even though he had washed them a few days ago.

The stable door served as a clothesline for his pants and his yellow and red shirt. Dipping the soap into the water, he worked up a lather over his skin and rinsed. After wrapping a croker sack around his torso, he went back to the hayloft to snooze the day away. At evening milking time, his pants were still wet. They'd have to dry on him.

As soon as he milked and did chores the next morning, he went exploring. He knew nothing about the Taylorsburg community, but he had to start somewhere. He headed east.

Aha—a clear little creek.

He hung his clothes on a bush so he could immerse his body for a proper bath. His gray-streaked black beard spread out in the water when he rinsed his nostrils.

Wandering about, he looked for something or somebody he could use. All sorts of opportunities awaited his skillful approach. A church sign pointed south.

"Let me go check this here church out."

He followed the road up the hill and to the right. Across the street from a gigantic cemetery a white plank-board building welcomed him with an unlocked door. Near the pulpit stood a cabinet.

"Here's lunch." He wolfed down the communion wafers. There had to be some liquid to quench his thirst. On the lectern sat a glass half-full of water.

"Stale, but it's wet. I've tasted worse. Lord, I know you're watching me. I have to be one of the vilest critters you've got your eyes on today. Excuse me— I was hungry."

He retraced his steps back to the main road, which he followed east until he arrived in the little village of Taylorsburg.

He'd hang around the store till he understood the lay of the land. Without anybody to talk to, he spoke to himself. "Howdy, Mr. Trutledge. You're the smartest man around here. Bet they've got a dominoes game going on somewhere. I'd like to know where the needy widows are, the rich old folks, the stupid."

~Chapter Seventeen~

Zoe wasn't sure where she was or why she was there. Her eyelids lifted with effort in the bright daylight.

"Mama, does your back feel better after taking a nap on the floor?" Trudy, eyes fixed toward the rafter, lay supine.

"Why do you ask about my back?" The question irritated Zoe. "I never complain."

"You hold it and groan." Billy lowered his book.

"Stop fussing over me." Zoe stood and stripped to her slips and bloomers.

Trudy followed suit, and Billy removed his shirt.

Zoe inserted her hand into the washtub of water. "Nice. It's not too hot or too cold. Brother, you were smart to fill it earlier in the day."

She stood on the side of the porch so she could scoop water into a bucket. After she poured water over her children's hair, she bent over for Billy to pour water on her hair. They shared a bar of last winter's lye soap.

"I don't see a trace of ink, Trude." She rinsed Trudy and Billy's hair as they stood on the ground. "It took several shampooings. Don't ever let anybody do that to you again."

"It wasn't my fault." Trudy blew out a sigh as she climbed onto the porch to pour a bucket of water onto Zoe's hair.

Billy mounted the porch steps. "I guess we're clean now, but I want to make sure." He scooped a bucket of water and slung it at Trudy. She didn't say a word, but when he turned his back, she returned the favor. To get even, he popped her with a wet face towel on her arms and legs.

"That stings." Trudy squealed as she dodged.

"Stop." As soon as the children calmed down, Zoe, feeling the mischief bubbling forth from her inner being, dipped the bucket into the washtub and slung water on them. They chased one another until she gasped for breath. "That really is enough." They sat on the side of the porch and washed what was exposed.

She checked their backs for chiggers.

"Buy alkie rub tomorrow, Mama," Billy said. "It drowns the red bugs."

"I will. Now, take a bucket of water and a towel and washcloth to the kitchen. Close the door behind you. Bathe your private parts, dry thoroughly, then put on clean underwear and outside clothes."

Zoe and Trudy finished their baths and wrapped themselves in ragged towels. As soon as Billy completed his bath, he came outside.

As soon as everyone dressed, Zoe ran her fingers through a pile of corn shucks. "Checking them for weevils. Next time, I'll cut your hair, Billy."

He removed his book from his school satchel. While she rolled Trudy's hair, he arranged a towel as a pillow and lounged on the porch. King slept at his feet. Soon the boy fell asleep again.

"Brother is too tired." Zoe wanted her son to stop thinking he had to be the man of the house. "He works all the time."

"You need to get more rest." Trudy, sitting on the floor between Zoe's legs, patted her mother.

"And you need more play time." Zoe hugged Trudy.

"You too, Mama."

"I haven't thought about it much lately." Zoe rolled her hair. "Fixing our hair is play for me."

Trudy fastened the corn shuck rolls in the backside of Zoe's hair.

"Let's find me something to wear to town." Zoe stirred the pile of clothes.

Trudy held up a dark gray trumpet skirt. "Here we go."

"Very stylish." Zoe modeled a fancy white blouse embellished with tucks, rows of lace, and ribbons with the wrinkled skirt.

"Perfect," Trudy said.

The hand laundered blouse and skirt dried fast in the summer heat, and a fire in the stove heated the flat iron. While they waited, Zoe said, "Let's make a fresh batch of biscuits for supper."

"Mama, I'll get that for you." Trudy stood on a chair to pull a pan half-full of flour down from a high shelf.

Zoe sifted a mountain of it in the middle of the pan and mixed in two pinches of baking soda and a pinch of salt. Then she made a little hole where she added a ball of lard and a spoon of bacon grease. She greased the pan. Into the lump of dough, she worked buttermilk in increments with her bare hands. She shaped the biscuits and placed them with their sides touching inside the pan.

By then the iron was hot enough to press the skirt and blouse, almost dry in the heat. While Zoe ironed, Trudy shelled butterbeans. After weeks covered in the gray clouds of grief, it was good to feel a light moment.

The cows and the livestock fed, the Camerons ate beans, sliced tomatoes, green onions, and biscuits with butter and honey. Zoe provided for her children. Life was good. The nausea had let up. They had joy, tasty food, and fun. One day, the one she had, was all she needed.

~Chapter Eighteen~

Morning came. With the chores done and preparations for the adults to go to town, the day had promise for some mischief. Trudy tried to look innocent.

"Remember, Son. You're in charge." Mama pointed her finger.

Dressed in clean clothes, Trudy and Billy stood ready to greet their guests. Mama was elegant in her outfit complete with the hat she wore to the funeral and a used reticule.

The Model T full of Bentons arrived on time. Mr. Sam honked the horn at King lounging in the sandy roadbed. When he reached a good stopping place, he hopped out and chinked a wheel. Bouncing around in a frenzy, the twins emerged from the automobile.

Trudy noticed Mr. Sam had a new short haircut. The only hair on his face was a neat little moustache between long well-trimmed sideburns. The razor scrapes on his red face would heal in a few days. If not, she had caused the poor man permanent hardship. It was amazing to see what he looked like underneath. She had no idea Mr. Sam was such a nice looking man.

"Papa went to the barber shop yesterday," Buddy announced.

Bailey didn't say anything, and neither did Trudy. She looked at Mama with a question on her burning face.

Mama lifted a box of wrapped eggs. Billy took them from her and placed them in the Model T.

"Be careful with those," Mama said. Good morning, Samuel. Young man, remember you're responsible for the group. We're glad to have you visit us, Bailey and Buddy. We won't be gone long. King, stay out of the road." Then she cut her eyes toward Trudy. "Missy, we'll have a talk when I return."

Oops.

"Bailey and Buddy, behave. Do what Billy Jack says." Mr. Sam added to Zoe's admonitions. He looked at Trudy from the corner of his eye. Did he know her potential for monkeyshines?

"Bailey told him what I said. Bailey's right. Her papa and my mama have sweet feelings for each other."

Admonition was a big word Miss Eleanor Anne taught the class. Even though she struggled to forgive the hussy teacher, Trudy had to admit the woman taught well.

No wonder Mama didn't like that woman.

Wide-eyed, Trudy looked up at Mr. Sam and Mama, then concentrated on looking down and away.

The children stood on the porch until the automobile left. As soon as it was out of sight, glee burst out of Trudy.

"Bailey, you're too skinny. I'm going to fatten you up today." She issued orders to the boys. "Watch for Mr. Sam and Mama. Holler if you see or hear them coming."

Bailey followed Trudy into the kitchen. "What are you going to do?"

"Cook. What do you want me to cook for you?" Trudy didn't have many choices, but she saw no need to point out the obvious.

"I like eggs."

Trudy had little else to offer. "How do you like them cooked?"

"Scrambled."

"Sit down." Trudy pointed to a bench at the table and placed Mama's medium-sized round iron skillet on top of the stove, still hot from the breakfast fire. She spooned some bacon grease into it, cracked eggs, and dropped them into a bowl one at a time to check for freshness before loading them into the hot grease. Six—that was plenty. Oops. Spills. After pulling down a plate from the shelf, she stirred the eggs until they were cooked solid.

"Now eat 'em." She served the plate to Bailey.

"I changed my mind." Bailey looked dubiously at the eggs.

"Eat."

"I ain't hungry." Bailey slipped away from the bench at the table.

"You have to eat 'em. Mama will get after me for wasting."

"I said I ain't hungry," Bailey shouted.

"Try," Trudy shouted back.

"I can't." Bailey rubbed her tummy.

"Eat 'em."

While the girls' argument progressed, the boys entered the kitchen.

"What are we going to do?" Buddy asked.

"Make biscuits."

"You don't know how to make biscuits." Trudy snickered.

"We're going to learn." Billy pulled down Mama's biscuit making pan.

"I'll tell." Trudy gave him the look she'd practiced to put him in his place.

He found the sifter. "No, you won't." He looked through the few groceries on the shelf. "I can't find the sody."

"We ain't got none. There's a little in the flour already," Trudy said.

Buddy stayed nearby as they started their project.

"We just bought sody the other day." Billy moved the objects around on the shelf.

"I used it to whiten my teeth." She smiled to display her pearly choppers. Trudy broke into a fit of giggles. "Mama—she's been polishing her teeth too."

"We probably got enough left in the flour. Small detail not worth worrying about." He made biscuits with his hands the way he had seen his mother do it. "Buddy, you can help." The boys dipped into the wet flour up to their elbows. Soon the flour spilled out of the pan, across the table, and onto the floor.

While they played with the flour, Trudy worked on Bailey. "Eat 'em, Bailey."

The little girl opened her mouth and inserted a big forkful. She chewed and swallowed. "These eggs are tough. Papa makes 'em soft."

Buddy was white with flour. The boys patted out enough terrible looking lumpy biscuits to fill a pan. They had leftover dough. "This is fun." With no warning, Buddy slapped a wad into Billy's face, and the big boy showed similar courtesy. Back and forth, globs of dough flew while Trudy continued to stand over Bailey.

"Eat 'em, Bailey. You got to." Trudy was disgusted at her brother. "Are you going to cook your biscuits?" Ignoring her, the boys slung dough. She took a second to put the biscuits into the oven. "Bailey, eat them eggs. They'll make you pretty."

"I'm already pretty."

"They'll make you prettier. Now, eat 'em."

While Trudy placed the biscuits in the oven, Bailey slipped away from the table and grabbed a glob of dough. Giggling, she threw it at Trudy.

Pinching off a ball of dough, Trudy reciprocated. Strings of it whirled like the tail of a comet.

Giggling and running through the kitchen, everybody was slinging dough at everyone else.

Trudy and Buddy rounded the table in a wild chase.

Bailey slid on the floor on her way back to the biscuit-mixing pan. "Oh, no."

While Billy tried to catch her, she took advantage of the slide by grabbing all the leftover glob, which she smacked into Billy's face.

Out of ammunition, they stopped the war. Billy started cleaning up. They peeled the dough from their faces and arms and brushed off as much flour as possible.

"I'm going to my house to wait for Papa." Buddy walked toward the kitchen door. Bailey following.

"Bailey, get back to eating your eggs. Sit."

"It's hot in here." Buddy wiped his forehead with the tail of his shirt.

Billy headed Buddy off at the door. "Come back here. Help clean up."

"I'm tired of cooking." Buddy placed his hands on his hips.

"All right." He stood in front of Buddy. "Sister, you told us to listen and watch. You started all this anyway. Now, clean up."

"I'm telling." Trudy stuck out her tongue.

"Your papa expects you to stay here. You can't go home by yourself," Billy told Buddy. "I know what you can do. Stand in the doorway and listen for the Model T. If you hear them coming, holler."

"I'll help my brother." Bailey tried to slip out of the kitchen.

"Nope," Trudy said. "Come back and sit."

When Bailey moved to another side of the table, Trudy placed the plate of eggs in front of her. Bailey, having pushed the plate away, folded her hands on the table. "You can't make me. I want my papa."

Billy and Trudy hurried. The more they wiped, the more flour they smeared.

"I know a good activity," Bailey said. "Papa mixes water with flour and makes paste. We can cut out colored paper and make pictures."

Buddy ran back into the kitchen. "I think I heard 'em."

"Oh, no." Billy moved faster.

"Eeeat 'em, Bailey, eat 'em." Trudy shoveled, but Bailey clamped her mouth shut and shook her head. The Model T was percolating along the road not far from the cabin. Trudy opened the kitchen door and tossed the eggs. At least King appreciated her cooking, even though the eggs were overcooked.

Mr. Sam parked the automobile. He and Zoe unloaded their purchases. "Exciting news—I ordered a sewing machine." Mama talked as she gathered packages. "Hugs."

The children stood in silence.

"Isn't anybody going to give me a hug?" Mama asked.

Bailey broke rank. Crying, she hugged Zoe and then Sam. "Papa, I thought you'd never come back. What did you bring me?"

"Children, why are you not talking? You have flour and dough all over yourselves." Mama zeroed in on Trudy. "You will need to give a report of your activities, young lady."

Mr. Sam leaned down toward the twins. "Little Miss Bailey, you look entirely too innocent. Those are crocodile tears."

"I didn't do nothing." Bailey held her hands out as she continued to shake her head in innocence.

"What's cooking?" Zoe asked.

"Biscuits." Billy's voice was soft as a whisper.

"Better check them. You don't want them to burn." Mama covered her smile with her hand. "Trudy, what has been going on here?"

"Billy's in charge." Trudy shrugged and threw up her hands.

"I need to make sure you little urchins don't burn yourselves." Mama rushed back to the kitchen and pulled the biscuits out. "Who made these?"

"We did." The boys spoke up.

"Samuel, come have a biscuit."

Trudy chewed one of the funny looking hard biscuits. *Not bad.* Mama and Mr. Sam sat on the porch in the worn-out straight chairs like royalty and ate biscuits while the children cleaned the kitchen.

"We'll tell them about the surprise bags when the kitchen is as clean as I left it." Mama spoke loud enough for all of them to hear.

~

At supper time, Zoe dropped butter into her iron skillet and layered it with the boys' leftover biscuits, sliced. She served them with honey and fried ham.

"I thought we were out of ham." Trudy reached for a slice.

"This was a gift."

"A gift from Mr. Sam." With a knowing look on her face, Trudy fluttered her eyes. Her tongue made clicking sounds.

"Yes." Zoe didn't look up.

"Mama." Pounding the table with the handle of his knife, Billy commanded attention. "I seen some tracks what don't belong."

"Where?" Zoe asked.

She shivered to think how far Billy strayed from the house. She believed he made a practice of patrolling the entire farm. The narrow sandy road passing near the burned house and through the barnyard extended southward down the long sloping hill to a point where it divided. To the left on the west was a road to pastures and timberlands. Eventually it led to the neighbors' property.

The folks living in the Esco Settlement walked through the Cameron farm because this road was the shortest way home. The road to the right, the east side, led to the shack where the Camerons lived. The road passed within inches of their house, wound down to the well and pear orchards, and passed by the Bentons' house.

Admiring his skills of observation, Zoe beamed at Billy. William Cameron's mother, a tan-skinned woman with intense blue eyes and almost black hair, was one-half Choctaw. She passed her prominent high cheekbones down to William, Billy, and Trudy

William inherited a deep respect for the land and a close relationship with his surroundings. He had noted every detail on the farm and encouraged his son to do the same. From his grandmother and father, Billy inherited uncanny powers of observation.

"What did they look like?" Zoe asked.

"All the neighbors to the west have large wide feet. They don't wear shoes much in warm weather. The Hayses to the north have smaller wide feet. The new shoe prints I've seen are thin and long with separate heels that dig into the dirt. Cowboy boots, I think. Some good-for-nothing's been snooping around," he said.

"We need to help you keep an eye on them," Zoe said. "I don't mean to baby you, but I wish you wouldn't roam all over the edges of the property. I worry about you."

Ignoring her concern, Billy touched his face with all his fingers. I see the tracks, but King don't bark. Must not be a stranger."

"Promise me you won't wander far." Zoe forked the last slice of ham onto Billy's plate. "We don't want to waste this."

"I wonder why King didn't bark—who could it have been?" Billy gazed out the window into the twilight.

"You aren't paying attention." Zoe grabbed his arm.

"At least nobody's stolen the corn sheller. I seen a bunch of footprints in front of the door of the crib. Some of them are neighbors' and some of them are strangers'. These folks ain't got no business going inside Papa's shed."

"What's to keep an invader from climbing in the window of the cabin and killing us?" Trudy's eyes wanted to pop out.

"King," Billy said.

"Angels." Zoe laughed. "Besides, we don't have anything anybody would want."

~Chapter Nineteen~

Trudy had supposed the two families would stop their long-standing tradition of playing games now that the best player was in heaven, but they sat at Mr. Sam's dining room table as always. After a few rounds of dominoes, Samuel brought out his checkerboard, and the children scooted the dominoes to the other end of the table.

Mr. Sam's face wasn't red like it had been. Mama couldn't hide how much she liked his new look. It was a good thing he didn't stay splotched. Another good thing was he took the boys for haircuts. Brother looked a mess when his hair grew the least bit.

"It's strange to be here without William." Bother. Was Mama crying again?

"I miss him too." Samuel reached for the beard he no longer had. "The next few days we men need to plow that last field of corn. We'll have to keep working with the mule. It's a fine crop. No skips in the rows."

"We're beholden to you, Samuel."

"It's the least I can do. Next year—" He gave her one of those looks that said something important was coming.

Not a checker had moved. Trudy and Billy stared from their end of the table while the twins stacked the dominoes in towers. "Soon you need to look into something else to do with your land. Row-crop farming is too hard."

"We'll make some money somehow." Mama sat still as a stone. "I don't know yet what to do."

Trudy and Billy stood behind her. How could they play when worry paralyzed them?

"A part of me wants to keep the fields the way William did. Changing what he left makes me feel disrespectful."

"You seem afraid."

"No. Let's talk about it later." Mama spoke in a soft voice.

"I'm sorry. I said too much." Mr. Sam placed his elbow on the table and rested his chin in his hand.

The twins built the tower so high it fell over. "When they're lying down, they're dead," Buddy said.

"Like Sarah Bailey Benton and William Jackson Cameron." Bailey arranged the dominoes in new stacks.

"Sell some timber," Mr. Sam stacked the checkers in the box and folded the board. "Get some beef cattle. Stop all that milking. I'll help you reorganize when you're ready. Stop working so hard. Your profits will be more certain even though you'll put forth less effort."

"William didn't plant any cotton this year because he said the boll weevils would eat it up."

"Smart man. I don't know what he planned to do with all that corn this year. A lot of things we talked over, but we never talked about his bumper corn crop. Maybe he just needed to plant something in place of the cotton." Mr. Sam looked intently at Mama. "Here's what I think you need to do."

All three Camerons leaned toward him. "If you get some beef calves started, you can fatten them up and sell them a little later."

"I need some time to think." She looked at him with her sad eyes. "I can't now. It still hurts too much. I must keep up with each day as it comes. Something crucial."

Mama stopped talking for a long minute. "Something always demands our attention."

"What are you talking about? What is crucial now?" Sam asked. "I want you to understand I care what happens to you and your children."

"I have to mend the fences."

"Buddy and Bailey, you may serve your cookies now." Mr. Sam poured lemonade.

"The cookies tasted better than anything I've had in weeks. I love these." Mama ate three. After a polite passage of time, she said, "Thanks. It's been an enjoyable evening. Now we have to get going."

"See you bright and early for the plowing." Billy started toward the door.

"We'll walk you home." Mr. Sam motioned to the twins.

"We'll be fine. Thanks though." Mama stood to go.

He grabbed a lantern.

~

When the morning glories spread colors on the fences, the guys in overalls and the girls in everyday dresses went to work. Mr. Sam and Billy hitched the big plow to Bob Mule. The others dug juicy clay-colored worms in loose loam near a log and scooped them into a jar. As they skipped to the pond, they sang about being happy and free. Soon Trudy felt happiness all through.

The fish couldn't resist the worms.

By suppertime they had a luscious array of vegetables along with a pile of fried bream and hushpuppies. Lanterns and lamps cast soft lights throughout the cabin.

"Papa, I caught a big fish," Bailey held up her hands to show him how long it was.

"Eat some." Trudy spoke in a stern voice.

"I don't want to eat the poor fishies." Bailey pushed her plate away. "I ain't hungry."

"We're about to get the plowing done." Mr. Sam piled food on his plate. "Sunday, the Lord's day, of course, we'll rest."

"Church." Mama cried again. When would she run out of tears?

Billy pushed his untouched plate away. He leaned his head against his hands.

"What about Saturday? Papa never worked on Saturday except for the milking and chores." Trudy couldn't allow them to forget all of William Jackson Cameron's traditions. "He always took us to town in the surrey."

"Trudy." Mama gave her a look that told her to hush.

"We'll go to town as always. We'll pile into the auto and go shopping."

"Lately we've been going to town on weekdays whenever we wanted to." Mama replenished everyone's tea. "We'll see if we need anything this week."

"Miss Zoe, what do you do with them buckets and old cans in the corner?" Bailey asked.

"When it rains we catch the water from the leaks." Mama tousled Bailey's hair.

"Why?"

"So we won't have a mess all over the house."

"What do you do with the pile of tools in the corner and those pieces of wood?" Bailey asked.

"Sometimes we store our tools inside," Billy said. "I think Mama keeps the stuff in the corner in case she needs to fight off anything or anybody King doesn't run off first."

~

Saturday the two families, dressed in their good clothes, piled into the Model T and traveled to the Mercantile. Mr. Sam kept Jake MacGregor busy with purchases.

Trudy spoke in a timid voice. "Mrs. Bently, can I look at that pretty red cloth?"

Mrs. Bently placed it on the counter. Trudy's hands caressed the soft fabric.

"You would look pretty in a dress made out of it," Mrs. Bently said.

"Thank you."

"Some lace at the neckline would look nice." Mrs. Bently laid two cards of white lace next to it.

"This one." Trudy pointed to the one with dramatic points.

"I'm sure Miss Zoe knows this, but let me explain to you. Sometimes red cloth fades. It would be wise to make a dress with a detachable white collar trimmed with the lace. That way she wouldn't have a laundry problem."

"What's this? A white lace collar already sewn to fit the neck of a dress?"

"That's a collar made entirely of Irish lace. It's a pattern of roses. We have these in different sizes. A little expensive though. All you have to do is wear it on top of your dress. The red color would be lovely underneath."

Trudy had never seen such a fine thing. Mama walked over to where Trudy stood. "You're taking up Mrs. Bently's time." Her voice was brittle.

"But, Mama, what are you going to sew on your new machine?" Trudy wiped the tears spilling from her eyes.

"I'll remake some clothes to fit us from the nice used ones." Mama leaned over and whispered into her ear. "I'll make us some cute things out of flour sacks. It'll be fun. You'll see."

"Okay." With a clean but second-hand handkerchief, Mama wiped the tears from Trudy's face.

Bailey shifted from one foot to the other.

Mr. Sam walked toward them. "Bailey, do you like this fabric?"

"I love it." Bailey reached out and rubbed her hands over it.

"Maybe we can work out a deal with Miss Zoe. I'll buy enough to make both you girls dresses just alike if Miss Zoe will sew them." Mr. Sam looked at Mama with a question on his face.

Trudy and Bailey pulled their hands up in fists and squealed for joy. Mama's face broke into a slow smile as she reached for two lace collars.

After Mrs. Bently cut the cloth, the girls drifted away to look at other things. Trudy peered at the jars of spices. She loved the smell of nutmeg. She wished Mama would buy some for cookies.

Jethro McKenzie, the store handyman, stirred up dust everywhere they went. When he finished sweeping, he stocked new merchandise from the back room. He popped up first in one place and then in another.

"Mr. Jake must be adding some new leather goods for horses to his store stock. We could go run our hands over them, but Jethro put those things out a minute ago. He may not be through. He'd show up in that part of the store again," Trudy told Bailey.

Trudy believed he hung around to listen in a way her parents had cautioned her not to do because it was rude.

"Bad manners," she added.

"Does Jethro know my family?" Bailey asked.

"Maybe. He used to work as a farmhand for us. My papa said he was a hard worker. Mama used to feed him lunch on the back porch."

~

With liquid eyes Jethro gazed at Zoe. His long-fingered hands encircled the broom handle as he stood idle.

Jethro had never seen a more beautiful woman. She needed someone to protect her and her children. William was a great man, but he'd moved on to his reward. Zoe Cameron needed a man around. He wished he could change what she was going through. Samuel Benton—always Samuel Benton. He deserved to die.

~

A motley assortment of men sat at a crude table in the back corner on the west side, where the door was propped open to let in the breeze. They drank Coca-Colas, played dominoes, and laughed at what they said to one another. Trudy had seen all the men before except for the new one who had joined the group—the one with a big heavy beard, coal black with streaks of white hairs. His beard reminded Trudy of a skunk. His funny-looking red and yellow shirt hung loose from his skinny frame.

As Mr. Sam pulled his leather money pouch from his pocket to check out, he had only a fifty-dollar bill. "I'm sorry," Sam said.

"Let's see what we can do." Jake laughed. "You could always spend some more." He shuffled through the cash drawer. When the cash register went ka-ching, the weird man in the red and yellow shirt jumped. The other men fell silent.

"All right," Sam said.

"I was kidding. I have some coins in here, but I don't have enough folding certificates. Let's see." In order to supply the required change, Jake pulled out various gold coins.

Buddy ran over to stand by his father, and Billy followed. "Is that bucket money, Papa?"

"Some of it is."

The boys walked away to have a talk. Trudy with Bailey tagging along followed so she could hear. She didn't mean to be impolite, but she didn't want to miss significant information.

"What's bucket money?" Billy spoke in a soft voice.

Having something important to tell, Buddy talked too loud. "Papa has a bucket full of money."

Billy's eyes grew big.

"A big old bucket." Buddy spread his hands. "He lets me and Bailey help him count the money. We put unusual coins in it. Some of the coins are from other countries. He takes out the collectibles and saves them in special folding books."

"Where does he get it?"

"Sometimes he gets it here. Sometimes he goes to the bank and trades plain money for it."

"When you get rich, what are you going to do with your money?" Billy whispered.

"Lots of things." Buddy couldn't make himself speak softly. "When the bucket gets full, we're going to do something important with it, like take a trip."

"That's stupendous. Your papa is so smart," Billy whispered.

"Guess where we keep it." Buddy's voice became more intense.

"Hmm," Billy said.

Buddy cupped his hand over his mouth. "Papa said not to tell this part. He won't care if I tell you I don't think. I have to talk soft." But he didn't. "We keep it in the utility closet on a shelf."

When Billy whispered something into Buddy's ear, nobody in the store seemed to notice them.

"Papa said we might go to New York." Buddy was shouting. "Maybe we can go to Niagara to see the waterfalls."

"Wow."

"We call it the dream bucket." Buddy's eyes sparkled.

"I'm surprised you never told me this before," Billy said.

"That's because the subject ain't never come up." Buddy looked earnestly at his older friend. "You never asked me about it before."

~Chapter Twenty~

Bedtime. It had been an exciting day, and now Trudy needed to rest her mind, but she couldn't turn off her thoughts. For weeks she'd lived through more good days than bad.

Lord, this is a special prayer. Help me put up with Billy Jack. You know how he irritates me, but he is a smart brother. Besides, I need him to help take care of Mama. After all, he is my brother, and I love him.

Without Papa she and Mama were growing closer. Mama managed the farm better than Trudy expected. Lying on her mattress, she arranged her pillow in a comfortable position.

God bless Mama. Give her the strength she needs.

The Benton twins were fun. She couldn't love them more if they were her brother and sister. She and Bailey had hoped Mama and Mr. Sam could become romantic, but Mr. Sam got on her mother's nerves. Maybe Mama was mad because she needed him to help her. Maybe Mama was too proud to let him do things for her. Mama seemed to think she had to fuss every time.

Marcie. Trudy missed holding her doll when she went to bed although Marcie was nothing more than a bunch of yarn Mama knitted and shaped like a monkey stuffed with cotton. Still it seemed sad her little monkey had to face the fire all alone without her button eyes.

I'm too old to have a doll. Right, Lord? Sleep would be sweet. Thank you for this house. At least we don't have to sleep on the ground.

She drifted off.

"Stay here in the wagon, Trude," Papa said. "I need to go into the Mercantile for a minute."

It had to be a dream.

"Stay here and watch Bob and Molasses."

"Yes, Papa."

They didn't go to town in the wagon. They always went in the surrey. Papa never left her, but why was he leaving her now?

Papa walked into the store. He wouldn't look at her.

"I'll bring you a little bag of horehound candy."

He was talking but he wouldn't turn around.

"Come back, Papa."

All day passed. She drove the mules over to look at the town schoolhouse. Then she tied them up back at MacGregor's Mercantile. Nobody knew or cared she had gone.

"Come back, Papa."

He was lying inside the wagon under a black blanket. She drove the wagon to the flat black house no taller than the ground except for the columns and the coils of bedsprings sticking up. Mama was there wearing a black dress. The columns looked abandoned, and the porch steps led to nowhere.

She hated the times when it happened. Once again she awakened Mama and Brother with her wild screams. Mama hugged her and sent her back to bed.

Sleep approached but drifted from her. When Papa's body lay in the pine box, she was sure he had already gone to his new home in heaven. After each disturbing dream, she wondered more about life after death. Where was Papa? Between stints of sleep she wondered if Papa existed anywhere at all, but she'd never tell Mama what she thought.

~

Elvin Trutledge sat in the back of the Mercantile in Taylorsburg in the middle of the day. He loitered there all his spare time except on Sunday, when Jake MacGregor closed the store. Every day he watched the other men while their time away at dominoes, and he played enough to be included in the group.

Now and then, he played a game of checkers. Thinking about ways to locate money, he listened for clues.

After not having the opportunity to collect his wages from working on the river, he was entitled to money. People had it stored up under their mattresses and in Mason fruit jars. They didn't spend it, didn't need as much as they had. It didn't seem right for his children to go hungry when other people had more than they knew what to do with. Some streak of luck would come along. As soon as he acquired what the community had to offer, he'd hop on a freight train to Florida. He listened intently to every conversation for something he could employ to make his fortune.

A more urgent problem than the need for cash was his incessant itching. He didn't want to talk about it in front of the other men, who were always looking for a good laugh. He waited until the men left and approached the store owner. "Hey, MacGregor, what are them tiny little red bugs that chew the daylights out of me?"

"Chiggers." Jake grinned.

"Can't stop scratching. They leave bloody sores. You got anything to stop the itching?"

"Rubbing alcohol. I keep it poured up in bottles. What you need to do is drown the critters in it."

Elvin Trutledge fished in his pocket to find money, which he slapped onto the counter. As soon as MacGregor handed it to him, he held it high to study the clear liquid.

"Now whatever you do, don't drink this stuff. It'll kill you."

"You must think I'm a fool."

"Where did you come from and what are you doing here?" Jake asked.

"You keep up with everything, don't you? I worked in the coal mines till one day I couldn't take it no more not seeing the sunshine. I'm on my way from Paradise, Kentucky, to Orlando, Florida. I stopped here to work a few days."

"I see," Jake said.

"Tell me about that woman with the dark red hair. Is she the widow I heard you folks talking about?"

"What's it to you?" When Jake bristled, Elvin realized he'd overstepped his bounds. MacGregor could ask questions but not answer them.

Hanging around in the Mercantile with a bunch of ill-advised hayseed farmers and a meddlesome merchant grew tiresome. Elvin Trutledge told all of them where he had been and what he had done, including his life in Paradise and his swim in the Mississippi River. They looked at him as if he made it all up so he could tell something more ridiculous than the rest of them.

The fresh countryside called him. He could cover ground with his long legs as fast as he wished. He'd check out the environs. It had taken several days with baths in Lost Creek for the leech scars and the bug bite sores to heal, but now he was as good as new. The rubbing alcohol helped.

It was time to go exploring. Oh, he'd return to the store, but meanwhile he'd see what he could find. Opportunity called.

He headed south. Next to the sign marking the county line, he found an insignificant deserted building constructed of logs. It could have been a church at one time. Maybe it was a school sitting vacant throughout the summer. At any rate, the roof was starting to sag in the middle. When he tried to open the lock, the board holding it in place fell off. He walked inside.

"Here's a good spot to eat lunch in the middle of the day. Then I can stretch out on a bench and take a nap. Maybe the schoolmarm will show up. I could teach her a lesson or two."

He walked out and closed the door. "I've got a private building to eat my lunch in. Heh heh, I'm rich."

He went walking up a steep rocky hill. It rounded and rolled sometimes through sandy ground and sometimes through red clay. At the top he found the most luscious watermelon patch he'd ever seen. Standing in the middle of it, he gazed all directions. To the north he saw the remains of a fine house. Nothing stood but columns and doorsteps.

"Must be the red-headed widow's house they was gossiping about. With a house like that, she's bound to have money. I wonder who all's courting her. I seen her in the store. If she's the one I'm thinking she is, she's a real beauty. I remember when Betty Jean was pretty like that before she let herself go. Seems like that widow-woman and me needs to strike up an acquaintance."

To the east of the front yard of the house was a big garden full of green plants. So much luscious food going to waste, he decided to have watermelon for lunch. Another day he could have tomatoes. He thumped until he found a ripe one. After twisting the vine loose, he hoisted it.

The heavy load sank into his bony shoulders. He wouldn't waste his energy carrying it back to the schoolhouse. He decided to walk through the grass-covered pastures stretching east of the watermelon patch. He liked the looks of the well-groomed paddocks. Some farmer kept his stuff in top-notch shape. Such a farmer might have money to spare. While he was up that way, he could do some reconnoitering. Besides, if he crossed the pastures, he could get back to the schoolhouse quicker because it was a straighter course than the road. He saw all sorts of possibilities worthy of investigation.

He found a shady spot with a thick log nearby. Since his knife was not long enough to separate the melon, he slammed his lunch into the log and sat to eat. Enjoying the good life, he failed to see a Jersey bull with intimidating horns. In a scratch of time, he had no choice except to climb the shade tree.

After what seemed at least an hour, the bull moved on in response to a man's high-pitched voice calling him to the barn down the way. Elvin's legs and arms were so numb he could hardly climb down. By then he needed to get back to his late afternoon milking job.

How about the little brat with the bucket of money? Where did he live? South of town one of the men said. Came into the store with the widow woman and her young ones. He'd keep listening. Maybe he could follow them simpletons home from the store. He wasn't sure if the brat's pa had a wagon or a Model T.

~

Samuel wrote a note to Eleanor Anne:

It's good you are having an enjoyable summer. I think you should take the position to teach near your home. I read in the newspaper that the governor wants to consolidate the schools. Chances are we will not be able to maintain our little Gravel Hill School another year.

Samuel

He sealed and posted the note.

~Chapter Twenty-One~

Restless nights with frightening dreams drifted into days filled with farm work. With the coming of a sunrise, Trudy tried to guess what Mama was planning for the day ahead. In the bright morning, the milking chores soon moved behind. Mr. Sam and the twins drove up with lumber hanging out the back of the Model T. Having stopped in the middle of the road down by the well where Mama was drawing water, he killed the engine and blocked a wheel. Buddy popped out carrying a hammer, and Bailey followed with nails.

When they appeared, Mama paused from turning the crank of the windlass. Holding on, she dug her face into her arm to push her hair back before she resumed drawing water. She poured the water from the tube into the bucket and wiped her hands on her apron. Trudy waited to help her tote the bucket up the hill.

"Morning, ma'am."

"Good morning, Samuel."

"The well stand is about to collapse." As soon as Sam chocked a wheel, he took the bucket of water.

"Among other things."

"I'll help my widow neighbor with the most pressing problems first."

"William didn't use the well down here at the cabin much. He didn't take the time to repair it." Mama looked confused.

"I understand." Sam started up the hill.

"If this well is too dangerous, we can get our water from the well up at the house place." Mama followed him.

"No, no, no. That's too much trouble. It's dangerous even if you don't use it."

When the Camerons and Bentons reached the cabin, Mama plopped on the porch floor to rest. Panting, she sat without talking while Sam stared. Mama scratched her ear and wiped her hands on her apron. She fidgeted with her sleeves as she gazed into the distance.

"Samuel." She didn't look at him. "Don't you have things you need to fix at your place?"

"Not as urgent as this."

"Do you think you might need some time to mind your own business?" Mama spoke softly. She didn't want the children to hear her, but they always listened when she lowered her voice.

"Oh? You're being abrupt, Mrs. Cameron. The safety of your children and mine is my business."

Mama stood as though she weighed five hundred pounds. As she walked back toward the well, Sam held onto her arm. The boys, obviously ready to work, walked along close by.

"Can we play, Mama? Come on, Bailey. Let's go see the ducks." Mr. Sam and Mama acted peculiar, but Trudy was tired of trying to understand grownups. She seized the opportunity to go to the little pool north of the well. That's where the mother and her babies stayed—way off limits. Since the adults would be working close by, she knew it would be all right to go see the ducks as long as she and Bailey remained in view of Mama.

Mr. Sam used his important voice. "We have to keep the children away. I'm getting ready to tear down this frame. This well will be an open hole."

"I won't go near it, Papa," Buddy promised.

"Mr. Sam, I'd like to help." Billy rolled up his sleeves.

"For starters you boys can tote those rotten boards to the edge of the woods." Sam stacked the decayed wood far from the well. He unloaded the lumber as the boys toted the old wood away. "Watch for nails."

After dropping off a load, Billy walked along the path back to the well. "Come here, Mama."

"What is it?"

"Look. I ain't never seen this footprint before. Look at the crease across the sole of the right shoe."

"That's odd." Mama frowned.

Billy worried Mama. Maybe the mysterious footprints needed to be worried about, but it was a beautiful morning, Mr. Sam was taking care of one of their big problems, and there had to be some time to play.

Hand in hand, the girls skipped off to explore. While the boys helped Mr. Sam, Trudy and Bailey scampered near the edges of the tiny pond. The baby ducks hovered near their mother in the shallow water. When they approached, the little ones scattered.

Bailey broke away from Trudy to chase them. "We've got to catch the babies and take them back to their mother." Bailey followed the ducklings up the little hill toward the well, and Trudy ran after Bailey.

Back turned to the well, Mr. Sam sawed a board. Trudy sprinted to try to head Bailey off, but the little girl ran dangerously close to the big hole. Without paying attention to where she was going, she kept running until she zipped straight toward the gaping well, which dropped deep down to the stream of cool underground water. The circumference of the hole was big enough for Bailey to fall into. Trudy grabbed her.

"Let me go. I have to get the ducks back to their mommy." After squirming out of Trudy's grasp, Bailey started running again. Up the short hill and closer to the well Bailey went. What if Bailey didn't recognize the uncovered hole for what it was?

"Stop," Billy yelled. "You're headed toward the well hole."

Buddy screamed. Without the familiar wooden stand, it must have looked different to Bailey. What was she thinking? She dashed toward the ducks without seeming to hear anybody. She ran so fast she couldn't stop.

"Oh no, Bailey," Buddy jumped as he yelled, but she paid no attention. The shouts roared, leaving no distinct words. Bailey ran straight toward the hole.

When Trudy yelled, "Be quiet, everybody," she merely added more noise.

The two ducklings fell into the shaft, and Bailey threw on the brakes. With rocks and sandy dirt flying into the hole, she skidded toward the edge. She lost her balance and fell.

Trudy was too breathless to formulate words. A grunt lodged in her throat.

Bailey struggled to her knees. Sliding in the loose sand around her, she stood. Flailing her arms, she leaned over to look for the ducks. "The poor little ducks."

"Move back." Who said that?

She emitted an ear-splitting shriek as she leaned forward to look for the ducklings in the well. Before anybody could reach her, she fell again.

Trudy took giant steps—the biggest and fastest she had ever taken in her life—toward her friend Bailey, who was slipping into the hole. The six-year-old tried to save herself by jumping to grab the grass on the far side. Instead of gaining a hold, Bailey pulled the grass up by the roots. She slipped toward death's grasp.

Mr. Sam lunged toward her, but Trudy reached her first. With more strength than she should have had, just in time to keep Bailey from dropping toward the deep dark pool, Trudy grabbed one of Bailey's arms and brought her other arm around Bailey's waist. She pulled so hard she tore her little friend's dress. Bailey's weight, coupled with the force of pulling, knocked Trudy down. The two of them rolled away from the hole.

Trudy held onto her until Mr. Sam lifted his little daughter into his arms.

"Bailey." His voice quivered. "We could have lost you in the well."

"But what about the ducks?" Bailey said. "Get them out."

"They're probably alive. As soon as we fix the well, we'll draw water to help them out."

"No, Papa. Do it now."

Billy brought two lengths of thin rope from the Model T. "Let's play a game."

"What kind of a game?" Buddy asked.

"The rope game." He tied one end of the rope around his own waist and the other end around Buddy.

Mama Zoe took Bailey from Mr. Sam's arms. Trudy followed them to a shady spot up the hill from the work area. Mama rubbed Trudy's shoulders. "I knew I could count on you, Trude."

Five minutes later, Bailey wiggled to free herself. "I'm ready to get up now." She stood. "Billy, can we play the rope game too?"

He tied Trudy and Bailey the same way. They remained tied until Mr. Sam finished the job. Bucket after bucket of water failed to reveal any evidence of the little ducks. He drew water until the well was dry.

"Let's go eat some lunch." Mr. Sam left with the twins.

~

Zoe had no appetite. That morning she'd planned to cook some fresh vegetables, but Samuel's surprise visit consumed every moment. Trudy and Billy would have to make do with cold cornbread and hard-boiled eggs. Afterwards, all three of them reclined on the porch until King barked.

"Samuel," Zoe muttered as she sat up. She smoothed her hair, wiped her sleepy face, and righted her dress.

"I'm sorry I woke you up." Samuel and the twins bounced on the ground beside the porch. A solid round green watermelon rolled back and forth in front of him.

"Look what we've got," Buddy shouted.

"Could you hold this a minute, Billy? I need to get those old newspapers out of the Ford." Samuel brought a long sturdy knife from the auto. Trudy fetched an assortment of spoons and forks from the kitchen.

The cracking sound of the melon in Samuel's expert hands drew the others to look. "Our first watermelon of the season."

The meat, the inside of the watermelon, would it be red, or had Samuel's ears fooled him when he thumped? Samuel didn't need to be disappointed.

Snap—the melon was perfect. He opened it into two equal pieces of red mouthwatering sweet fruit filled with black seeds. For each child, he cut a thin slice to be eaten without silverware. He cut two large pieces for him and Zoe.

The juicy melon was a melody of flavor. No other food could smell fresher, taste better, or look prettier. In the yard, they spat the seeds onto the ground.

"Maybe some watermelons will grow here," Trudy said.

Billy rolled his eyes. "Silly sister."

"We're going to take some to sell at the Mercantile," Buddy said. "We've got more than we can eat."

"What do you want us to do with our rinds, Miss Zoe?" Bailey asked.

"Sweetie, I'm not making preserves or pickles this year. Not enough time. Son, get a bucket. We'll feed them to the pigs."

Samuel cleaned the mess with skill.

"Tomorrow I thought I'd take you boys out with the bird dogs to get some off-season practice. We'll go to town and buy some ammunition. All right, Zoe?"

"Fine."

"For a few hours we'll swap Bailey for Billy," Samuel said.

Zoe reached a loving hand toward Bailey, who didn't know how close she had come to drowning in the well that morning, or perhaps she was too young to understand. Trudy wouldn't be able to deal with the aftermath of the trauma so easily.

"If you girls have time, you can ride with us. We won't be in town long."

"I suppose we girls could take time off to shop," Zoe said. "We'll finish the chores by seven in the morning. As soon as we put the milk away and wash up, we'll be ready."

Zoe's day ended with hopes for a break in the routine the following morning. After chores, supper, and prayers, she waited hours for sleep to relax her weary being. Although she had worked harder most other days, she hadn't been as tired since the day the house burned. Two months had passed without her monthly visitor. The first month she blamed its absence on all she was going through. Having to sleep near her children, she was glad not to have the curse—one more problem to solve. She would have needed more privacy than she had.

The second month she was sure. Even so, she didn't expect to bear another child. Once she delivered a baby boy after six months. By the time she saw his perfectly formed little body, he had already gone to heaven. Since Trudy's birth, she had conceived four other babies she lost within the first three months. She believed five little Camerons lived in heaven with William.

Zoe and William had hoped for more children, but disappointment brought suffering. Each time, she had been careful not to lift, not to get too tired, not to get upset, and to eat healthy meals. Still she couldn't carry another baby to term.

As a widow with no one to stand by her, she knew her womb wouldn't support another fetus to full development. That summer she didn't have time to take care of herself. She would lose the baby any day now not because she neglected her care—there simply was no opportunity to pamper her body.

After this miscarriage, she wouldn't fuss over herself. She'd keep working to take care of Trudy and Billy. As with four of the other losses, she wouldn't tell them. It wasn't proper to talk to her children about such things. Too bad William would not be with her to comfort her.

Beyond her concern over being with child, she experienced generalized uneasiness. She tried to turn it over to the Lord, but she kept taking it back. Shadows, which seemed to her unusual, passed in her peripheral vision as she sat on the upended bucket at the window. She must have imagined she saw them. If someone had walked by, King would have barked. She went back to bed.

As soon as Zoe drifted to sleep, Trudy cried out, "I'm afraid."

"I can't get any sleep," Billy said. "Tell Sister to be quiet."

"Come here, Child." Zoe took Trudy to the porch, where they sat snuggled close to King. The dog didn't have his usual musty odor. He must have bathed in the fishing hole earlier.

"It was awful, Mama." Trudy sniffled.

"I loved the way you saved Bailey's life."

"But she could have died like Papa and Miss Sarah. Horrible."

"Not really." Zoe sat up. "We never die."

"That's not true. Papa died in the fire. Miss Sarah died giving birth to the twins."

"If we know Jesus, our spirits live in heaven with him forever." Zoe pulled Trudy near. "What I mean is if we let Jesus into our hearts and know him as a friend."

"Oh."

"When our lives end, we just go be with Jesus," Zoe said. "It's sad for the people left here on earth, but the ones in heaven aren't sad. No tears in heaven. Remember? 'And I shall dwell in the house of the Lord forever.'"

"Why didn't Papa fix the well?" Trudy asked.

"None of us can do everything we should," Zoe said. "He tried."

"Mama."

"Yes, Trudy?"

"I love you."

"I love you too. Let's get some sleep. Tomorrow we're going to have fun."

~Chapter Twenty-Two~

After the morning's work, Trudy washed the milk smells away with lye soap. She changed her dress, softened her hands with rosewater and glycerin, and sat still for Mama to braid her hair, Mama was right: the day would be good. Rarely did they go to town with no purpose except pleasure. Being careful not to kick the watermelons, both families loaded into the Model T.

After Mr. Sam unloaded the watermelons, he announced, "Coca-Colas for everybody." They lined up for their sodas. Jethro McKenzie stared at them, but Trudy wasn't in the mood to let him dampen her spirits. He cleaned with his feather duster while she stood in line.

Creepy. She couldn't let him see her roll her eyes; so she looked straight ahead.

"What can I do for you today?" Mr. Jake wiped his hands on his apron.

"We need some shotgun shells for my twelve gauge. Number eight shot."

"Okay, Sam." He got the shells.

"These boys need some shooting lessons. I'm taking my bird dogs." Mr. Sam walked over to tell Bailey goodbye. Mrs. Bently was giving Trudy a lesson in fabric selection in case Mama would purchase some at a future time.

"Time to go, girls."

"Already?" Bailey said.

Mama took a deep breath. "Would you girls like to walk home? It's kind of far. If you get tired though, we can stop and rest."

Trudy looked at Bailey. "What do you think?"

"Let's do it."

After checking out the new merchandise in the store, the three ladies went outside to stroll up and down the boardwalk. Trudy couldn't believe what her mother did afterwards. Even though they had already had a treat, Mama went back inside and bought three hand-rolled ice cream cones.

"Please put those on my ticket, Jake."

"I love days like this when the grownups act like kids," Trudy said.

"Miss Zoe, I wish you could be my mommy." Bailey beamed up at Mama.

"How sweet," Mama said.

They walked two miles down the road and turned right to go up the hill toward home. The guineas shrieked, "Come back. Come back. Come back. Chi, chi, chi, chi!"

"Something's wrong. The guineas are fussing," Bailey said.

"What's happening?" Trudy asked.

"I don't know, but the guineas tell us when strangers come to our house."

They reached the Bentons' house. "Miss Zoe, I'm so tired," Bailey said. "Let's stop here at my house and rest."

"All right." The door was not locked; so they went inside. Nothing seemed to be out of order.

~

A few days later Zoe looked up to see Samuel driving with the twins to the cabin. "I've come to be neighborly. What do you need help with?"

"It seems I always need something," Zoe said. "The lawyer sent me a letter. He wants me to come discuss the estate."

"When?"

"Today."

"How were you planning to go to Taylorsburg?"

"I was planning to walk. It isn't as hard to do as I thought. I decided not to take the wagon. I was going to stop by and see if I could leave Billy and Trudy at your place. I was afraid they might get upset about the meeting."

"Zoe, anytime, I'll be glad to give you a trip into town."

"I know, but I get tired of imposing on you."

"How many times do I have to explain that I want to help you?" Samuel had an exasperated tone.

"I wish I could do everything for myself."

"I can take a few more watermelons to the Mercantile," he said.

"I don't know about leaving these four at home. Things didn't go well the last time."

"We'll behave." Billy spoke for the group. As he slung his tuft of dark hair back, he wrinkled his nose, which was spotted with a few fresh freckles,

"Son, I can't believe your hair grows so fast."

"You can go to the barber shop with Buddy and me next week," Samuel said. He pitched his next remark to the children. "Miss Zoe, let's give them one more opportunity to see if they can stay by themselves for a few hours without getting into trouble. What do you think?"

Zoe looked dramatic. "Okay, I hope the misadventures of the previous time we left you have depleted Trudy's stockpile of mischievous ideas for escapades."

"This time, why don't you stay at our house?" Samuel laid down the rules. "No food fights. No playing in dangerous places. Don't even touch the stove. The guns are locked up. They're off limits. Don't try to use a knife for anything."

"Yes, sir," Buddy said.

Watermelons waited in a neat stack in his shed. Samuel transferred a load of them to the back floor of the Model T.

"I want all of you to understand. Billy is in charge." Samuel wiped his face with his handkerchief. "He is twelve years old, and I respect his judgment. See that you do too."

"We'll be good. We understand. We'll behave. Promise." All four of them chimed in.

~

"What fun can we do?" While the four children wandered through the Bentons' front yard, Trudy considered the possibilities. Maybe it was time for her to allow Brother to take charge since Mr. Sam and Mama wanted him to.

"Chase the guineas," Buddy suggested.

"I don't think so," Trudy said. "They are our friends."

"When I grow up, I'm going to be a detective." Billy moved to the top step of the front porch. "I'm practically grown now."

"I never thought about having a detective for a brother."

Billy rubbed his face to see if anything was growing on it yet.

"I was planning to be a piano teacher, but since I don't have a piano maybe I can be a detective too." Even if she'd owned a piano, she had no time to practice.

"I want to be a mommy. So many children need one. When I grow up and get married, I can find some children who want me to be their mommy. I want lots of children." Bailey looked dreamy-eyed. "Y'all want to know a secret? I want Miss Zoe to be my mommy."

"I want to be a detective like Billy," Buddy said. "You're my best friend, B.J." To the girls he added, "Him and me know everything. If I don't know something, just ask Billy. If he don't know something, ask me."

"I can be a detective and a mommy too," Bailey said.

Zeke and Spot licked the children's fingers.

"Go back to bed under the porch." Buddy poked the dogs. "Y'all can't play. This is business."

Tails tucked in disappointment, the bird dogs returned to their usual spots.

"Let's all be detectives. We can start now." Billy, assuming the role of boss, stood on the porch as he looked down at his subjects.

"I want to play." Bailey rushed up the steps and stood by him.

"We're not playing. This is real." Billy folded his arms in front of them and stuck out his chest. "We're forming a private investigators' company. Cameron and Benton, Pinkertons."

"We need a crime," Trudy said.

"That's all right. We can investigate until we find a crime. Just do as I direct."

"Oh good, we're detectives." For once Trudy allowed her brother to be the boss.

"Great." Billy laid the groundwork. "We'll find some clues. Listen up. You must report any evidence you find to me, the president of the company and the chief detective."

"How do we start?" Buddy looked up through his blond curls covering his sincere blue eyes.

"We'll look for clues." Billy shook hands with Buddy.

"Like hunting Easter eggs," Bailey said.

"Right. We'll work in teams. Buddy is my assistant. You girls can be another team."

"Where do we start?" Trudy took a practical approach.

"Right here. We'll work all over the yard. The boys will go this way." Billy stepped down into the yard and pointed. "The girls will go that way. If you're not sure about a piece of evidence, collect it all the same. When we stop, mark the spot you checked last with a circle of rocks."

"Yes, sir," Bailey said as the first investigation began.

Before the others had time to focus their eyes on the grass, Buddy held up a coin. "I've already found something—a piece of bucket money."

"I'm not believing this," Bailey said. She inspected it. "Yep, it's bucket money all right."

"We ought to put it in the bucket." Buddy held it tight.

"First, we'll put it inside a little bag so we can show Mr. Sam which one it was." Billy gestured with his hand the way Reverend Black did in sermons.

Buddy led the group into the house. "Come on. I know where Papa keeps stuff like that. He'll be so glad. Here we go."

He flung the utility closet door open. The shelf where they kept the bucket of coins . . . was . . . empty.

"Maybe your papa moved it to a safer place behind some of the big supplies." Trudy made a practical suggestion.

They looked behind the cleaning buckets. Opened the pantry. Not behind the flour, cornmeal, sugar, or lard. Looked behind all the other containers large enough to hide a bucket behind. Nothing. Lifted the tablecloth. Not under the table. Checked all the cabinets. Where did Mr. Sam put the bucket? Why did he not tell the twins?

Buddy gave the group a couple of bags to hold evidence.

"Thank you, Detective Buddy." Billy sounded more important than ever. "There's no reason to keep tearing up the house. Mr. Sam wouldn't be happy about it. One more idea though. Is it too big to fit in the gun cabinet, Buddy?"

"Oh, yes. It's a regular size big bucket."

"Is it too big to fit under a bed?" Trudy asked.

"Our beds is low."

"Hmm. We can't do anything else in here," Billy said. "We need to get back to work in the yard. No time to waste. No telling what else we'll find."

They rushed back to the yard. "Come on, Bailey. We've got to try hard. They're ahead of us," Trudy said.

"No, Sister. It ain't a competition. What's important is doing a thorough investigation," Billy said.

"How do you know all this?" Trudy placed her hands on her hips.

"I read detective stories at school."

"I didn't know you were so smart," Trudy said.

"Billy is fantastic smart." Buddy looked annoyed.

"Let's don't fool around."

"Chief Detective Billy, shall we resume combing the area?" Trudy laughed at herself.

Billy held up a piece of red and yellow fabric about three by four inches in size. "I don't know what it means, but it may be important."

"I saw that cloth. A stranger was playing dominoes in MacGregor's Mercantile. He was wearing a yellow and red shirt just like that." Trudy had an epiphany.

"Aha, what did he look like?" President Billy probed.

"He was skinny, thin skinny. He had a long beard and beady eyes, all sunken into his head." Trudy tried to visualize every detail.

"What color were his eyes?"

"I'll have to think about that. His hair was black, and his beard was sort of like a polecat—mixed black with gray. What looked so unusual was his beard. It was the biggest thing about him."

Billy requested another of Buddy's bags. "Let's place this inside here. It's more evidence. Now, back to work."

"I found something." Bailey held up another coin. They all scurried about the place where she found it. All the Pinkertons found coins.

Billy counted. "Seven coins."

"Something weird is happening here," Trudy observed. It was both unsettling and significant.

"It hasn't rained lately," Billy said. "Look for tracks. They'll be faint ones in the sandy dirt where the grass don't grow."

Trudy found some. "These are too narrow to be Mr. Sam's shoe prints."

Billy studied them. "There are two people's tracks here. Notice some of them look like cowboy boots. See how the heels dig into the dirt? See how they are long and pointed. These others have a crease across the sole of the right foot."

The other Pinkertons paid attention.

"These are the tracks I've been seeing by our house and barn. Let's cover them with washtubs so when it rains they won't be washed away." The boys fetched galvanized tubs.

~Chapter Twenty-Three~

When Sam drove into his garage, all four children stood nearby. With grave expressions, they waited in a line.

"What now?" Sam asked.

"They all look well and intact," Zoe said.

"Papa, Papa," Buddy shouted as he jumped up and down. "Some of the dream bucket money got spilled in the yard. Where did you put the bucket?"

The color blanched from Sam's face. With the other five close behind, he bounded inside to open the utility closet.

"We wanted to put these coins back in the bucket," Buddy explained.

It was a tense moment. Sam's jaw worked. If they could have heard his feeling, it would have been a high-pitched-single-note sound tangling his brain like steel being filed. Sucking air through his teeth, Sam made a whistling hiss.

"I didn't move the bucket," Sam said. "Come show me where you found the coins."

They loped to the place in the yard.

"Good job, boys and girls. I'm upset but not with y'all. What's under the washtubs?"

Billy spoke up. "Footprints. Shoeprints in fact."

"Show me."

"They're narrow." Trudy turned a washtub over to show him. Bailey turned another one over.

"I feel violated." The rage swelling from the core of Sam's body turned his face red. He worked his fist as he clinched his teeth and the muscles of his jaws hardened. "Anything else?"

"A scrap of cloth." Billy dug into the other bag.

"A man in the Mercantile was wearing a shirt like that. He was a fellow I don't know. He . . . had a great big black and white beard." Trudy paused. "Skinny, and he had snake eyes, purple blue I think."

Samuel, walking away, reached for his nonexistent beard. "I need to think." He walked back toward the four children. "What were you kids doing when you found these things?"

"Being Pinkertons."

"We're detectives," Buddy said. "We looked for evidence in case crimes have been committed."

He placed his arm around Buddy. "Son, it looks like you found one."

"Samuel." Zoe caught up with him.

"Yes?" He looked at her from a face made tight with a frown.

"Let's load into the motor car and go back to town. You need to discuss this with Jake," Zoe said.

"Mama, you're right," Trudy said. "That would be the next logical step. You are smart."

"What if Jake? No, I know there's not a more honest man anywhere," Sam said. "You're right. I need to pull him aside and talk with him."

"It's not safe to leave the children alone anymore," Zoe said.

"Besides," Sam said, "they are the ones who found the problem. They deserve to be included. Load up, everybody." Samuel cranked the Model T. "Let's go."

Trudy snuggled close to Zoe; Bailey sat in the back between the boys.

Men—especially daddies-- weren't supposed to cry, but how could Sam fight the tears when someone violated his precious children?

Driving back into town, he set his jaw like a rock. The trip gave him time to formulate his thoughts.

"Y'all wait in here a minute. This won't take long." He blocked the wheel and killed the motor.

Inside he said, "Come out here a minute, Jake."

He and Jake MacGregor stood and talked outside the Mercantile. When they finished, Trudy swapped seats with Bailey. "It's your turn, to sit up here."

Sam cranked the Model T and drove the two families back to his house.

~

Trudy buried her head in her arms. It didn't sink in on the twins how bad this was. It was like the day they lost Papa and the house all at once, but not as bad. It took time to get stuff straight in folks' heads.

As soon as they piled out, Billy said, "We've got to get back to work."

"Yeah," Buddy agreed.

"From now on we're Pinkertons no matter what we're doing," Billy said.

"What does that mean?" Buddy asked.

"Even when we don't look like we're working, we will be," Billy said. "It's good to work when we're just acting like regular kids. People won't suspect us."

"Good point, Brother."

"We now have an important case," Billy explained.

Mr. Sam turned toward Mama with what appeared to Trudy to be a boyfriend look. It was more evidence she could use in another investigation in the future.

"Yep," Buddy said. Back at the Bentons' house, the children returned to the yard, Zeke and Spot came back out, Buddy fussed at them. "Dogs, how did y'all let a burglar steal the dream bucket?"

"Don't jump, Zeke. I'm tired," Bailey said. "Can we do something else?"

Billy looked as though he were lost in thought. "I know. Let's make our business cards. Bailey, would you go and ask Mr. Sam for some paper?"

"I'll go with you," Trudy said. The girls went inside while the boys leaned against the porch.

One of the magnificent things about Billy was the way he changed into a problem solver when the family needed him. He was all right even if he got on Trudy's nerves sometimes. He was the best big brother a girl ever had.

Bailey led Trudy to the north parlor, where they kept their school and office supplies in the roll top desk. It was the room where the Bentons sat on special occasions when they had guests.

Trudy couldn't believe what she saw. Mr. Sam sat with his head on a table. Her mother placed her hands on his shoulders. He stood, turned toward her, and placed one arm around her. A one-armed hug. They kissed—her mama and Mr. Sam kissed. It was a light kiss, a little peck, not a big mushy one like Mama and Papa shared the night before the fire. After they finished the kiss and hug, Mr. Sam moved away.

Trudy looked at Bailey, and Bailey looked at Trudy. Their eyebrows went straight up, and they snickered in silence as they backed out of the room.

"Oooh, Trudy. Can you believe they kissed? It makes me sick," Bailey whispered.

"I thought it was sugary sweet." Trudy beamed as she spoke in a soft voice. "What do we do now?"

Bailey cleared her throat. "Papa, could we have some paper and pencils?"

Seeming startled, Mr. Sam and Mama jumped farther back from one another. "Sure. Let me help you." He looked for the supplies while Mama looked out the window. Did Trudy imagine she saw a dreamy look in her mama's eyes?

Mr. Sam handed them some paper and four pencils. Outside Trudy led the group away from the house.

"I thought we'd work here on the porch," Billy said.

"First, we have to talk," Trudy whispered. She led the others away from the house.

As soon as they reached the edge of the yard, Bailey said, "Guess what."

"Yeah," Trudy said. "Guess what. We done some more Pinkerton work. We discovered something big."

"Tell us," Buddy demanded.

With a look Trudy told them she was in the know. "Your papa and our mama were . . . were . . . were . . . k-i-s-s-i-n-g."

"Nasty." Buddy said. He curled his lip, twisted his nose, spat.

Billy took a contemplative stance. "We need to file this information away. It may be evidence for a future case. Right now, we have to get down to business on this. While y'all were gone we found a bunch of buttons."

"You're right, Brother. We're supposed to stay on this main case," Trudy said. "It's important, not just little kid important either. Come on. Let's work on our cards. Who knows when we'll need to present them to a new client?"

They went back to the porch to work. "What to put on the card?" Buddy asked.

"First, get some scissors, Buddy, and then we'll talk about it," Billy said.

"Okay." Buddy rushed inside. A moment later, walking like a cat, he sneaked back out the front door.

"Where are the scissors?" Billy asked. They needed to cut the paper into smaller sections to make cards.

Buddy's eyes were huge with surprise. "I forgot." He looked around at the others. "They were holding hands, and Papa kissed her on the cheek."

They giggled. Buddy returned to get the scissors.

"Don't run with the scissors," Trudy reminded him. He slammed the door when he went back inside. "Papa, we need some scissors." Buddy giggled as he returned.

"It don't mean nothing," Billy explained as he folded his paper. "Mama's sad about losing our papa, and your papa's upset about losing the bucket of money. He's always sad about losing your mama. She feels bad about losing the house. She worries about money for us to live on. I catch her crying. They're just comforting each other. I know it's weird though. Now let's get back to work."

In her mind, Trudy gave him credit for growing up. He'd be thirteen before time for school to start. Soon the twins would turn seven. She hoped they all had better birthdays than hers was.

Billy held up his paper to show them how to fold it to make four cards. "Print your name on each card. And then 'Cameron and Benton, Pinkertons.' "

"I can't do all that." Bailey held her pencil up and blinked. "I'm just a little kid, but, but I'm a smart kid. I'm big enough to be a Pinkerton."

"It's all right. Write your name and 'P' on each card. Make at least four cards."

"I asked Jesus to help us find the dream bucket," Buddy said.

"You're a good artist." Bailey squinted at Trudy's fancy borders.

"Do y'all think Mama is pretty?" Trudy asked.

"She's beautiful." Bailey put her pencil down.

"Yes." Buddy nodded.

"You know, I never supposed she was until the day of the fire. Up till then she was simply Mama. It's like I saw her in a whole new way." Billy said.

"I know. Maybe Mr. Sam started seeing her in a different light that day. He seems to think she's a fine lady," Trudy said.

~

"I feel violated," Samuel told Zoe. They sat beside each other, and he leaned against her.

"I'm so sorry this happened." Zoe held his hand.

"My children don't seem to understand the loss we're going through. They're still innocent enough to believe I can fix anything. I built hope in their little hearts. When the disappointment sinks in, it will be overwhelming."

"Yes," Zoe agreed.

"One minute everything is good, and then it's all gone."

"It's things, Samuel. Just things. You still have Bailey and Buddy."

164

"And I have enough to live well—to provide well for the twins. The bucket money was our extra."

"Do you ever think about what *you* need, what you would enjoy?" Zoe asked. "All you do seems to be for other people."

"To see the ones close to me happy gives me joy."

They sat for a long time.

"Zoe, I don't want to let the children see how broken I am."

~

Zoe felt kindheartedness for Samuel, her best friend. With the closing of the afternoon, he and his children followed her and her brood to the Cameron farm to milk. Having been allowed by Trudy to take a turn milking One Horn, she balanced herself on an inverted bucket in the privileged spot adjacent to the udder of the matriarchal cow. Thanks to Samuel, One Horn now wore a bell.

She was aware that her feelings extended beyond kindliness. She wanted the touch of his strong arms around her during the times when the challenges of the night overcame her. In the moments when she was honest with herself, she knew she was in love with her neighbor, but she couldn't afford to allow her emotions to guide the steps of her life.

Guard my heart, Lord. Right now I want to hold this precious man in my arms. Please wrap him in your love, since I'm not able to.

As she emptied her thoughts to the Lord, she filled the huge bucket with hot frothy milk. Gingerly she stood being careful not to spill the milk or wrench her aching back.

"I'll carry that for you." Opening the stable door, Samuel reached for the heavy load.

She hoped she didn't speak her thoughts.

~Chapter Twenty-Four~

Zoe longed to rejoice in the Lord's house on Sunday despite all their losses. She placed her hands on her middle. No one would be able to see she was carrying a child if she stood straight and wore loose clothes. Nothing mattered to her as much as her children did, even if people suspected her condition and even if tongues wagged about how she had no right to go out in public when she was in the family way, especially without a husband. Furthermore, she kept showing up with a man during the time when she should be mourning.

She wanted to comfort Samuel. His heart was broken. She wondered what she could say to make him feel better. She longed to hold him the way she held Trudy and Billy when they needed comfort, but he would get the wrong impression for good reason—her feelings were like a loud musical composition being performed by the town band. How could she keep him from noticing? She didn't know how to silence her heart.

She had another serious problem for which she knew no solution. Billy's feet had outgrown his shoes. Only impoverished children went to church barefoot. William Cameron would never have allowed his son to appear in public on Sunday without shoes. "Wear these thin socks, Billy." His development over the last few months had amazed her.

"My feet hurt, Mama." He yanked at his shoes.

"I'll take you to the Mercantile and work out something with Mr. Jake."

"I can take more corn and peas." The boy's words ripped into her brokenness.

Samuel had all the pain a person should have to bear, but he still wanted to help her. He was a good neighbor giving them a ride to church. She wished she didn't have to depend on him. Pretty soon she wouldn't be able to accept a ride from him.

Her feelings were like a run-away horse. She couldn't trust them. What she felt was wrong. She needed to use common sense.

She considered other ways they could go to church. They had two other alternatives: to walk through the woods or to hitch up the wagon. To walk to Taylorsburg and then to Friendship Church was too far. If they walked through the woods, they'd have to rely on the angels to protect them. They'd have to walk a log to cross Lost Creek. It was impossible to go over Logans' Ridge. The unruly dogs would tear into them. If they took the farm wagon, they'd arrive too dirty to be comfortable in God's house.

Billy, sitting on the bench by the table, stared out the window.

"We could go to Calhoun Church in Hot Coffee, but we've always gone to Friendship. It wouldn't feel right," Zoe said.

Billy dropped his head between his knees and sobbed audibly.

"Son, the Lord is going to get us through this. I promise you'll have a new pair of shoes by next Sunday. Get up and wash your face."

Trudy crept from person to person. Billy elbowed her. Zoe failed to hug her.

Quarter of an hour later, Mrs. Zoe Cameron with the Bible in her hand and new life within her womb stepped toward the Model T. She knew more reasons to go than to stay home. Trudy, carrying a little second-hand purse, followed. Each child used to have a Bible.

Lord, thank you for insulating us from pride.

~

Walking out of church, Samuel let his eyes caress Zoe. He was blessed to have Zoe as his friend. He could never do as much for her as she'd done for him.

"That breeze feels good," he told Zoe as he drove back to the cabin after church. "It's a little cooler today than it has been."

When they reached the cabin, King ran along beside the auto, until a rabbit enticed him to go on a chase through the cornfield on the south side of the road. Bailey sat in the front, Trudy sat in the back between the boys. "Just curious. Where's your honey tree?"

"You can see it if you drive to the edge of the front yard where the cattle gate is," Zoe said. "Look straight to the right."

"Oh, okay. We'll drive down that way. Bailey, don't go near it. Remind the others to stay away from it." Puttering along, Samuel stole glances at Zoe. He wished he could fathom the pools of darkness within her mind. If she'd tell him more, he could help.

She pointed toward the tree. A black shadow loomed over the honey hole. A giant black mass moved on the trunk of the tree. Samuel caught a glimpse of Zoe biting her bottom lip and looking sideways at him. With as little noise as possible, he circled in the yard and back to the road. As fast as he could, he drove toward his house. King followed him from the front porch to the well before returning to the cabin.

"What's going on?" Billy asked.

Neither Samuel nor Zoe answered. The bear, a happy animal, fulfilling his purpose in life—eating all it could find—represented in Samuel's mind a threat to the nearby people. He doubted there could be co-existence. Without a sense of morality, the bear would enter Zoe's cabin to devour whatever he could find. Samuel felt he had no choice but to shoot it.

~

"Bailey, Sweetheart, as soon as we stop, I need you to get in the back seat," Zoe said. "I know it's crowded, but you'll have to sit in a lap."

"We're in too big a hurry to get out. Don't kill the auto." He hopped out, chocked a wheel, and ran inside his house.

Samuel returned a minute later with his Swedish Mauser rifle and a Remington hunting rifle, along with ammo for each.

"I can load those for you," Zoe offered. With nimble fingers, she went to work as they rode.

"What is it?" Buddy asked.

"Shh. Let's keep quiet." Samuel returned to the cattle gap. With his gun in his hand, he climbed out of the Model T and scotched the wheel. Through the scope, he took aim at the black bear in the beehive.

Pow! The bear catapulted upward before falling. On its way down it emitted a prolonged bawl. When it hit the ground, it ran with a limp. Meanwhile, Samuel cocked his rifle. It ran away from them but abruptly circled back their direction. Leaving a trail of blood, it ran on all fours with its head slightly lowered, his eyes intense. Approaching the Model T, the wounded bear growled.

"Be quiet," Zoe whispered. Buddy, Bailey, and Trudy squeezed Billy. He encircled them in his arms.

Zoe stepped onto the running board and down to the ground. She moved clear of the Model T, cocked the weapon, and aimed at the bear. She had the target fixed in her sight in case Samuel's shot failed to stop the beast. She edged to the right while she kept beside Samuel without walking behind or in front of him. Her father had taught her as a young girl to shoot. Self-assured with a gun, she didn't hesitate.

The bear was too close for Samuel to rely on his scope with absolute accuracy. As the snarling bear moved closer, she steadied her hold on the gun.

"Shoot, Zoe!" She didn't have a second to delay. In Samuel's command, she heard the strength of the voices of both her father and her husband. She couldn't allow her hands to be nervous. Steady. Blood dripping behind the wounded beast continued to mark the zigzagging pattern as it approached, moaning in angry pain.

When she fired, the bullet whistled straight toward the bear's head. She hit the spot where she aimed, but the rifle kicked her shoulder. Blood gushing from between its ears poured over its brown muzzle. In the meantime, Samuel fired another shot, hitting the animal's side. Within twenty feet of Zoe, it flew up again before it collapsed. The adults returned to the front seat. No one said any words, nobody breathed aloud.

King, fresh from chasing another rabbit, waited under the cabin. Despite the dog's bravery, he was gun-shy. When they drove by, he emerged from his safe place with his head down, tail tucked, and body slinking to the side. As usual, he followed the automobile to the well before going back.

Zoe adhered to the rules of gun safety as she held the weapons. The children sat speechless in the back seat. From the corner of her eye, she saw Samuel wiping perspiration from his face with his handkerchief as he shook his head. He beamed at her.

"All of you are coming to our house for lunch," he said when they arrived at his home. He didn't ask—he told. With face muscles hard as granite, Zoe forced a smile.

"Why don't you relax a minute while the kids help me get lunch ready?" He unloaded the ammunition before locking the weapons inside his gun cabinet.

Zoe said. "All of you be sure to wash your hands."

"Just sit here." Returning to the kitchen, he pointed toward a chair at the kitchen table. "You look a little pale."

"I'm fine," she said.

With the children's help, Samuel served the meal promptly.

Zoe picked at her food. She stared at her plate of baked chicken and vegetables in stony silence. On a normal Sunday, she would have marveled at Samuel's ability to cook. That Sunday afternoon she sat with her eyes closed.

How could she keep these children safe the way they'd been living? She wasn't ready to leave the farm. They had nowhere to go, but she'd put them in danger. She didn't even own a gun.

She didn't want one without a way to lock it away from Billy and Trudy. Both of them inherited their father's impulsiveness.

How could she teach them to respect a gun when it took all her time to keep them from being malnourished?

The baby needed her to eat, but she couldn't.

"I'm proud of you, Papa." Bailey left her place at the table to go hug Samuel.

"It all happened too fast for me to believe it," Trudy said.

"From now on all of us need to be much more careful. Who knows how many bears roam through this area?" Samuel said. "Did you all see the way Miss Zoe shot that bear?"

"Mama, I think it's time I learned more about how to use a gun," Billy said.

Zoe barely heard them. Her mouth full of the one bite she tried to swallow, she bolted from the table. She walked until she left the room. When she reached the kitchen, she broke into a run. Perspiration chilled her face as she leaned from a porch post to retch.

Trudy ran to her and placed an arm around her waist. "Go back inside, Sweetheart." She couldn't have her daughter see her disintegrate.

~

"Mama's sick, and she won't let me help her. Mr. Sam, please take her a wet rag."

Bailey, with her arms on Mr. Sam's shoulders, stood clinging. The boys kept their places. Trudy went to the right side of Mr. Sam while Bailey maintained her position on his left.

He rose. "Girls, go back to the table. Stay inside."

~

Samuel rushed toward Zoe with a clean wet dishtowel for her face. Holding onto the porch post, she continued to heave.

"It's all right, Zo."

Her eyes rolled back as she fell limp. He took her gently into his arms and laid her on the porch to recover.

"Girl, let's prop your feet up." He turned over a straight-back chair to support her legs with the back of it. After turning her head onto her right side, he placed the cool cloth on her neck. He cradled her head with his hands.

"Go back inside, kids." All four faces left their spots in the doorway as they backed up. "Miss Zoe needs to be quiet. Oh, uh, Trudy, could you hand me a pillow?"

In a tiny voice that seemed to come from somewhere far away, Zoe said, "I have to be strong for the children."

He slipped the pillow under her head. Sitting on the floor beside her, he stroked her with the cool cloth until she recovered.

"I fainted?"

"Yes," he said.

She closed her eyes again.

Samuel looked at the emaciated frame of his cherished neighbor as she went in and out of consciousness. Was malnourishment causing her belly to pooch a bit? Her respirations were shallow. Her pulse was fast and thready. Sadness mingled with fear as he sensed how wasted she had become in a few weeks. Her eyes were sunken, and her eyelids were the color of orchids.

"I've tried to take care of you, Zoe, but I've failed." His heart ached for the person who was the best friend he had, his tutor through the time of caring for two infants, who soon became toddlers, and eventually first graders. Zoe taught him to diaper, helped him feed the two babies, sewed clothes for his little girl and boy. He had fond memories of the way she loved to present the little garments she made. During the first year of his grief, William and Zoe kept him from going out of his mind.

I don't even know if I handled the bear problem the way I should have. I knew she could back me up with a gun, but it kicked her hard. She must have thought I wasn't much of a man, having a woman back me up. I want to take care of her, but she seems to resent my help. Dear God, what am I supposed to do?

For starters, he'd reassure the children. He called them in the calmest voice he could muster. "Buddy and Bailey, change to your play clothes. Trudy and Billy, come here please."

The Cameron children tiptoed to the porch. Both tear-stained faces looked down at him. Trudy mouthed, "Is Mama going to die?"

"Your mama's fine. She just fainted. We're going to have to make sure she gets enough to eat and drink from now on." He gave them a moment to absorb what he said. "I'll sit here on the side of the porch with her a few minutes."

The children stood in the yard while Samuel watched Zoe.

"I'm all right," she said after several minutes of rest. "Let me help you clean the kitchen."

"No, I'll do it. You just come in here and sit down to keep me company."

She sat leaning on the kitchen table and nibbling from a small bowl of potatoes and carrots.

An hour later he drove the group back home. "Let me go inside and check things over."

"If you insist." Zoe, pale and dazed, spoke in a weak voice.

"This place is not safe," Samuel said. "You can't tolerate the heat with the windows closed, but if you leave the windows open, a bear can hop inside. Furthermore, he can undo your door latch."

"We'll stay here and harvest the fields and garden," Zoe said. "We'll tend to the livestock and milk the cows."

"You're being foolish, Zoe."

"No, Samuel. I'm trusting God."

"I need you to stay here with the girls." He looked around. "Trudy, Bailey, come here. Keep an eye on Mama Zoe."

"Yes, sir."

"Billy and Buddy, come with me." Samuel looked around at Zoe. "That okay with you? We're going to see about that carcass."

"Sure." Zoe's eyes fluttered.

"I want to go, Papa," Bailey said.

"Next time, Sister." Samuel bent over and kissed her cheek. "I need you to help Trudy watch after Miss Zoe. She doesn't look like she feels well."

"Okay," Bailey said.

Samuel and the boys went to the barn. "We're taking the tractor." He threw some croker sacks and rope into the trailer. His hog-killing knives and axe remained on the floor of the tractor away from the boys. As soon as he hitched the trailer to the tractor, the boys climbed into the trailer and stood near the front to ride. When they arrived, they found King sitting by the dead bear.

"Are we going to eat the bear meat, Mr. Sam?"

"If the weather was cold, we would," Sam said. "We don't need to risk eating spoiled meat."

"But it's a little cooler today," Billy said. "You said so."

"Reckon I'll risk it."

Sam sliced the jugular vein to drain blood from the bear. Next he used the long sharp knife to cut off the head. "Do you want to keep the head?"

"No, my mama and Trudy will think it's spooky."

"Boys, you're going to need to help me pull." Starting at the rear, he removed the hide. He sliced it loose by sliding the knife between the hide and the flesh. He pulled as Billy and Buddy held the skin taut. With his axe, he whacked off the legs below the knees and split the breastbone. Next he field dressed the carcass by splitting the bear's belly so he could gut it. Out came the bear's heart and liver. The animal was much too big for one man and two boys to load into the trailer in one piece.

"Step back, boys." With the axe, he chopped out the spine to cut the animal into halves. Then he quartered it with his sharp long-handled knife. By placing portions of the meat in the sacks, he made it manageable so he could lift it.

"How much do you think this bear weighed?" Billy helped him scoop the remains of the bear into the trailer.

"I'd say about two hundred pounds."

"That's heavy, Papa." Buddy also tried to help.

"We'll scrape it and tan it. Billy, if you want to, you can make a rug. That is, if it's all right with your mother."

"All right." Billy sounded pleased.

They took the carcass to the pond. Sam dropped it into the water not only to clean it but to cool the meat. Intently working on dressing the bear, Sam lost track of time. He knew he'd need to cook the meat to preserve it. Maybe he could can some of it in Mason jars.

As soon as they finished dousing the bear in the pond, Sam returned it to the trailer. "All right, boys, let's do the chores. I want Mama Zoe to rest. Maybe she's asleep or maybe she won't know we've gone."

He drove back to his house, where Trudy and Bailey sat on the parlor floor surrounded by Bailey's corn-shuck dolls.

"Mama's resting in Bailey's room," Trudy said.

"Oh, hi." Zoe, smoothing her hair, walked into the parlor.

"Mama and Bailey and me already milked," Trudy said.

"You're one stubborn woman." Samuel looked at her with concern. "We'll walk you home."

As they walked along, the boys shared the details of preparing the bear hide. Billy asked, "Mama, can I have the hide for a rug?"

"Sure."

When they reached the cabin, Samuel took Zoe's hand and pulled her toward him. "Goodnight, my friend." He kissed her forehead. It was an innocent little gesture, but he could not hide his emotions. Zoe, his best friend, was no longer simply a friend.

He'd no right to feel the passion that for an instant captivated him. He admired her strength and her love for the children. He found her vulnerability alluring. Standing too close, feeling her breath, nuzzling her luxuriant hair, pressing his lips on the soft skin of her face—he didn't intend to linger so near the woman who had been his mentor and the wife of his beloved friend—he lost himself in the moment.

Her expression, tense and disapproving, called him back to reality.

"May God send your angel to watch over you." He gently released her calloused hand.

~

"Billy, go wash off while I fix supper. Trudy, set the table." Zoe felt wilted. She scrambled eggs and kneaded biscuits. From the shelf she pulled down a jar of blackberry jam Caroline MacGregor had sent them. To keep Trudy happy, she ate.

Forcing a pleasant expression on her face, she went through the motions of mothering. When she was sure her children were asleep, she wept and continued to weep until deep into the night. As much as she feared bears, she feared more that Samuel would hover over her and her children. Early on, she had expected him to blame her for William's death—could she have prevented the accident by being a better wife? Knowing she thought that way too often, she asked God for a release from such thoughts.

Then she moved on to the next worry on her list, the fear he might take the children and place them in an orphanage. What would he do if he realized another child was on the way?

He had tried to convince himself he was in love with her. He wanted to protect her from the challenges she faced. Romance would be convenient. Perhaps she had been too forward, too affectionate.

Fear, anger, and regret took her back to her life with William. She had tried to reason with him, but he wouldn't listen. If he had given her information she needed, their lives would be simpler. She should have been gentler, not nagged him.

But, Lord, I prayed not to think this way, and here I go again.

Before she tried to sleep, she prayed for safety, and she begged for money to buy Billy a new pair of shoes. She hoped the children didn't hear her sniffling. Crying cleared her mind.

No work she did to help Trudy and Billy was ever too tiring or too boring. She was thankful for all they had.

Thank you for protecting us from all kinds of dangers, including black bears. I don't know what I'll tell them when I lose this child. I'll do all in power to keep them from knowing. Lord, I have to leave my problems up to you.

In the darkness, Zoe heard the wild sounds of a screech owl, coyotes, whippoorwills, frogs, crickets, and unidentifiable critters. Somewhere nearby, a skunk perfumed the air. She placed her head on her pillow and slept.

~

In the meantime, Sam had work to do. He fed the twins leftovers from lunch. He cut out hams and shoulders, which he would cure in salt. Zoe was sure to enjoy the hams. He filled as many pots as he could on the top of the stove and parboiled chunks of meat, which he placed in roasting pans in the oven, he filled more pots with meat and poured brine over them. Outside he built a small bonfire and fired up his two wash pots, filled with bear meat and salted water. He put the twins on pallets on the back porch.

Zoe didn't want to accept gifts from him, but she needed meat to feed her children. He'd do what he could to save the meat, which she could add to vegetables to make stews.

He dragged the bear's hide into the back yard not far from his children. He scraped all the meat off. After scrubbing it with lye soap, he stretched it fur side down over a rack from his salt house.

"Time to salt it, right, Papa?" Buddy popped up from his pallet.

"You're right. I'll coat it in salt now." He'd wait a few days for the fur to absorb the salt. Then he'd coat it with alum.

All through the night, Samuel Benton cooked and canned bear meat. While he worked, he spent time contemplating. Who took the dream bucket? What would become of Zoe and her children? Was Eleanor Anne happy? What had he ever done to make her think he was interested in her?

~Chapter Twenty-Five~

Before the rising of Monday's sun, Zoe jumped up from her mattress.

Father, I'm persuaded you will take care of us in the face of whatever obstacles we may face. I'm trusting you.

The children awakened. Trudy filled three cold biscuits with jam and distributed them. Zoe, sorry for the hard lives her children led, thanked her daughter. As they walked to the barn, Zoe forced herself to eat.

"I have a plan," she told Billy and Trudy.

On the way back to the cabin from milking, Zoe, Billy, and Trudy found the ground black with buzzards eating the carrion left there—intestines and internal organs. Zoe wondered what Samuel planned to do with all that meat. The thought of cooking meat brought on a wave of nausea. She could manage chicken, ham, and fish; but the thought of beef and wild game repulsed her. Leaning against a pear tree, she emptied the contents of her stomach.

In the pea patch, she gave her children a refresher course in selecting peas mature enough for them to pick. Customers would not object to a few immature pea pods, which could be snapped like green beans, but people weren't accustomed to eating too many snaps. Bending over gave Zoe a severe ache in her low back, but she didn't stop to rest. They picked until they had harvested all the mature peas.

"We haven't looked at our watermelons." Zoe pressed on with determination. Her son would have shoes by the following Sunday. "It's time we should."

"I checked them. I think they're ready." Billy's comment reminded her that he roamed all over the farm. Most of the neighbors were trustworthy, but some of them frightened her. Billy had identified shoeprints of two strangers. Human predators posed more severe threats than bears and rattlesnakes.

Lord, we've had our share of tragedy for now. In the name of Jesus I ask you to keep an angel near my Billy.

"Son, I wish you wouldn't go off by yourself all over the place."

"I always have, and you've never said one word about it." Billy shook his bushy hair out of his eyes. "Why should I stop now when you need me more than ever to check on stuff?"

"I don't think it's safe. With William gone, people are coming around for no good." Zoe didn't want to think about the dangers facing her and the children. She tried to maintain a delicate balance between cautioning her son and daughter about danger and not frightening them. "Let's go see the watermelons."

They hid their sacks of peas behind some bushes by the gate at the entrance into the pea patch. Zoe knew how to thump watermelons with accurate results. "If the watermelon has a *bonk* sound when you thump it, it's ripe. If it goes *thud,* it isn't ripe." After checking several, she declared the watermelons ready.

"William Cameron's last crop of melons would have made him proud," Zoe said.

"Oh, wow." Trudy ran from one watermelon hill to the next. "We've got a big crop of them. Let's take some to the Mercantile."

"Sweetheart, we mustn't do that. Samuel has been taking his to the store. Jacob would put ours in front. We'd feel sad. I refuse to compete with our friend."

"You're right." Billy, chewing his nails, paced back and forth.

"We're going to peddle our melons and peas." As the daughter of a prominent Natchez planter, also as the wife of a prosperous man—both who enjoyed financial blessings while their impoverished peers suffered the oppression of Reconstruction—Zoe was not accustomed to going to town and peddling from a wagon, even though other farmers sold produce that way. Yet she would do what was necessary to buy Billy some new shoes.

"Here's what we're going to do." As they walked back down the hill, she placed a hand on Billy's shoulder and held Trudy's hand. "We'll hitch up the wagon and come back to the top of the hill to get a load of watermelons. In the morning, we'll go to Taylorsburg and offer our produce from door to door. Right now, let's go back down to the peas. We'll tote all the peas we can to the barn and come pick up the rest."

"Mama, it's too far. Let me stay here with King and guard the peas," Trudy said.

"I don't think that's safe," Zoe said.

"I'll keep my hand on King's collar so he won't follow you. Nobody's going to bother me or the peas with King guarding."

"I think she's right," Billy said. "Me and Trudy have come up here to pick peas lots of times."

When they reached the gate, the four full bags remained where they left them. "No, I can't leave you here." Zoe pointed at the thick growth next to the gate. "We'll hide these peas behind a bush."

"Let's try something. I've taught King to stay, but I've never gone off and left him this far away before." Billy pointed his finger at the dog. "King, stay."

Being careful not to talk lest King might think they were calling him, they walked away. He stayed.

They pushed the wagon out. Zoe wished she could devise an easier method to remove the wagon from the shed. Her right shoulder, bruised from shooting the rifle, ached, her belly felt heavy, her mouth was dry. Trudy pushed, but there was nowhere for a third person to stand and help. Zoe wouldn't dare tell her. Billy, growing stronger each day, amazed her with his ability to move the heavy wagon.

Although Trudy had a way with Bob and Molasses, Zoe was afraid the mules would kick the girl. She wouldn't be able to forgive herself if her children were injured. Billy led Bob Mule to the wagon, and Trudy led Molasses.

She hoped an angel would watch over her children and the crops.

"We'll load up the peas and then pick some watermelons," Zoe said. "Tomorrow morning if we get up extra early and do the chores, we can take off to Taylorsburg soon after daylight."

"We can make enough money to buy you some shoes, Billy. Trude, if we have anything left, I'll either get you something or save the money for you."

"I don't need nothing, Mama." There was sweetness in Trudy's voice.

As they traveled up the road in the wagon, they heard King's deep bark alternating with persistent throaty growls. When they rounded the corner, two men ran away from the pea patch gate. King continued to voice his threats. In the middle of the road, he took a guarding stance with his hackles up. As he looked toward the west, he scraped sand with his feet.

The bags were as the Camerons had left them. After loading the peas into the wagon near the front, they piled back into the wagon to go to the watermelon patch, which was on top of Cameron Hill. Zoe whacked Bob Mule and Molasses with the reins. She guided them to make a turn as sharp as the wagon could tolerate.

"Anyone has permission to walk on this road," Zoe said. "Your pa's people gave everybody the right. When Great Grandfather Cameron settled this hill, he made the road through his property and gave it to the public to use."

"So, those men were just walking by?" Trudy asked.

"Probably some of the Milfords," Billy said.

"I think so, Son. Trudy, baby, you are growing into a pretty young woman. You're vulnerable."

"What does that word, *vulnerable,* mean, Mama?"

"You're not able to defend yourself," Zoe said. "You're just a little girl, but some young, and old, men want to hurt little girls."

"Do you really think so?" Trudy asked.

"You'll just have to believe me. I don't trust the Milfords. You are too precious to me to risk leaving you where they could find you alone. If I did something that would allow you to be hurt, I don't think I could endure the pain."

"Aww, Mama," Trudy said.

"Nothing matters to me as much as what happens to you two." Zoe extended her arms. "Now, don't you understand why I didn't want to leave you here?"

"Yes, ma'am."

The mules managed the sharp right and pulled the wagon up the straight narrow lane. "William's grandfather, Max Cameron, laid out the roads." They climbed to the top of the hill. The edge of the property to the south was the Schmidt and Covings County Line. It formed a perfect right angle with the little lane between William's fence and his brother's fence.

"See how straight this road is?" Zoe said. "Your great grandfather planned it this way. It is like the kind of stuff Camerons are made of. Boundaries not to be crossed, like these lines."

It sloped downward with flat places along the way. "These rows curve around this hill perfectly. Your pa and his pa worked at this. Notice this field has no washed out spots. Camerons don't have erosion in their fields. Look behind you. The place where the house stood was a large almost flat area, you know. Your grandpa picked the best house site possible." The columns and chimneys stood as reminders of their former life.

The trees prevented their seeing the cabin on another flat spot farther down the hill. Sitting in the wagon on top of the hill, they could see for miles in all directions where their ancestors and the forebears of their neighbors had carved out fields from forestlands. Looking straight north, they could see the housetops of the little village of Taylorsburg.

"I don't believe God created a sweeter spot on earth," Trudy said as the mules pulled them slowly up the hill. "I know I haven't seen the rest of the world, but nothing could be any prettier than the view from here."

"I won't ever leave here." Billy spoke in a dreamy voice.

"Time will tell," Zoe said. "If I can get the money, I plan to send you both off to college. Who knows where your lives will take you? Whatever happens to you, don't forget you are God's children and you are the children of parents who love you. And don't forget to dream big."

Zoe moved her eyes off the expansive sky as she snapped back to the urgent problem at hand. "Son," she asked, "Where did William turn the wagon?"

The children laughed at what seemed to her an inside joke. The road was narrow all the way down the south side of the hill to the county line. They used to ride up to the watermelon field with their papa. For some reason they never knew, William constructed an invisible gate.

"You won't notice the gate unless you're looking for it. After you get inside, you'll see he left enough space to ride along the edge. We'll pass the spot where he didn't plant nothing. He left it that way so the wagon can turn."

"This makes me feel stupid," Zoe said. "Maybe William didn't want thieves to have an easy time coming inside this field."

Billy hopped out to unfasten the gate. He pulled it open so the mules could make a sharp turn to drive inside the field.

"I'll thump the melons and let you two listen with me," Zoe said. "Then we'll twist them loose from their stems. Don't you go pulling any till I say so. We don't want to waste the crop."

William had allowed a clump of wild plum bushes to grow on the edge of the field. "Look, Mama. The plums are red." Trudy pointed toward the plum thicket.

The thought of the plums ripening brought Zoe new remorse. William loved wild plums. What he loved most was taking her to the tree and helping pick them so she could make plum jelly for him.

"I bet we could sell some tomorrow," Trudy said.

"Go ahead. Get a bucket out of the wagon and start picking while we harvest the watermelons."

"Watch for snakes," Zoe said. "Remember they like to hang around in the plum bushes. Look high and low."

Lifting the watermelons, Zoe thought her back would break. She sat on a terrace row and fanned with her bonnet.

"I can lift these," Billy said.

"I need to rest a minute," Zoe said.

"You don't look so good."

After a brief rest she resumed lifting. They lifted some of the larger ones together.

With a high pile of watermelons, they faced the problem of turning the wagon. As soon as they finished the turn, the mules dug into the dirt to go back up the hill along the inside of the fence.

"From now on we'll turn the wagon before we load," Zoe said. "Hop out and walk."

"I have to close the gate anyhow," Billy said.

"This is one time we don't have to worry about Bob Mule running away," Trudy said.

Upon command, Bob, pulling on the left side, led the team into a sharp turn. In a left turn, Molasses had no choice but to move faster than Bob. "Whoa," Billy hollered. "Stop, Mama."

She brought the team to a halt. "What is it?"

"Look at them shoe prints. There's that broken shoe sole again."

"You know, I thought it looked like some trespasser had been picking a few melons," Zoe said. "It's not unusual for the neighbors to steal a few from the patch."

"We're going to have to be extra careful," Billy said. "A stranger is trespassing."

"I'm glad you realize that," Zoe said. "Let's get going." Down the hill they rode through the barnyard. "We'll park under a shade tree in the yard."

"Why?" Billy asked.

"Two reasons. No three. It gets hot in the shed. Two, we're going to leave early in the morning. I hope to save time. Three, we'll spread the peas and plums out in whatever containers we can come up with on the porch so we can keep them from getting too hot."

Bob frisked at the change in their routine, but Molasses didn't waste the energy. They took the mules back to the horse paddock between the cabin and the barnyard.

After Zoe drew a bucket of cool water, they ate fresh watermelon.

~Chapter Twenty-Six~

The day of farm work delivered a red sunset with time to rest. As soon as her children's heads touched their pillows, there were sleepy breath sounds. After Billy and Trudy went to bed, thick clouds blackened the night. Zoe knew the watermelons would be fine, but if the rain came she would need to spread out the peas and plums so they'd dry. King would guard the produce from any four-legged predators. Morning, which would come hours before sunrise, was not far away.

Even though she was as tired as she had ever been, Zoe sat by the window to review her plans. Moments passed. She loved the purple-black velvet of the night sky. The twinkling star that peaked through the cloud covering reminded her that God made the world. He had his eyes on her. Whatever fell upon the Camerons, the Father would handle. As a widow, she was one of his favorites in all his creation. The sweet peace of the night comforted her weary body as she admired the wonder of the night.

She didn't know how long she'd rested on the bucket when King's tentative barks transformed into menacing growls. The tired children continued to sleep. Danger loomed somewhere outside the window. In a quiet dash, she moved to stand near the wall on the corner side so she could peer out without being observed by the predator. What was it? Possibly a raccoon, maybe two, wanted to climb inside to raid the kitchen. Maybe another bear? In the blackness, the hairy form looked like a skunk, but it smelled different.

Were claws scraping over the wood of the window seal? Abruptly the noise stopped. A solid grip? Realizing the invader held onto the bottom of the open window, she reached for William's hog-butchering knife. Billy and

Trudy—she dared not risk cutting them with the knife—she couldn't imagine a more horrible outcome. Their soft snores indicated they were in their beds, so she pulled the weapon from its leather scabbard. It was sharp enough to use for a razor. She would defend her children at all costs.

In the dark of the clouds, she couldn't see much at all. With both arms, she drew the knife back until it pointed straight up. The momentum would compensate for her lack of strength.

Thwack! With all the power she had, she forced the blade down onto whatever the creature was. What sounded like a paw or two fell to the floor. Until then, she had been convinced it was a raccoon, but the instant the blade made contact with the intruder, a human scream curdled her blood. In a flash, she removed the stick holding the window. With the force of gravity, it slammed.

Billy sat up. So did Sister. "What was that, Mama?" Trudy whispered.

"Some animal trying to climb into the cabin through the window."

"That was somebody!" Billy whispered.

"Think so?" Zoe asked. She felt along the wall until she found one of Trudy's rags, yanked it from a wall crack, and ran it across the floor to pick up that which she knew was not a claw.

"Let me see that," her son said.

"No, I don't want to light a lamp. Whatever it was will see us. Go back to sleep. We have a big day ahead of us."

She wrapped what felt like the tips of three fingers with incredibly long nails in the rag and secured them inside a croker sac, then tucked the bundle near her mattress. Careful not to slice herself in the dark, she wiped the knife. Crouching on her bed, she tried to still the surroundings zooming past. She didn't know whether she was fainting again. In time, dreams came.

Before dawn, they began their chores; first, they fed the mules and horses. While the children were busy milking, Zoe slipped into the thicket on the west side of the barn and made her way to the clearing by the dense bushes. By one corner, she held the blood-stained croker sack. To give herself the necessary momentum, she slung the package in circles. On the third sling, she released it so it lodged on top of the high flat part of the roof. Nobody would climb on top of the barn. With the passage of time, weather and buzzards would annihilate the evidence.

She didn't have an opportunity in private to look into the sack; neither did she have the stomach.

Dear God, what have I done? Please forgive me.

When they returned to the cabin after completing the chores, King chased a buzzard from beneath the window by the road. "Blood," Billy said.

"Where?" His observation jolted Zoe.

"Blood splattered on the outside wall and soaked into the sand. That's why a buzzard was here."

Zoe rushed to the well and drew fresh water. She heaved with nausea. Beads of perspiration flowing down her face blinded her as she stumbled back up the hill with the water bucket.

"Mama, I would have done that for you." Billy ran to take the load from her.

"Thanks, Bill." He seemed like a little man instead of her boy Billy, but the knowledge of what she had done would burden his soul. She'd never tell him.

She rewashed her hands before she changed to a loose blue dress and a floppy bonnet. "I feel much better." She let out a sigh.

"Mama, why did you scrub your hands so much?" Trudy asked.

"I didn't realize I did."

Billy selected his best work clothes but went barefooted to town. Trudy squeezed into the dress she wore the last day of school. The skirt of it was too short. She took her time putting on her shoes.

"Billy, wear your hat. Trudy, don't forget your bonnet. You know we've got this Irish skin that blisters in the sun."

"I've got enough Choctaw in me not to have to worry about it," Billy said.

"Don't count on it. You have new freckles on your cute nose." Zoe packed the big sharp butcher knife Jake MacGregor had given her, two blue speckled enamel pans, and some croker sacks.

They were on their way to town. "Let's develop a sales strategy," Zoe said. "The watermelons are too heavy to tote."

"So what do we do?" Billy asked.

"I'll cut a melon. You two'll walk up to people's houses and knock on their doors. Each one of you will carry a slice of watermelon as a sample. When people see it and smell it, they won't be able to keep from buying."

"All of a sudden I feel bashful." Billy squirmed on the wagon seat. "What do we say?"

"Good morning, Mrs. So-and-So. Then she'll say, 'How much do these cost?' "

"Ten cents apiece," Trudy chirped.

"Is that too much?" Billy asked.

"Son, I think you'd give them away and thank people for taking them. As soon as the people get interested, they'll ask you where the watermelons are. All you have to do is point to me sitting in the wagon. Then you say, 'I'll go with you.' "

"I don't know," he shook his head. "I doubt this'll work."

"It will work. Ask the Lord to give you courage. Now, Miss Trudy, you keep quiet until they get back to the wagon. Then you can shine. Show them the peas and plums. After they buy something, always say, 'Thank you,' and remind them to check the produce at MacGregor's Mercantile."

Zoe reminded Trudy and Billy the reason behind her plan to mention MacGregor's. "You see we don't want to compete with Samuel or Jacob. We want to promote them. That's why we're reminding them to shop at the Mercantile."

"So folks'll buy watermelons from Mr. Sam," Trudy said. "They'll select whatever Mr. Jake is selling, whether it's our stuff or not."

"You've got it." Zoe went through all the steps again as they rode to town.

They parked under a red oak tree on the southwest corner of the village. Zoe knew other farmers parked in a row somewhere on the northeast side of town, but she wanted to have a unique place. With skill, Zoe opened a watermelon and placed two thin slices of the rich red-meated melon on trays.

Before they left the wagon, Trudy said, "Mama, please cut us some little rashers so we can tell people how good it tastes."

Zoe ate a thin slice too. The flavor delighted her taste buds. Here was a food she didn't have to force herself to eat.

"Whatever you do, don't allow it to have flies on it when you go to a lady's door."

Zoe watched them walk away and then she tidied up the wagon. The morning dragged on. Minutes passed between the customers. She couldn't resist the impulse to lie on the bench of the wagon. Exhaustion overcame her pride. Two folded croker sacks served as a pillow. With her skirt spread over her legs, she curled on her side. The bench was hard, but she was too weary to care. She would rest a few minutes with her eyes wide open to make sure no one found her lying down. Trudy and Billy would come back soon with another customer.

She didn't know how much time passed. She felt something, maybe a bug, on her hair. It moved onto her face. She realized she must have napped. When she swatted her arm, a hand with long fingers grasped her wrist.

"Relax, Miss Zoe. You had a fly on your face."

Jethro McKenzie.

"Let go of my arm so I can sit up."

"I'll help you." Jethro's voice was smooth as jelly spread with a spoon onto a hot biscuit.

"No, thank you. Let go so I can balance myself."

"I was passing by here on the way to Mr. Jake's farm. He give me some chores on his place today. I seen you stretched out here on the wagon seat. At first I thought you was dead. Then I caught you breathing."

"I didn't mean to fall asleep."

"It was all right," Jethro said. "I've been watching over you so nobody could harm you."

"Not necessary. The kids are nearby. I guess you'd better get going."

"See you later, Lady." As he walked toward Jacob MacGregor's wagon, he looked back at her.

She turned away.

The children returned with more customers. Not long after lunchtime, they sold all their produce.

"The mules are hot and thirsty." Trudy wiped sweat from her face.

Zoe drove the mules to the watering trough. After they drank she drove them toward the Mercantile. "Don't say a word to anybody about what we've been doing or how we got this money. We'll go buy sodas and something to snack on. Then we'll get your shoes, Son."

"My feet are dirty," Billy said.

"We'll tell Mr. Jake you need to clean up so you can try on some shoes. I'm sure he'll take you to the back and let you wash your feet."

In the store when Billy stood up in his new shoes, the look on his face made the effort worthwhile.

Zoe counted the coins stacked on the counter. As Jacob pulled out the money for their lunch and the shoes, she said, "How much is left?"

"Two dollars," Jake said.

"Let's see what we can find for you, Missy."

"Shoes," Trudy said.

When Geneva Bently pulled out the foot-measurer, Trudy's shoes grabbed her socks. Red marks indicated that the shoes pinched her feet. As soon as Trudy slipped her socks back on, Mrs. Bently tried one pair, another, and another on Trudy's feet.

"I want this pair." Trudy admired herself in the mirror.

~

At sunrise Sam cleaned out his smokehouse. He didn't smoke meat in the summer, but he decided to make an exception. He removed the shoulders and hams from the salt water where he'd kept them and strung them from a rack. In the dirt pit, he started a fire.

The kitchen was a mess. Having consumed eight cups of coffee since midnight, he lifted a jar with trembling hands and admired the chunks of canned bear meat. When he sat down to rest a minute, his head fell onto the table.

It was ten o'clock when the twins shook him, and he straightened his head. "Oh, my neck."

From the garden he picked mint, rosemary, and different varieties of peppers. With the twins' help, he also brought an assortment of vegetables inside. He peeled and chopped carrots, potatoes, onions, and tomatoes. All this he cooked in a pot with bear meat smothered in gravy.

All three of the Camerons looked too thin. Poor Zoe was starving. She had gone without enough to eat so often she'd lost her appetite. Perhaps she had some kind of stomach disorder causing her to retch. One day he'd go to town and ask Jake to look in his medical book. She had a disease of some sort. Jake could help diagnose it.

After he fixed lunch, he took a nap, along with Buddy and Bailey.

Later, with effort to stay awake and with Bailey and Buddy's help, he stirred up a yellow cake. He removed it from the oven and set it aside to cool while he made a pan of cornbread. Next Sam cooked chocolate fudge frosting in another iron skillet. He was on a mission to nourish his neighbors.

~Chapter Twenty-Seven~

The Bentons went to help the Camerons with the evening chores. After the milking, Sam said, "Supper's cooked at my house."

"You shouldn't have gone to the trouble," Zoe said.

Not accepting a negative response, Sam herded the group and marched them to his house. Although the loss of sleep had left him punchy, he felt a sense of accomplishment. As soon as his guests and children sat at the table, he ladled up bowls of stew. He expected positive reactions. Everyone but Zoe relished his creation. She sat munching cornbread as she sipped buttermilk.

"Excuse me." She rose from the table halfway through the meal and rushed to the back porch.

Sam threw down his napkin and bolted from his chair. "Stay here, children. Enjoy your supper."

He stormed out to the porch in time to see her leaning on a porch post and losing the cornbread. "What is going on with you?"

"Oh, nothing." She sounded nonchalant. "Just need a little fresh air."

He rushed back inside to fetch a wet face towel. "What's wrong, Zoe? I'm worried about you."

"I'm fine. Lately, the smell of red meat makes me sick. It's the hot weather I suppose."

"It's not that hot tonight. We've had a little cool front blow in. I canned enough meat for you to last until I butcher a steer after the first frost." He said the wrong thing.

She responded with projectile regurgitation. "I'm sorry. Please keep the bear meat. I can't."

"You need a doctor." He stomped back inside to serve his cake, which turned out to be a masterpiece.

With her head down, Zoe returned to the table. "Samuel, do you have any canned peaches?"

Trudy put her arm around Zoe.

Bailey, her mouth full of chocolate frosting, left her place at the table and went to pat Zoe's shoulder.

"Why are you crying, Mama?" Billy asked.

"I'm not," Zoe said. "Something just went down the wrong way. I choked."

After the meal and cleanup, Sam said, "I think we need to call it a day. We're all tired."

"Yes," Zoe said.

As he and the twins walked the neighbors home, he insisted Zoe keep her arm in the crook of his.

"I'm fine," Zoe said, but she was weaving.

When they reached the cabin, Sam went inside to light the lamps.

"You are so kind," Zoe said.

"We'll go to the Mercantile and get shoes for all the boys and girls. My treat." Sam's face felt hot.

"I can't let you spend your money on us." Zoe hugged him. "You've just lost your gold coins. Besides Trudy and Billy don't need shoes because—"

"It's my responsibility to help the widows in our church, remember? So there." Samuel held her hand for a moment.

"Look, Mr. Sam." Trudy held up her new shoes. "Billy's got new shoes too."

"Those are high-quality shoes." Sam smiled. "I'm happy for you. Here's the problem. I promised Bailey and Buddy new shoes."

"I want shoes like Billy's," Buddy said.

"Them's pretty," Bailey inspected Trudy's new shoes.

"It looks like you all will need to go to town with me tomorrow to shop for shoes," Sam insisted. "Oh, I've been so inconsiderate. I bet your watermelons are ripe. I'll take a few from your patch with us."

The following morning while the Camerons milked, the Bentons visited the Camerons' watermelon patch. In the Mercantile, Sam lined up the new shoes for the twins on the counter so he could pay for them. "I'd still like to get Billy and Trudy something."

"But you've lost your dream bucket," Zoe protested.

"Let me worry about it."

"How about new hats for each child?" Zoe suggested.

"Brilliant idea," They selected hats and lined them up on the counter by the shoes.

Something was more exciting than new shoes and hats. The children whispered among themselves as they looked in the back of the store at a thin man with a long, thick gray-streaked black beard. The yellow and red shirt with buttons missing hung from his slack frame. As they watched him, he stood. When he turned, they realized a plug was missing from the back of his shirt.

Before Buddy could say something, Billy cupped his hand over the little boy's mouth. Trudy and Bailey walked near him, but the man didn't seem to notice.

"Let's go out now," Billy spoke in a soft but distinct voice. The families followed him. As soon as they went through the front door, Billy tugged on Samuel's ear and whispered. The others huddled nearby. "That's the thief."

"What makes you think so?" Samuel asked.

"He's wearing that shirt, Mr. Sam. He lost a plug out of the back and some buttons in your yard. I bet old Spot took him down with Zeke right in there backing him up."

"Just because the dogs tore up his shirt in the front yard, we can't be sure he took the money, but he's a suspect."

Buddy jumped up and down. "We got to *do* something, Papa."

Sam stood still in need of a minute to collect his thoughts. "Y'all wait here in the Ford. I'll get Jake to come outside. The cracker barrel club will be listening to whatever I say; so we can't talk about it in the store. By the way, you kids did a fine job of not letting on. Otherwise, he'd have run out the side door."

"You have to say something that won't perk up any ears," Zoe said. "Hmm . . . let me think. Tell him I want to speak to him in private about the supper you are planning for him and his wife."

Sam laughed. "Only if you'll help me cook it."

"I'll do it," Zoe said.

Sam went back inside.

Jake walked to Zoe's side. "We want you all to come eat at my place Friday night," Sam said.

"I'll check with Caroline." Having removed his spectacles from his shirt pocket, Jake wrote a note on a pad.

"These children, also known as Cameron and Benton, Pinkertons, have made some significant observations." Samuel waved toward the children. "We need your help."

Four detectives' cards found their way into Jake's brawny hands. "Oh?"

"The boney man in the red and yellow shirt, who is he?" Samuel asked.

"Trutledge, Elvin Trutledge. He's a vagrant from Muhlenberg County, Kentucky. Got tired of coal mining and left home. He jumped out of a boxcar near here. When he wears out his welcome in Taylorsburg, he'll hop another train, I suppose. He says he's headed to Florida. What about him?"

"These investigators found a plug of his shirt and some of the buttons from it in our yard." All four Pinkertons sat like stones ready to topple. "We suspect he's the burglar, but we don't have enough evidence to accuse him of stealing the dream bucket."

"What's the dream bucket?" Jake asked.

"It's our bucket full of gold coins. My children have helped me with it since they were two years old."

"Oh, no. Such a letdown," Jake lowered his head, and a few seconds of silence passed. "I hate it for you."

Sam chewed his lip.

Jake looked down the street. "I'll get Marshal Canterbury down here. I saw him up at the Covington Hotel dining room a while ago. Y'all wait out here."

"Okay. We'll keep an eye on the door." Sam spoke on the behalf of the Pinkertons.

"I don't think he'll walk out the side door," Jake said. "He would attract too much attention from the other men. They'd know he's trying to escape from something, and they'd go after him for the fun of it. He's not the kind of man people like."

A few minutes later Jake returned with the town marshal.

"Stay here in the Ford till I tell you all to get out." Sam joined Jake MacGregor and Marshal Canterbury on the side of the store by the front corner, out of sight of the window and front door.

Canterbury and Jake leaned toward Samuel, who recounted the children's observations.

"Excuse me," Jake said. "I need to get back inside."

"Okay, kids," Samuel called. "Come over here. We don't need to call attention to ourselves."

The marshal stood waiting by the corner.

"Marshal Canterbury, these are the Pinkertons. You know, private investigators. Billy Jack and Trudy Cameron, Bailey and Buddy Benton."

Marshal Canterbury shook their hands, and each Pinkerton handed him a business card.

"I have the evidence with me." Billy fished two little bags from his pants pockets—one containing the piece of cloth and the buttons, another holding coins.

The door of the store flung opened as Jake returned with Elvin Trutledge in his grasp.

Trutledge tried to jerk loose, but Jake MacGregor, still in great shape from his football playing days at Ole Miss, was a force the thin man couldn't manage.

"Hands off me, store clerk. You've got no right."

Trutledge's coal black hair streaked with a few white strands in his beard accentuated the pallor of his face, so chalky he looked dead. His sunken cobalt blue eyes, perhaps once good-looking, added to his ghastly look. Something else bizarre about his appearance begged for attention: he covered his left hand with a clean white work glove.

"Yes, he does. I deputized him on the way down here a minute ago." Canterbury eased closer.

Trutledge continued to try to squirrel away, but Jake held on.

"Missing some buttons?" Marshal Canterbury asked. He held the buttons next to the ones on the shirt. "Turn around please."

"Why?"

"Perhaps these fellows have a piece of your shirt. We need to look to be sure."

"What are you talking about? Leave me alone."

The marshal assisted Trutledge to turn around. "Yep, the cloth matches the hole in the back of your shirt."

The run-away coal miner turned to face the group. "You can't prove nothing. It's circumstantial evidence."

"Trespassing," the marshal said. "Come with me, Trutledge."

When Jake loosened his grip, the man bolted, but Jake grabbed him again. Canterbury reached for a pair of handcuffs.

"Careful. My left hand's sore. I had an accident tending to the cows the other day."

After the lawman applied handcuffs, the two walked away.

As they rode out of town, Billy asked, "How's the bear skin doing, Mr. Sam?"

"Quite nicely. After most of the salt soaked in, I brushed off the excess and coated it with a thick layer of alum. In a few days, it'll be ready to use. We need to leave it on the rack for now."

~

Trudy thought Papa would have enjoyed the meal. . . .

The MacGregors came for supper at Mr. Sam's house. He fixed a chicken pie with dumplings and a buttered crust. Also baked a pan of bear meat with onions, potatoes, carrots, and peppers. Mama cooked creamed corn, peas with fresh relish, and some fancy eggplant dish. She made a pound cake, and he made ice cream to go with it.

Bailey rolled out dumplings while Trudy stirred the cake in a real mixing bowl. The boys took turns turning the ice cream crank.

After supper, Trudy and Bailey played in the floor with Baby Katelyn, the boys played checkers, and the adults discussed new evidence.

"Did you have any Canadian money in your bucket?" Mr. Jake handed Mr. Sam a coin.

"Where did you get that?" Sam asked as he handed the coin back.

"We want to see." The Pinkertons gathered around.

"It showed up in my cash register." Holding it up to the light and wearing his spectacles, Jake turned it around to look at both sides.

"That's a two dollar piece minted in Newfoundland." Mr. Sam spoke with the certainty of a coin collector.

"I've been watching every coin that comes in since your money disappeared."

"It looks like something from the bucket," Mr. Sam said.

"Only one other person helps me with the cash register."

"Mrs. Bently?" Mama asked.

"Yes."

"Of course you trust her," Mama said.

"As much as I trusted my own mother. Let's watch a few days and see if anything else develops."

"All you Pinkertons, keep this quiet." Mr. Sam looked at Buddy especially. "Don't mention this to a soul. Don't even talk to each other about it. We don't want anyone to know we have this clue. If you say anything, a person may overhear you."

"Could I ask something? I just thought of a problem." Billy abandoned the game of checkers. "If a thief had all that money, wouldn't the only way he or she could spend it be to leave town?"

"Good observation, Billy," Mr. Jake said. "Until this coin showed up, I had no way to solve this except noticing who hasn't been in the back of the store lately and checking at the depot to see who's left Taylorsburg. The men drop by for a few days, and then every once in a while some of them quit coming to the Mercantile. I don't keep up with them."

"Most people leave town on the train even though a few local folks have automobiles," Sam said. "I'll go talk to James Harrison before anyone leaves. He can be on the alert."

"And I'll put Marshal Canterbury on notice. I can talk with him in the private conference room at the hotel," Mr. Jake said.

"Something else," Buddy said. "It's really, really heavy."

"Yes, Buddy." Sam smiled at his son. "Whoever took it had to have been strong or fast. Maybe that's why he spilled money in the yard."

"Maybe it was more than one person," Buddy said.

"Maybe he divided it and made more than one trip," Trudy added.

After the MacGregors left, the Bentons and Camerons cleaned. Papa—Trudy didn't need to think about him. She listened as Mr. Sam told her mama something in a hushed tone. "We need to do our Christian duty by this man, Elvin Trutledge. Could you spare a little time one morning?"

"Sure. What do you want to do?"

"Go talk to him in the calaboose."

"That's not a place where a lady should go, but I'll stand by the door and mend his shirt while you go inside."

~Chapter Twenty-Eight~

The night fell heavy on Zoe as she sat by the window, stared into the sky, refused to give up. The cool breeze on her face refreshed her after another day of gathering produce to take to the Mercantile. The man who tried to climb inside was in jail.

Billy slept under the kitchen table. Trudy was quiet on her mattress nearby. The moon, a new sliver, was going down. Clouds covered all the stars. In the blackness, Zoe sat on a bucket.

Here we are, Lord in heaven—two fatherless children and a widow. What about William's baby? If this baby lives, it will be a precious reminder of my beloved, but how can I mother an infant in this shack in the winter? Thank you for taking care of us this far, but I've gone almost as far as I can go. Help me put up a front for the children. Teach me not to do rash things. Father, if I caused all this, please forgive me.

One more thing: I rely too much on Samuel. He has his problems. Please bring back his bucket of dreams.

Something made a rustling noise outside her window. In an instant, she stood against the wall as before. From her assortment of weapons and tools, she grabbed the sharp-bladed ax. Holding it overhead, she waited but dared not reach for the window prop in case the new interloper would be able to reach her arm.

King emitted a low throaty growl. The next second, he charged. During the ensuing scuffle in the road beside the window, she removed the stick that held the window open. The dog was fighting a small thing close to the ground.

"I smell a billy goat," Trudy mumbled.

"Be quiet," Zoe said. "You must be dreaming."

"No, Mama. I do."

"Go back to sleep. Don't talk."

Too tired to care, Zoe placed the hog-killing knife beside her mattress and went to bed.

"What's King doing?" Trudy asked.

"I'm not sure and I'm not going to see."

"I think one of Uncle Stuart's goats is in our yard."

"He wouldn't wander off this far. Hush, girl." Zoe was too tired to smell or listen. Nothing mattered but sleep.

Trudy's heavy breaths showed she was asleep again.

At least I know it isn't Elvin Trutledge. Whatever it is, King can handle it. Lord, I've already turned it all over to you.

~

"Where's King?" Trudy asked on their way to the barn to do morning chores. They called, but the dog didn't appear.

"Son, go look for him. We'll finish up here," Mama said halfway through the milking. When Mama and Trudy finished the chores and returned to the cabin, Trudy ran ahead.

"He won't come out," Billy called from under the house.

"Be careful. Watch for snakes," Mama said.

"Come on, boy." He spoke in soothing tones.

"Try to nudge him," Mama said.

"I'll come help you," Trudy offered.

"Don't. You'll scare him. Stay out of here." No matter how much Billy coaxed, the dog didn't move.

Trudy ran inside and returned with an old ragged quilt.

"Good," Mama said. "Try to scoot this under King. Be careful. He may try to bite you."

"He'd never bite me," Billy said.

"The poor thing is hurt or sick," Mama said. "He wouldn't do it on purpose."

Billy slid the dog onto the quilt. King emitted a low growl.

"Now pull him out. Let Trudy help you." The two of them slid the dog out through the soft bare dirt. His eyes half-open, King remained flat, pushing out shallow breaths.

"What's wrong?" Billy asked. "Boy, your neck and legs are enormous."

They had stuff to trade in town. "I need you to help me hitch up the wagon. Let Trudy watch King."

"Aw, Ma." Billy kicked the side of the doorsteps.

~

Half an hour later Zoe and Trudy sat on the front seat of the wagon with Billy and King in the wagon bed. Despite the heat of the day, Zoe shivered. A stabbing sensation lingered in her lower back. At least, she didn't have to help push the wagon out of the shed. The time was coming when she'd need to leave the wagon in front of the cabin every night.

She cringed at the thought of facing Mrs. Bently and Jake MacGregor. They should have put the cash on the bill instead of buying shoes. Sometimes it would have been easier if they had called her something hateful, like "frivolous" and" irresponsible," in her earshot as she walked away. Or they could have made snide remarks. Then she'd been able to bow up against them.

As soon as they tied the mules, Trudy took the basket of eggs inside and removed the rags. "None of them is broke, and they're all fresh," she told Mrs. Bently.

"Jacob, I hate to ask you this, but could you come out here and look at our dog?"

"Sure." He removed his soiled apron before going outside.

"Out here." Trudy showed him the wagon as if he wouldn't recognize it.

Jake placed his hand on the dog's nose. "Warm and dry," he said. "Fever."

"Please, Mr. Jake. You've got to help me," Billy pleaded.

"There's nothing we can do. Just try to keep him comfortable. If he wakes up, give him plenty to drink."

"That's all?"

"I wish there was more we could do." Jake shook his head and patted the boy's shoulder.

Meanwhile, Zoe tried to rock a ten-gallon can of cream toward the edge of the wagon bed.

"Hold on. I'll get that." Jacob rushed to take the job away from her. "We'll stick this in a barrel of water. I have a shipment going out today to the cheese plant in Newton."

"We picked these blackberries," Zoe said. "Could you use some in the store?"

"Big and juicy." Jake tasted one. "I'm sure customers will buy them quick. If not, I'll take them home to Caroline. She'll make me a cobbler."

"Fresh roasting ears." Zoe looked solicitous as Billy presented two full sacks. "I don't know how much of a demand there is for corn."

"Fresh food is hard for us town folks to come by." Mrs. Bently looked inside one of the bags. 'Some of us need more than we can grow in gardens. This corn will go fast."

Plums, wild cherries, a large eggplant, a bunch of washed carrots. "Can you apply the proceeds to my account? I'll pay the rest of it as soon as I can."

"Stop worrying about it," Jake said. "By the way, feel free to bring your watermelons here. I'm selling them as fast as you and Sam bring them in. Come on, Trudy. Let's go check the dog again."

Mrs. Bently walked toward Zoe. "I know you're busy, but do you have time to take in sewing?"

"Oh, yes." Zoe didn't know how she'd manage, but she'd budget her time.

"Here's an order for some curtains. The window measurements are written down on this sheet of paper." A stack of fabric and two spools of thread waited on the counter.

"Thank you." Zoe's eyes burned. "When you collect the money, put it on the account."

"Now what do you need?" Mrs. Bently asked.

"Just a box of baking soda, and some lime."

"For pickles?"

"No, a sack of lime for the outhouse." Zoe was relieved not to see any men in the store.

"Sit down and talk to me a minute," Mrs. Bently waved toward the bench. "It seems you are trying harder than any human being is required to."

"I'm sorry." The tears flowed from Zoe's eyes as she grabbed her handkerchief.

Mrs. Bently put an arm around her. "It's all right. I've been meaning to tell you to call me 'Geneva' instead of 'Mrs.' You may not realize it, but I consider you a dear friend."

"Thank you, Geneva." Zoe spoke between sobs.

"You're still young."

"Thirty-one, too young to be a widow," Zoe said.

"What do you want to do the rest of your life?"

Zoe paused to think.

"Go ahead," Mrs. Bently placed her arm around Zoe. "You can tell me your true feelings. This won't go anywhere."

"Before I can think about the rest of my life, I need to get my head straight." Zoe chewed her lip.

"I see."

"I'm afraid." She caught her breath. "Of several things. William's always on my mind. "

"Samuel."

"Samuel tries to help me. He feels pity for me. He might mistake our friendship for romantic love. Could be I've unintentionally led him on."

"You have to be sure how you feel, don't you?" Mrs. Bently said.

"Yes, I have to be sure of his heart and mine. That will take time. Right now all I can think about is the dog. I thought he was dying, but he seems to be a little better."

Geneva squeezed Zoe's arm.

"I've got to carry on for Billy and Trudy no matter what. People will talk because Samuel and I are together so much. We come to the Mercantile and go to church together. They may get the wrong impression."

Geneva nodded with a look of acceptance. "Who cares?"

"I do, but I shouldn't. Now, back to your question. I want to be independent. I don't want any man to take me on as charity, some woman he's obligated to take care of. I'll work till my fingers bleed to get a life back together for my children."

"You already have, dear girl. In the meantime if love comes your way, don't turn your back. William wouldn't want you to be lonely."

Zoe smiled. "Thank you a thousand times. I've been needing a lady to sit down and talk with me."

On the way home Billy lay down in the back of the wagon next to the dog. "Mama, drive slow."

After lunch Zoe and Trudy picked the field peas and butterbeans while Billy stayed with King. Then the three of them set up their workstation on the porch: Zoe rolled the new sewing machine from inside, Trudy and Billy shelled peas.

Billy, not fond of shelling peas, stopped to give King a light touch. "The swelling's not going down none."

King held his head up and opened his eyes wide. Whimpering, he moved over to recline on an accustomed spot.

"Mama, is it all right if I give King some buttermilk?" Billy asked.

"Sure."

He returned with the buttermilk and hovered over the dog. King sniffed the milk, lapped up one mouthful, and lay down again.

"It's a clue about the dream bucket," Trudy said.

"What do you mean?"

"King is." Trudy continued to shell peas as she talked. Zoe wondered whether being a good little helper or shelling more than Brother did was Trudy's goal.

"That's a crazy notion of yours," Billy said. "What does King have to do with the bucket disappearing?"

"He would protect us no matter what. If we weren't home, he would defend our place till he chased some burglar off or ran down dead from trying."

"And? What's your point?" Billy asked.

"Zeke and Spot would do the same thing, but they are always inside the fence."

"Unless they are not." He pinched her arm.

Zoe saw him. "Billy, let Sister say what she has in mind. Be nice to her."

"The next time you pinch me, you'll be sorry. I've got too much on my mind right now to deal with your childishness." Trudy fluttered her eyelids. "The bird dogs almost never leave the yard. Everybody closes the gate."

"Maybe that's how we know Elvin Trutledge didn't steal the money," Zoe said.

"I see. He managed to sneak into the yard while the dogs were asleep," Billy said. "When they woke up, he had to get out of there. He came within an inch of losing his shirt. Them dogs could've eat him up."

"That's the clue," Trudy put more beans into her shelling pan. "Even if Mr. Sam and the twins left the gate open when they went to their watermelon patch or came over here, Spot and Zeke would go back home to defend the house."

"That's right," Billy said. "They don't follow their people off the way King follows us. They always go back to the house."

"Except for only one time in a coon's age when the dogs weren't at home, so far as I know," Trudy said. "The day Mr. Sam took you and Buddy to practice shooting."

"Correct," Billy said. "Whoever it was had to know Mr. Sam and the twins were gone with the dogs. I get it."

"Samuel bought bullets at the Mercantile that morning," Zoe said. "An eavesdropper in the Mercantile knew the house was going to be unguarded. Billy, when we walked back home, Bailey noticed the guineas were squawking. She thought something was wrong."

"We've got to think. Who heard us? Mr. Sam told Mr. Jake. Mrs. Bently could've overheard. Seven or eight men were sitting in the back of the store. Jethro McKenzie was cleaning up," Billy said.

"You can strike Mr. Jake off the lists you both have in your minds. He is a good man. Besides, he wouldn't risk hurting his business by stealing a customer's money, even if he were a bad man," Zoe said.

"Mrs. Bently wouldn't do it either," Billy said. "She can't move that fast. She don't seem like the kind."

"She doesn't." Zoe darted her eyes at Billy.

"Jethro McKenzie," Trudy said. "He gets on my nerves always standing nearby and staring at us. He's creepy. He could have heard us talking."

"He don't, he doesn't seem keen enough to be a criminal." Billy breathed a deep sigh.

"You're right, Son. Besides, he couldn't have received enough information that day to do it, unless he had been studying us and accumulating other information. He's a good boy, just a little weird."

"All those men in the back, Mama," Trudy said. We don't even know who they were."

"Mr. Jake will," Zoe said.

"I'm going to draw some fresh water for King." Brother took the bucket that sat on the porch shelf to the well. Seconds later he returned. He flew into the house to grab a hoe.

"What is it, Billy?"

"Come see." He was breathless.

Zoe and Trudy followed him. Near the backside of the house was a dead rattlesnake as long as a hoe handle.

Billy chopped the rattle off. "Buddy will love this."

"So that's what I smelled last night," Trudy said.

"Come on, you two. Let's get to work." Zoe made the sewing machine hum. She marveled to think King recovered. Should she tell the children King should be a memory?

King arose from his resting spot and lapped up the milk. "He was waiting for it to warm up," Trudy said.

When the Model T pulled into the yard the following morning, Samuel chocked the wheel but didn't kill the engine. The twins dragged out. The problem of the missing bucket was obviously causing their emotional kites to dive toward the dirt.

"We're going to do our Saturday shopping. Would y'all like a ride into town?" He had no spark in his voice.

"Yes, that would be nice." Zoe began gathering the things she wanted to take to the store. "I don't need much, but I do have some trading."

Trudy brought out the shelled peas, Billy brought out the unshelled peas, and Zoe toted the curtains to the auto. Then Billy went back inside and lugged out a croker sack full of corn still in the shucks.

"Can you make room for all this?" Zoe asked.

"I think so." They loaded into the Model T with produce in their laps.

"Mr. Sam, a snake bit King, but he's better now. King killed it. At least I think it was the same snake I found." Billy said. "It was a diamond-back rattlesnake."

"Big?" Buddy asked.

"As long as a hoe handle."

"Buddy, I've got something to show you." He pulled the rattle from his pocket.

"Wow," Buddy said.

"Don't say nothing in the Mercantile. Just listen. We're going to study everybody and figure out what's going on." Billy said.

In the store five of them had hard faces. Only Zoe showed a flicker of joy. She couldn't suppress the pleasure she felt when she handed Geneva Bently the finished curtains.

"Already?" Mrs. Bently said.

"Let me remind you. Put the money for them and the peas and corn against my bill."

After shaking Sam's hand, Jake turned to Zoe. "Come to the back a minute, Zoe. Let's look at the books."

Zoe sat at the side of Jake's desk so he could show her the ledger. She opened her mouth in shock.

"It isn't as bad as you thought, is it? Look. The balance is coming way down."

A slow smile spread over her face. "I'm good for this. It'll take a little time."

"You're doing fine. I haven't applied the stuff you brought in today to the balance."

Geneva led her over to the fabric department. "Here's another project. I believe you can take this dress and make another one like it the same size."

"Sure. I'll be glad to do it. I'll change the neck and sleeves a little so it'll look different."

Mrs. Bently cut the length of fabric from the bolt and selected thread. As she took the ticket to a box beside the cash register, Jake showed Samuel another Newfoundland coin.

"Where did you get this?" Samuel asked.

"Jethro," Jake whispered.

"This hurts." Samuel rested his forehead on his hand.

"He's running an errand, but he'll be back in a few minutes."

"You sure he's coming back?" Sam asked.

"Oh, yes. He thinks he's in the clear. He thinks we all believe Trutledge is the thief."

"I told James Harrison to be on the lookout for odd coins at the depot," Sam said. "Also whenever anybody buys a ticket to leave town, he is to let Canterbury know."

"Good. I haven't had a chance to speak to Canterbury in private yet."

"That's okay." Samuel took a deep breath. "We don't really have enough evidence, but I want to press charges. If we're wrong, we can always back away."

Jake cupped his hand over his mouth and turned his face to the wall. "Central, get Marshal Canterbury on the line." The pause was short. "Marshal, meet me at the back door of the Mercantile. It's urgent." Jake threw his hand over the speaker to muffle Canterbury's booming voice. "We've found our guy."

"Who?" Marshal Canterbury asked.

"Jethro." Jake puffed the name into the telephone mouthpiece. "Hurry."

Moments later, Canterbury arrived and went to the room in the back, where a private door opened to the outside. This was the one Jake used to go to his horse stables. No customers ever used it.

While Jake was in the back, Samuel, Zoe, and the children moved toward the front door as if they were preparing to leave. Jake returned and busied himself near the side door.

When Jethro entered through the front door, Marshal Canterbury stepped out of the back room. Jethro tried to bolt first out one door and then another.

"You're under arrest, Jethro McKenzie," the officer said. Jake restrained him while the marshal handcuffed him.

"It was the guineas," Jethro shouted. "I'll kill every last one of them."

"No, Jethro," Jake said. "It was you. The trail of evidence you left."

"I'll get out on bail, and I'll murder Sam Benton." Jethro emitted a hyena-ish laugh. "That lowlife scum of a man needs killing."

~Chapter Twenty-Nine~

Zoe, recalling a bout of queasiness the last time she rode to town in Samuel's Ford, nibbled the crusty biscuit she'd brought with her. As she had hoped, chewing a morsel of dry bread assuaged the nausea. When she stepped onto the ground, she stumbled. Trudy and Bailey, walking behind her, grabbed her arms.

"What brings you to town today?" Geneva Bently asked as the Camerons and Bentons walked into the store.

"Our Christian duty." Zoe's eyes flashed.

"Could the children stay here a few minutes and have some refreshments? I'll pay when we get back," he said.

"Sure."

"What would you like?" Samuel asked.

"Ice cream cones." All of them spoke at once.

Outside, Zoe placed her hand inside the arm Samuel offered her, and they walked toward the calaboose.

"I'm a little uncomfortable doing this," she said.

He walked in his long-legged stride as she tripped along short of breath.

"I'll take care of you," Samuel said.

She let his arm go and stopped walking. "Just a minute."

"What's wrong?"

"Oh, nothing. I just need to make an adjustment." She tucked her scarf inside her neckline. "I didn't realize this blouse emphasized so much décolletage."

When Samuel laughed at her, she looked indignant. He offered his arm again as the walk resumed. "You look fine."

"Samuel, I can't believe you're doing this."

"It's what the Lord told us to do—visit prisoners."

"You're taking this too far." She caught her breath. "Please slow down."

They crossed the street. Passing the bank and a vacant lot, they walked west toward the little square tin jail.

"Where's Marshal Canterbury?" Zoe asked.

"I suspect he's watching from the dining room. He sits over there and drinks iced tea most of the day."

"That's fine. He can see everything going on here from the dining room except what goes on inside."

"You are a radiant Christian. You can show these poor sinners what it means to have God's love in your heart." Samuel patted her fingers.

Throughout most of her difficulties she was a young woman who radiated joy. She had a little inner light. When she entered a room, she made everyone in it glow in the reflection of the sparkle in her eyes.

"Yeah." Zoe felt no joy when they arrived at the jail. "I don't think I'm going in there." She backed away.

Taking her arm, he said, "Come on, my dear friend. I know you want to help these poor men get on the right track. You can't hold grudges."

"I forgive them, but I don't have to visit them."

"It's your moral duty." Samuel shoved her along.

She tried not to snarl as he threw back the door. On the right was Jethro McKenzie, recently admitted. On the left was Elvin Trutledge, soon to be discharged.

"Howdy," Samuel said as they stepped into the open space between the two cells.

"I don't have to speak to you," Jethro said. "Hello, Miss Zoe."

"What do you want?" Elvin asked.

"We came by to see if you guys need anything. Miss Zoe would like to mend your shirt."

"I'll step out while you remove it." Standing outside the calaboose door, she took the needle, thread, thimble, buttons, and the piece of his shirt from her bag. A moment later, Samuel handed her the stinky garment.

It was good the wind was blowing. She retched. What was this odor? Oh, that night at the cabin.

Her nimble fingers whipped the scrap of cloth into place with yellow stitches. It would just take a minute to sew on these buttons, but it would take a little longer to patch the back of the shirt. That yelling was driving her insane.

As soon as she finished, she knocked on the door. Through the uproar, Samuel heard her. Incredible that he could. After she handed him the shirt, she waited outside. Why did the maniacs scream? They were the ones who had violated *him*. One or both of them had taken his bucket of money. Their profanity made it difficult to understand what they said. Despite a strong urge to run back to the children, she stood outside and waited.

"Is Mr. Trutledge decent yet?" She cracked the door. She'd stick her head inside, say hello, and leave.

"Yes. Come on in." Samuel took her arm.

The loudest voice was Jethro's. She dared not make eye contact with him. Looking at his feet, she realized he wore cowboy boots. "I haven't seen you wearing those boots in the store, Jethro."

"Old Lady Bently don't like my boots. She won't let me wear them in the Mercantile. Says they make too much noise when I walk."

"So you wear them when you not working?" Zoe asked.

"Mama brought them to Marshal Canterbury. He allowed as I could wear whatever shoes I liked since he ain't furnishing me any."

"I see."

"Them's fine boots, my pride and joy."

Jethro reached toward her through the bars. She backed a step away. It was impossible not to stand too close to him, and there was too much space between the bars in the flimsy jail. He tried to grab her; so she took another step backwards.

"Miss Zoe, I'm in love with you. Don't you know?"

Her terror caused the baby to jump.

"Don't," Samuel said.

"I was just a kid working for Mr. William on y'all's farm. Way back then I had feelings for you I couldn't deny. You's got the prettiest hair I've ever seen on a woman." Jethro reached farther through the bars. "I adore you when you have it all curled up like that. Come over here, my sweet Zoe."

She continued to look down as she backed away. Terror chilled her spine.

"Look at me, little woman." Jethro leaned his face into the bars. "Let me see them eyes."

She grabbed the window frame to steady herself.

"I could make you happy. Mr. William liked me. He was good to me. It's clear he'd want me to have you now that he's gone." Jethro, shaking the bars, made the tin rattle. "This Sam jerk better keep his hands off of you, or I'll destroy his manhood."

"Samuel, let's get out of here." She inched farther back. The inside of her mouth turned to cotton. They could do no good for these two infidels.

Samuel's answer was lame. "I thought we should be kind to them, visit prisoners."

Jethro raged on. "Miss Zoe, I'll take care of your young'un's. Get me out of here so I can court you proper."

"Let's go, Samuel," Zoe headed for the door.

"When I get out of here, see what I do." He raised his voice to a higher level. "I'm going to nab Trudy."

"No." Zoe gasped.

"Got a sullen look about her. Attracted to me."

As much as she didn't want to hear him, she needed to listen.

"I'm taking her home with me to live with Mama. You and the boy won't be far behind. If I know you, you won't leave her with me. You'll join us. We'll be one happy family."

As she cowered farther away from Jethro and worked her way toward the door, she failed to realize her mistake; she moved so close to Trutledge he could reach her through the bars.

Seizing the opportunity, Elvin Trutledge grabbed a hunk of her hair and pulled her toward him with her back against the cell. His right arm came around her neck and held her in a vise-like grip. "Heh, heh, heh. I'll choke your little woman to death if you don't let me out of here."

With all the fiery power boiling inside her, she bit his forearm. Tearing his sleeve, she clamped down until she reached his hairy skin.

As he released his hold on her hair, she saw his left hand without the glove. He was missing the ends of three fingers. The scars were fresh, revealing red tissue not yet mended. Blood oozed from the nubs. Zoe's face blanched and her eyes widened.

First the boots, then the cut fingers. She knew . . . with her teeth she maintained her hold.

"Woman, you're killing me." Trutledge begged for mercy. "Let loose of me."

"You hurt her, and I'll slaughter you, Trutledge", Jethro yelled. "You deserve to die anyway. Let her go, fool."

"You ain't nothing but a windbag," Trutledge yelled. "Shut up."

"You ain't nothing but dead meat," Jethro said. "Buzzards wouldn't defile their beaks with your rotten flesh. My poor little pretty woman ain't got no choice but to dirty her mouth chewing on you."

In an instant Samuel grabbed Trutledge's arms with incredible force. "Let go of him, Zoe."

As soon as she loosened her teeth from his skin, she gagged. She willed not to faint. Keeping his voice calm but loud enough to be heard above the maniacal yells, Samuel said, "You both know Marshal Canterbury is the only one with keys to these cells."

"Go get him," Elvin Trutledge demanded.

"Drop to the floor," Samuel told Zoe in a soft voice.

"I'll choke your woman to death if you don't go get Canterbury now." The coal miner's voice was low and emphatic.

"She ain't his woman. She's my woman. Samuel Benton is the pitifulest excuse for a man in Mississippi." Jethro said. He cackled with insane laughter.

Samuel clinched Trutledge's arms. Writhing in agony, Trutledge released his grip on Zoe. Blood continued to drip from the wounded finger stubs.

Not taking time to pick up her scarf, which had slipped off, Zoe squatted to the floor. As soon as she was out of reach, she hurried toward the door. Samuel slammed Trutledge onto the floor before dashing out of the calaboose behind Zoe.

The hem of her skirt hiked in her hand, she ran toward the Covington Hotel. Samuel sprinted to catch up with her. "Are you all right?" he asked.

She stopped in the middle of the street. "Sure, I'm all right."

He grabbed her into a hug and pulled her out of the street. She beat his chest.

"I'm sorry. Zoe. It was my fault."

Zoe spat on the ground. "Uhrrr." She spewed Samuel's stupidity out of her. How dare this man placate prisoners at her expense! Out went the taste of Trutledge. She could not keep from vomiting in the middle of town.

Samuel reached for her, but she jerked away.

After helpless minutes passed, he said, "Come on. Let's get some water for you to cleanse your mouth." They went inside the hotel dining room. She rushed back to the powder room to rearrange her hair. A wave of nausea overwhelmed her. She splashed water onto her face and into her mouth. She loosened her skirt to tuck in the tail of her blouse.

At a table Samuel waited with a glass of water and some lemonade. He stood until she sat. "I'm so sorry, Zoe. I shouldn't have taken you there."

She sipped the cool liquid. The room seemed dark. Unaware of what had happened, she found Samuel sitting near her and her head leaning on his shoulder.

"It's all right," he said. He was stroking her face with a cool wet cloth as the waiter hovered over them.

"We can't stay here long. We need to get back to the Mercantile," she said. The fire within cooled fast as she thought about the children. Also she couldn't resist his gentle look.

As soon as they swigged down the lemonade, he left a tip on the table and paid for the drinks at the cash register on the way out.

Once they were out of earshot of the people in the hotel, she grabbed his arm and pulled his ear toward her. "Samuel." She spoke in a breathless whisper.

"What is it?"

"I want to tell you something," she said.

He looked at her with expectation.

"I cut Elvin Trutledge's fingers off with William's hog-butchering knife."

"No." Samuel was incredulous.

"He tried to climb into my window the other night. No one knows but you, me, and Trutledge, that is, unless he told. He wouldn't because I could press all kinds of charges. Please don't tell a soul. Trudy and Billy would be frightened."

"You're an incredible woman."

"Just defending my kids," she said.

"I want to hear all about this, but right now I have a plan to get rid of Trutledge. I don't have time to explain it all to you. We need to move fast. Canterbury is about ready to let him out of jail."

"Do as you wish as long as it doesn't involve me."

"It doesn't," he said. "Could you keep the twins a few hours?"

"Sure. I'd love that. At my place, okay?"

~

What mattered more to Sam than losing the dream bucket was the realization that Elvin Trutledge would soon leave the calaboose. All Elvin's demands to be released were absurd since he was due to be let out of jail anyway. Having that wild man roaming the countryside was a threat to the ones Sam loved. Revenge against Zoe was inevitable. After delivering her and the four children to her shack, Sam rushed back to town. Too bad his Model T wouldn't go faster.

At the depot, Agent Harrison raised his visor over his head and looked at Sam. "What can I do for you?"

"When will the next passenger train come through?" Sam asked.

"Which direction?"

"It doesn't matter." Sam broke into a sweat.

The agent checked his schedule. "We've got one headed to Jackson at five o'clock."

"Perfect." Sam instructed the agent to fill out a ticket book. "Here's enough cash to cover it. You can give me my change when I come back here in a few minutes. I have to hurry."

Over his shoulder as he opened the door, he added, "Could you mark it 'irrevocable' in red letters?"

Leaving the depot, he ran to the hotel.

Marshal Canterbury sat at his accustomed table. The time was 4:15.

"Marshal, we've got to move fast. Come with me."

They rushed over to the marshal's office behind the calaboose. Canterbury pulled his chair up to his desk. With his glasses perched low on his nose, he stared at a sheet of paper. Holding his pen in his hand, he seemed to muse over what he would write.

The tension grew within Samuel. He held his pocket watch in his hand as he paced. What if the train was early? Watching Marshall Canterbury dip his pin in ink, Sam bit a fingernail to the quick.

The marshal took a deep breath and stared out the window before he scratched a few words on the page. He blew the paper to dry. "Look at this. I think I've said it."

"I'll take your word for it. You know what you're doing. We have to go." Sam was breathless.

As they entered the calaboose, Jethro activated a tirade. "Samuel Benton, I'll kill you. Keep your hands off my woman." He shook the bars of his cell so hard the walls rattled. "Don't ignore me, unless you want a slow, painful death."

Canterbury selected the key to cell A from his ring and handed Sam the handcuffs. Elvin Trutledge, wearing Zoe's scarf on his hand as a bandage, had no possessions but his clothing. He tried to break away, but Canterbury placed a big meaty hand on him. The two men handcuffed his wrists behind him.

"You can't hold me without bail forever." Trutledge hunched his shoulder toward the marshal. "Where are you taking me?"

"To the depot," Marshal Canterbury said. "Sam Benton here has a generous heart. In spite of the way you've treated him, he has bought you a book of tickets so you can get out of town."

"What do you mean?"

"You're on your way out of Taylorsburg." The Marshal's tone was matter-of-fact.

"You're hurting me with those handcuffs. Take them off."

"Not yet." The train whistled in the distance.

"You can't do this to me," Elvin Trutledge said.

"Listen, Trutledge. If you *ever* come back to Taylorsburg, you'll be under arrest for assaulting Zoe Cameron."

"She bit me. Arrest *her.*" They pushed him along.

"In self-defense," Sam said.

Train cars clacking on the track drowned their conversation.

"Come on, let's go. Hurry." Sam was dragging Trutledge.

That moment the train pulled up, halted, and whistled. It would be a quick stop. They could miss the train. Sam lifted Trutledge, kicking in protest, and threw him over his shoulder. They seated him in the first passenger car. The agent rushed over to hand the ticket book to Marshal Canterbury, who handed it along with the note to the conductor.

"Go home and take care of your family." Canterbury removed the handcuffs.

"I'm headed to Orlando," Trutledge said.

"Not without your family. Work out something different."

"All aboard," the conductor called as Sam and the marshal walked sideways to the door.

"Sir, where am I headed?" Trutledge asked the conductor.

"Jackson, Mississippi, and then Memphis, Tennessee. You'll change trains in Memphis. Your ultimate destination is Paradise, Kentucky."

Trutledge squirmed as he tried to escape. He yelled, "Let me off here now."

"And face an arrest for assaulting a lady? Think about it." The conductor soothed him as Samuel and the marshal jumped off the train, which had already started rolling.

~

When Sam arrived at Zoe's house, no one was home. "Oh, the milking. It comes around way too often."

~Chapter Thirty~

I'm sorry. I took Papa's side. Mama needed to know where he kept his money. Heavenly Papa, I see now my parents aren't perfect, but help me forgive them and forgive me too when I mess up.

Trudy slept in dreamless peace.

~

In the fresh morning, Zoe rolled the sewing machine to the porch. Trudy and Billy were at Samuel's house with the twins. Feeding the cloth into the presser foot with the needle pecking the thread into the seam, she pedaled in a vigorous rhythm. It felt right to work her way through her problems one stitch at a time.

She didn't look up to see what excited King. "Thank the Lord you feel well enough to bark. That rattlesnake could have killed you."

The dog continued to communicate with the excitement he reserved to greet the children. The three youngest rushed onto the porch.

"Mr. Sam is having a party tonight," Trudy said.

Zoe, preoccupied with her sewing, didn't look up. "That's nice."

"Can we go, Mama?"

"May we?"

"You're invited too," Bailey said.

Zoe held up the dress to examine the seams. "I'm too busy shoveling away a mountain with a tablespoon to go to a party."

"Please, Miss Zoe. It's a cookout," Buddy said.

"A celebration," Bailey said.

Zoe continued to work. "What's to celebrate?"

"Don't you know?" Trudy, incredulous, flashed her eyes, whirled her head, placed her hands on her hips.

Zoe kept her eyes on her sewing. "I know I've got to finish this dress."

Trudy cleared her throat the droll little way she did when she had something important to say. "Marshal Canterbury did a search of Jethro's house. He looked all over the place."

"Jethro is in jail, but we don't know what he did with the money," Zoe watched her stitches.

Trudy continued her story. "Marshal looked under Jethro's bed, and he looked in the pantry, and he . . ."

"And he found the dream bucket." Buddy couldn't be quiet any longer. He jumped up and down.

"And the bucket is still full." Trudy nodded her head.

"Because it was so full it was spilling, but it's still heaped up," Bailey said.

"Jethro's ma and pa have a root cellar." Trudy recovered her role as storyteller in charge. "That's where it was."

"We got it back." Buddy couldn't stop jumping.

"And we're having a party tonight. Papa's having a wiener roast. He's going to buy one of them long weenie ropes." Bailey spread her hands.

"He's going to build a big old campfire in the front yard," Buddy said.

"He sent us to invite you and ask if me and Brother can ride to Taylorsburg with them."

"Brother and I . . . may. Yes you may."

"The cookout starts at five o'clock. You ought to come, Mama. You've got to."

Zoe silenced the hum of the machine. At last, her brain absorbed what they had told her. "You have the dream bucket back." She glowed. She jumped up and hugged the children. "That's wonderful. I'm so happy for you."

"Come go to town with us, Mama."

"I don't have time. It's all right for you and Billy to go. Where is he?"

"He's helping Mr. Sam stack the wood for the fire."

"Where's the dream bucket?"

Buddy took charge of the question. "Well . . . Papa put it on the dining room table, but he's going to put it in a secret place. I ain't supposed to tell."

"Good, Buddy." Zoe placed her hand on his shoulder.

Buddy looked as though he would burst. "He's going to wrap it up and hide it way down under our toys on Bailey's side of our box."

"We have to go, Mama." Trudy leaned against Zoe and held her cheek close for her mom to kiss it.

"I'm so happy for you." Zoe beamed as she hugged the children. "Be careful."

King jumped about and wagged his tail, but Zoe held his collar. "Stay here with me, King."

After the children left, she walked into the yard to take a little break from her work. She spotted some cardinals in a bush on the fencerow. Happy birds. She liked the way her face felt. The wrinkles of regret on the sides of her mouth smoothed into a new smile.

The birds, perhaps tired of being studied, flew away.

She walked inside. In three corners of the big room of the cabin, makeshift wires, which she had fastened with nails hammered into the walls, served as clothes racks. She laid out clothing suggestions for her children. For Trudy she selected a blue cotton dress, to which she had added a yellow ruffle on the lower edge. She had sewn a yellow strip of cloth together and turned it to make a tie for Trudy's hair. For her son she picked a green shirt, which she had mended, and some made-over trousers. For herself she pulled out a clean white blouse and a blue skirt, which she had patched in several places with contrasting fabric, giving it a quilted design.

Back on the porch, she resumed her work. She knew she couldn't sew enough and sell enough farm produce to make the money needed to solve her family's problems, but she intended to keep trying. Working was better than worrying. The sound of the sewing machine drummed, steady like the ticking of a clock. She sang as she pedaled.

Zoe sewed most of the day. Doubting the children would remember their chores—they needed a break so they could realize they were young—she began the barnyard work long before the sun started to dip toward the horizon. She fed the pigs. Since it was summer, she gave the horses and mules token servings of hay so they would remember to come when called.

Trudy's cow-poking stick grasped in her hand and King prancing by her side, she walked through the pasture to herd up the cattle. Nearing the thickets of brush and clumps of trees, where she heard One Horn's cowbell, she felt uneasy. The dark spots gave her a sense of foreboding. Whether the threats were real or imaginary, she was unsure.

This secluded part of the farm was where she'd been sending her little girl almost every afternoon. Evil people could lurk behind the bushes. The child's schedule seldom varied—it would have been easy to waylay her. Perhaps King had saved her life a few times.

"I'll go with her from now on."

Back at the stall, she filled a feed trough before she approached One Horn's udder. She could afford to be generous with last year's corn, a surplus.

Milking, she had a one-way conversation with One Horn.

"Why did Samuel plan to start the party in the middle of milking time? They aren't his cows. That's why. He doesn't have as many chores to do. My neighbor doesn't ever quite get it. Like taking me to the calaboose to see those two lowlifes. The man tries, but sometimes he has no clue about what I need."

One Horn chewed.

"What would he do if he knew I'm carrying my dead husband's child? I have management concerns. How will I butcher the pigs? I wonder who would buy some of them from me. How will I have time to maintain the smokehouse?

"Now that I don't have a surrey and don't plan to ride, I don't need so many horses. Furthermore, they're spirited. If we ever enjoy unhurried lives, would the children enjoy riding? Even so, I don't need six Tennessee walking horses."

How could she harvest hay in the fall? Maybe she could find a farmer who would cut and store it on halves. How would she winter so many animals? When she improved her fences, maybe Mr. Newton, a well-off farmer who lived five miles down the road, would swap cows for horses. They were worth at least three high-quality beef calves each.

The farming challenges vexed her, but with God's help she was handling them, if for a moment at a time.

To make matters worse, she couldn't can fruits and vegetables this year. What would she feed the children when the garden stopped producing?

She talked some more to the next cow. "The Gravel Hill School building is about to fall in. Who knows whether we'll have a teacher? William told me before he died he had heard rumors about school consolidation. Samuel will drive the twins into town, I'm sure. He'll want to take my children to and from school in Taylorsburg, but I don't want to be beholden to him for that. I can't let them drop out of school. They need their education."

She shuddered about the way Samuel would hover over William's baby. "It looks like I might carry this little one to term. I'm thankful but just don't know how I can take care of her or him."

"Mama, we're here." Zoe was milking the third cow when she heard Billy's voice.

~

Trudy prepared for the party. "Do I look okay?" she asked. Having taken a sponge bath, she outfitted herself in her blue dress.

"Sweetie, you look beautiful," Mama said. "Let me help you with your hair." Trudy sat on the porch until it was time to walk to the Bentons' party.

To see an uncontained fire blazing and crackling in the Bentons' front yard made Trudy so uncomfortable she wanted to turn around and go back to the cabin, but when she saw the twins helping Mr. Sam bring the food from the kitchen to the outdoor table, she decided she should be grateful.

"Samuel, I'm so happy for you," Mama said as she hugged Mr. Sam, who was holding a gleam in his eyes. He returned to his cooking.

"What are people supposed to do at a party?" Trudy asked Mama.

"Visit."

"I've been with the Bentons for hours. I'm with you and Billy every day. Now what am I supposed to do?"

"Celebrate." Mama smiled that way she did sometimes, sort of sad behind a half-way happy look.

"Sing. Eat odd food. Sit by the fire." Trudy shook her head. "We're supposed to have big fun."

The six of them settled in a semi-circle beside the blazing bonfire. In the brightness, their faces glowed. Bailey and Buddy gazed at the flames. Trudy could not remember when the twins had looked happier. She tried to read her brother, but he was a mystery. Was she imagining it, or was Mr. Sam staring at Mama? Lately, she had started to realize her mother must have had thoughts she kept as secrets.

They joined hands. "Dear Father, thank you for the return of the dream bucket. Guide us to use the money for your glory. Show me how to bring joy into our lives."

Everybody seemed to breathe at once as Mr. Sam paused. "Bless and forgive Jethro McKenzie. Help us to forgive him. Also Elvin Trutledge. We have so much hurt in our hearts. Thank you for the tears that are washing it away. Give us a time of healing. Bless our food. In the name of Christ."

Mr. Sam walked behind the table to help serve. "Come on. Let's get started." Trudy sat by Mama on croker sacks spread on the ground near the fire.

"I'm tired, Mama." Sobbing, Trudy laid her head on her mother's shoulder. Mama stroked her hair. "I'm supposed to be happy, but I'm not."

"It's all right, sugar."

"I miss Papa. The fire—I thought it would be all right. Mr. Sam made us a fine party. We need to try to enjoy it, don't we?"

"Yes, precious. Let's dry our eyes."

"Trudy, please watch the twins. Be sure they don't get too close to the fire. I forgot something," Mr. Sam said. A smile flashed across his face. With his long legs he sprinted back to the kitchen.

"Here we go." He returned from the house with a jar of pickles.

He cut wieners from the sausage rope and threaded them onto sticks. "Here you go, Zoe and Trudy. You ladies all right?"

Mama smiled. "We're fine. Thanks." As he turned his back, she said, "It's time for us to get busy having fun."

Biting her lip, Trudy stood by the fire to cook her supper. She looked at Billy. He pretended to have a good time, but he looked away with eyes full of liquid sadness.

Having a cookout was a new experience. They poured ketchup and spread mustard inside the buns. Slipping a hot wiener off the stick and placing it inside the bun challenged the party-goers' coordination. The sandwich was delicious, even though it was messy.

"It's called a hot dog." Brother could be such a smarty.

"Try some pickle slices in your sandwich." Mr. Sam loosened the top of the jar. With a fork, he served everyone pickles.

"Oh, yum." Billy spoke with his mouth full of food. "These are delicious."

"Crisp," Mama said. "Where did you get them?"

"The cucumbers came from your garden. No, I didn't steal them. Trudy suggested we help harvest them."

"I never taught you how to make pickles," Mama said.

"Mrs. Bently told me." He smiled.

Trudy busied herself being careful not to spill anything on her dress. For the moment, she didn't make eye contact with Mama.

"This is a joyful celebration. Zoe, thanks for sharing." Mr. Sam threaded marshmallows onto homemade skewers. "Be careful. No clowning. No sword fights."

"Samuel is a great man," Mama said. "It means everything to him for us to have a good time."

All of the Bentons and Camerons snuggled close together on one side of the fire to sing campfire songs and choruses. It felt good to be alive.

"Billy, your bear rug is ready," Sam said. "I'll bring it over to you in the morning."

"Sometimes I feel bad about killing bears and rattlesnakes, but if we don't, we can't live here in the woods," Trudy said.

"Duh. My sister says weird things."

~

As soon as Trudy and Billy breathed the sounds of sleep in their beds, Zoe crept from her mattress to her favorite inverted bucket by the window. A question formed in her mind.

~Chapter Thirty-One~

Zoe couldn't sleep. She faced another night without rest, no matter how tired she was. She gazed into the star-speckled blackness. Neither rattlesnakes nor prowlers could keep her from her consecrated place by the window. Some nights she came here to worry. Always the open window was a sentinel spot, most nights it was her altar.

Lord, I haven't trusted you enough. I've relied on my own little strength. It's time I listen to you for some significant answers to my questions. During the daytime, I suffer from the oppression of the urgent. At night, I want to snuggle my heart up to your glory and ponder over the situations facing me.

And I'm wondering about—

"Mama." Her son pulled up a bucket and sat near her.

She reached for his hand. "Yes."

"I'm the man of the family, but right now, I don't feel so grown up."

She hugged him. "I've been upset too. It takes time to sort out what happens to us. Sometimes I need to, I have to back up and think. *Contemplate*—wasn't that one of your spelling words?"

"Uh huh." He sat straight. "I'm mad." He beat his fist into his knee.

"About what?" Zoe asked.

"Papa . . . and the house."

"Me too. But when we get upset, we become confused. It's okay, but don't stay angry." Quiet moments passed. "Whatever we think about the things that happen to us is what we think about God. All the world is his."

"So if I get mad about what happened," Billy said. "I'm mad at God. Oh, no."

"He knows we feel this way sometimes, but we can't hold onto our anger," she said. "If we keep stewing about stuff, we don't honor him."

They sat. "Let's make up with him now." As they bowed in silence, she held his hand. After their prayers, she asked, "Feel better?"

"Yes, ma'am."

"Me too." She encircled his shoulders and gave him a quick hug.

She spoke soft words so Trudy could sleep, but the girl lay awake. "Funny how prayer can help us clear our heads." They shared a long silence. "I thought of something. We spend all our time making sure we have food to eat and clean clothes every day. And the farming gets done. I haven't had time to plan for the future."

"What are you talking about, Mama?"

"William—I mean your papa—used to hide money somewhere. I asked him where, but he never told me."

"We should look for it." Billy's emotions boiled into the sound of his words. "We need that money."

"Yes, Billy."

"Does anybody else know?"

"I hope not."

"Where do you think he hid the money, Mama?"

"I'm just now thinking about it."

"Folks coming around here. Leaving tracks. They might suspect money's here somewhere. It ain't natural for us to get stripped of all our money like this."

"It's high time we tried to find that money. If I started looking somewhere, I'd choose the locked storage crib behind the wagon shed."

"We ain't been inside of it since he passed away," Billy said. "Think about all them tracks around the corn sheller."

"He'd stash money. If he'd put it in the house, I'd have found it when I cleaned. I suspect he hid it in a safe place that was locked up. Sometimes I'd tell him we had to spend a little money. He'd always surprise me by going off toward the barn and coming back with gold coins to pay for whatever we needed."

Billy stood and groped for his outdoor clothes. "We've got to look for money in that crib."

"Don't go looking without me," she said. "That's an order."

"What will it hurt?"

"Snakes. All in the crib. Your papa kept king snakes in there to kill the rats."

"I can take a hoe or a pitchfork. King can help."

"We'll do this together." Mama spoke in a don't-cross-me tone.

"I'm not scared of king snakes, but what if I stir up a coral snake? Or a rattlesnake?" He sat down again.

"Like you said, some folks suspect he had money somewhere, and they can see we don't have it. We've got to keep our eyes and ears open. You've convinced me we've got trespassers. Do *not* go inside the crib without me. We're safer if we do this as the entire family group. Understand?"

"I get it," Billy said. He sat and stared into the night. "I'm sure those cowboy boot tracks are Jethro's."

"He has some wild notion he's in love with me. He's dangerous. I'm disappointed to find out he's not the man I thought he was." She lowered her voice and spoke directly into his ear. "The scariest part is he has threatened to kidnap Trudy."

"But he's in jail."

"For the moment. We don't know when he'll be released. We three need to stay as close together as we can."

Trudy popped up from her bed. "I'll kick him if he comes near me. I'll knock the daylights out of him. When can we get started looking for the money?"

"As soon as we do our chores and milk the cows in the morning. Now, let's get some sleep."

Billy returned to his mattress under the kitchen table. Zoe went to bed, and Trudy's head found her pillow. In a sleepy voice she said, "Mama, I'm glad we're happy again."

"I can't get no sleep." Billy slapped his hand against a kitchen bench.

"Mama," Trudy called.

"Yes?"

"Papa never let us play in there." Trudy's voice trailed off. "I always wondered why he kept it locked."

A few minutes later, sounds of sleep blended with the music of crickets, bobcats, and owls, but Zoe couldn't close her eyes.

Samuel thinks he has feelings for me. It's all over his face. Lord, please help me find the money William must have hidden so Samuel won't spend his children's dream money on us. And, if you are giving me this baby, help me find a better house for him or her.

She tried to shut down her thoughts.

I can't lie to you, Father. I'm in love with Samuel Benton. Please have mercy on me. With the new life inside me, my tender feelings are difficult to keep under control. I place this child in your care. Bless Trudy, Billy, Buddy, Bailey.

She drifted into sleep.

~

When the moon set and the sun brought a blush of light into the windows, the Camerons stirred. On the way to the barn, they ate cold baked sweet potatoes. Because they had done the chores early the previous evening, the animals were ready for the new day. The three of them worked at a higher level of efficiency than ever before.

In her revved up state, Zoe ran to the crib. She patted every crevice until she found the concealed key on the crib wall high behind an inconspicuous loose board. "Thank God nobody else has found it."

240

"Mama, we know they've been looking. I seen them tracks."

The key turned, but Zoe had trouble opening the stuck door. Billy charged his shoulder against it, and she yanked it open. The hinges squawked.

King jumped into the crib. Sniff, sniff, sniff—he wiggled his nose in a fast series of specialized movements. He rooted and pawed. Growling, he pounced into a pile of musty old hay on the right side.

"Critters," Trudy shouted.

"Listen at him barking." Billy laughed. "Go, King."

"Not so loud, kids. J. V. might be walking by. Hand me the pitchfork." Zoe pounded on the floor five or more times. She stamped hard. "Keep the hoe handy, but don't cut yourself."

"Sic 'em, King." Trudy pitched her voice low.

To the left of the crib door was an old metal trunk.

"Locked," he said.

"I don't have the key." Grunting, Zoe pried with the crowbar until the hasp popped.

As fast as possible, they pushed open the lid. In the bottom were a few old yellow papers. In slow motion, Billy and Trudy stepped back, but their heads craned forward. With reverence, Zoe lifted them.

"Let's go outside a minute." Memories absorbed her thoughts. She sorted through the pile.

Billy pushed Trudy back from Zoe's shoulder. "Mind your manners."

"You just want me to move so you can see better, Squint Eyes."

"Stop it." Billy reached his arm around Trudy. "It ain't a time for us to act like this."

"Both of you, come look over my shoulders." Zoe soothed them

"Documents?" Trudy asked.

"Yes, very important. This one is our marriage license."

"That ain't no good now," Trudy said.

"It could be if I had to prove we own this land. Let me see what else. This is the deed to our property and the bill of sale."

"How important is the bill of sale if you have the deed?"

"You're too young to hear this, but you have to. Uncle Stuart never forgave your pa. He believed we got the old home place through some unfair scheme. Here's proof otherwise. William paid for it with part of his share of the inheritance and some money he'd made."

"Working in Natchez before y'all married?" Trudy asked.

"Right." Zoe sighed. "Don't ever let anybody tell you otherwise. I'll find a safe place to keep these papers. For now, I'll leave them here."

"I know another reason Uncle Stuart stays mad at us." Billy broke into a chuckle. "Papa got five new calves this spring without owning a bull. That's because Bullbat jumps Uncle Stuart's fence. He walks across the road and then goes over our fence. He comes visiting our cows and goes back home."

"Careful there, Son." Zoe turned sharp eyes toward him.

"If we had a bull, he'd fight with Bullbat all the time. Besides—"

"Let's get back to work. Son, we don't need to talk about Stuart's bull."

They dug into the hay until they coughed in paroxysms. They shuffled through stacks of rusted tools. Dust flew in their faces. Inhabited spider webs loomed overhead.

"Papa told me what Bullbat did."

Zoe ignored him. She hung her head to one side. Nothing, not a clue, presented itself. "This is enough for now. I need to consider the possibilities."

Zoe locked the door and placed the key inside her pocket. "Let's go."

They walked home for a fresh drink of water.

"Where would Papa hide stuff?" Billy placed his hand on his forehead.

"We'll let this be our family secret for now." Zoe looked at Billy and then at Trudy. "We won't tell anybody, not Uncle Stuart and Aunt Melva, not Samuel or Bailey, especially not Buddy."

"Not Buddy for sure," Trudy said.

"Do we have to stop now?" Billy asked.

"I need to think before we go back."

~Chapter Thirty-Two~

While the morning glories were still open, Trudy went to the cornfield with Billy. She knew he'd fill his croker sack before she could fill hers. "Don't put any corn in mine. You'll make it too heavy."

"Beat you back to the house." He pranced ahead of her.

"You annoy me. I don't care if you beat me back." Should she remind him he could be such a child sometimes?

He slowed and walked beside her.

They poured the corn onto the porch floor. Its freshness invited Trudy to shuck an ear so she could pick the kernels and relish the raw taste.

"Sister, you're going to eat a worm if you ain't careful." He placed a dozen selected ears back into his sack.

They shucked the remaining ears and picked off most of the silks. "I'm taking this to Mr. Sam. I'll be back in a minute."

"Come on home and help me work," Trudy said.

"Save the shucks for the cows," Mama walked onto the porch. "They're going to love them."

Mama brought a knife and a large pan to slice off the tips of the grain and scrape the rich milk off the cob. "Bring out that jug and churn it so we can have fresh butter in the corn."

Trudy went to work shaking the make-do churn.

"We ain't—aren't canning this year, Mama."

"Yep. It's the first year we haven't. I don't have time."

"How're we going to live this winter?"

"We'll get by."

"We'll freeze in this shack." Trudy knew Mama was trying to do more than she could manage without a husband.

"All I can do is all I can." Mama's eyes filled.

"Maybe we can find Papa's money." They wouldn't find much cash. The idea that Papa hid something so important from his family—how was she supposed to accept it? She agreed with Mama though. If her mother lost hope, they'd be in deep trouble.

Mama kept working while she talked. "We've got a lot of work to do, but we have to keep all of our stuff in balance. We need time to dig through the crib some more. When Billy gets back, I'll send him to pick the garden. I'll need you to go help him."

"The ground is cracking beside some more of our potatoes," Trudy said.

"Take a stick with you and dig some up. That's what I mean by balance. We have to dig in the crib for the money but keep digging in the garden for the potatoes."

"I get it. Mama, lately you've been sticking out your belly. Are you spending too much time slumped over the sewing machine?"

'I haven't thought about that. I'll try to stand straighter."

"I just notice it when you seem tired," Trudy said. "You're always telling me to stand straight and not stick out my belly."

Billy returned to the porch. "Mr. Sam wants us to come to supper at his house."

"I should have told you not to go to his house this morning." Mama sighed as she threw her hands up.

For lunch they heaped creamed corn, fresh cornbread, squash, cucumbers, and tomatoes on their plates. They took their plates and sat on the porch with the hope of catching a breeze. With a bountiful meal on their plates, nothing else mattered for the moment.

"Papa would be glad we have something good to eat," Trudy said.

Billy glared at her. "You say some strange things sometimes, Gertrude. You must be a lunATic. I'm talking about moon struck."

"Stupid, it's "LUNatic" and you are one."

"Enough," Mama said. "After lunch we're going to put the dishes in water to soak and take a nap. We didn't sleep enough last night."

"Do we have to take a nap? Then what?" Billy asked.

"We'll see."

After naps they went back to the hot crib. Stirring in the rancid old room full of discarded implements covered with spider webs soon lost its glamour. Rats and snakes had dug trenches of hay and corn shucks in the battles of years past.

"I'm tired of stirring dust and rust and spider webs." The game to please Mama had gone on long enough.

"Let's start our jobs early so we can be on time for supper at Mr. Sam's," Billy said.

"Humph. You kids giving up so soon?"

After the milking, they washed their faces and changed to clean clothes. "I need to explain something," Mama said on the way to the Bentons' house.

"Have we done something wrong?" Trudy asked.

"No, not at all. I just want you to understand Mr. Samuel and the twins saved that money a long time. It's theirs. We're their friends. Until the house burned, we had as much material wealth as they did. We don't want them to think we're hard up."

"Why?" Trudy asked.

Billy elbowed her. "We don't want them or us to be embarrassed, stupid."

"No, that's not the reason. Listen to me," Mama said. "We don't want them to think they need to give their money to us. It's theirs."

"Lord, help us find Papa's money." *If he really had money.* Trudy doub

"Remember this, you two. We aren't poor. We're just broke."

At the end of supper, the four children cleared the table with careful politeness.

"Two nights in a row you've fed us." Mama seemed to be accusing Mr. Sam of something.

"Our pleasure." Mr. Sam smiled at Mama. "Tonight we want you to help us sort the contents of the dream bucket."

"You and the children can do that while I sew." From her bag, she removed a red dress she needed to hem.

Mr. Sam lifted the heavy bucket full of shiny coins onto the table. A roll of folding money lay tucked under a layer of gold near the top. He set the folding money aside before he poured the dream tokens onto the tablecloth.

Buddy and Bailey stacked similar coins. Billy and Trudy watched.

"Y'all can help." Buddy raised his eyebrows at Billy and Trudy.

The Cameron children sorted and stacked.

Mr. Sam counted and added, writing numbers on a sheet of paper. "Good job." When they finished, he totaled it. "First we take out a tenth of it." He stacked coins in a basket on the end of the table.

"Our tithe," Bailey said.

"Then we take out another tenth." Again, he placed money in a separate basket. "Does anyone know what this stack is for?"

Thinking hard but not finding an answer, Trudy looked at Billy. She saw nothing but confusion. Their papa had not taught them about money.

"Savings." The twins spoke in unison.

"Right. Always give a tenth to the Lord. It was all his beforehand. Also put aside a tenth to use later when times are hard."

The Camerons exchanged secret glances. What they'd learned about hard times that summer would fill an entire shelf of thick books. If Trudy ever had money, she'd practice Mr. Sam's method—it made excellent sense.

Mr. Sam continued his money lesson. "Ten percent plus ten percent. That makes twenty. All of it is one hundred percent. Take away twenty. That leaves eighty." The six-year-olds with their chins resting on their fists as they propped their elbows on the table sighed. "Normally we would budget the eighty percent to buy stuff we need, but since this is our dream money, we don't have to do that."

They pumped their hands up and down and rubbed them together. They hit one another's palms.

"We're going to use thirty percent for anything we want. We'll need new clothes and that sort of thing."

"Mad money?" Mama asked.

"Right," Mr. Sam said. "We can go mad, meaning wild, buying what we want."

The twins jumped up and down. Billy and Trudy, standing back, forced polite smiles.

"We'll have enough to purchase something nice." Mr. Sam's eyes beamed. "I was thinking about bicycles."

"We're too little." Bailey twisted her face.

"No, I saw some bicycles in a catalog. Made for children."

"Really?" Buddy was wide-eyed.

"Yes."

"I've got an idea." Buddy bounced with his thought exploding in his head.

"What's that, Buddy?" Mr. Sam asked.

"Could we get bicycles for Billy and Trudy?"

"That's an excellent idea. Zoe, what's wrong?"

Mama wiped tears. "I just do this since . . . you know."

Bailey flashed her eyes. "My turn." After she went over to give Mama a hug, she took a deep breath with a pause lasting long enough for everyone to look at her. Assuming a theatrical pose, she made eye contact first with one person and then another. "Papa." She paused with more drama. "I want to give you a bicycle, and I want to give one . . . to Miss Zoe." Bailey clapped her hands until everyone else cheered.

"What about the rest of the money, Papa?" Buddy asked.

"The other half—that's traveling money. Remember?" Mr. Sam glowed.

"We'll do some research about the places we'd like to see Then we'll make a final decision."

Buddy studied the pile. "That's a lot of money."

"We don't have to spend it all on one vacation," Mr. Sam said.

"While you're gone, we can feed your dogs and guineas and chickens. We'll watch your place and save your mail," Billy said.

~

On Sunday, Trudy and Bailey looked elegant in their new red dresses with white lace-trimmed detachable collars. Trudy had the smartest mama in the world.

Mr. Sam gave each of the four children a coin to place in the collection plate.

After church, Mr. Sam met at the front with Reverend Black and the deacons. He handed them a sack of money.

~Chapter Thirty-Three~

Starting the new workweek, Zoe sewed on her front porch. The cloth she held was sage green with no designs on it. She needed to be careful not to let the salt water pop from her eyes onto the fabric. Giving the project all she had, she raced against time. She wouldn't resign from the challenges of her life yet.

When William Cameron lived on the earth, he and Zoe dreamed big. He used to say, "Our children possess keen minds."

The boy liked farming. He had a logical mind that would make him suited to study law. There'd be enough money saved back to send him to college. He could go to Mississippi A&M at Starkville or to Ole Miss at Oxford. Maybe both. Perhaps he'd study farming at the A&M and law at Ole Miss.

Trudy was Papa's little darling. They'd send her to the Women's Industrial Institute and College at Columbus to study piano. William delighted in her talent.

Too bad, William didn't trust Zoe more. He must have thought he'd live forever. She was sorry she'd frustrated him. She could have been a better wife.

Zoe focused on her new project. She was sewing two dresses for a woman Geneva didn't identify. The more she sewed, the more efficient she became. Sitting at the machine provided convenient isolation that allowed her to concentrate on her dilemma.

She was sorry she had given Trudy and Billy false hopes about the money. She felt sure it wasn't in the house. She considered the little old log house on the south end of the property. William, however, didn't make a habit of going there. He didn't keep a lock on the door.

She doubted he'd buried it. If so, where? Who may have already found it? No, William was too shrewd to bury his treasure.

The money was in one of the buildings the Camerons called their barn. No doubt, he stashed it in the barnyard. If she could just think. She believed it was in the locked crib.

On the first day after William's death, she should have made the search for the money a top priority. With two needy children, she allowed the family's critical problems to overpower her. She'd failed to initiate her quest for survival

Lord, please direct my search. First, help me forgive my husband. As long as I hold grudges, I build a barrier between you and me. Help me to enter William's thought patterns.

Samuel and the twins appeared at her front porch. "We came to help Billy and Trudy gather the garden."

"That's nice, but you don't need to." She didn't look up from the fabric. She knew they came to help, but she needed her sewing time to disentangle her thoughts. Doing their chores in silence that morning, her children had seemed to understand her need for uninterrupted problem solving. Now Samuel would be interrupting her thoughts.

"It's a good chance for me to teach the twins."

With her private time demolished by all the discussion among the children and Samuel, she decided to cut out the second dress. As they were leaving, she spread a bed sheet on the edge of the porch and placed a piece of fabric on top of it. She laid the muslin template she'd constructed over the dress material. To hold the pattern in place, she used whatever flat objects, such as table knives, she could collect from the kitchen.

As Zoe finished cutting out the dress, Samuel and the children drove the wagon into the front yard. "How in the world do you hitch up that wagon? I keep trying to stop you."

"I'm used to it now," she said.

"What am I supposed to do with all this?" He pointed at the pile of produce, including a plethora of watermelons.

She shrugged her shoulders. She couldn't keep him from interfering with her schedule, but he would have to solve his problems. Why should she direct the activities of an adult man?

Samuel looked boyish with his hat removed. Tall and muscular, he stood in front of her. His soft blue eyes twinkled when he talked. Zoe knew she played with danger when she noticed such things about her neighbor. She lost herself in the magnetic attraction she tried to resist.

Sarah was never coming back to this earth. Neither was William. Still she felt guilty. She wondered if he knew she thought he was handsome.

"I asked you a question," he said.

"I'm sorry. Please take all you can use. Let Billy and Trudy decide how much we need. We'll take the rest of it to the Mercantile."

He sat on the side of the porch. "Do you have any cool water?"

"Oops, the bucket's almost empty. What's left is hot." She pointed with her scissors at her work. "The sewing—"

"I'll be glad to fill the bucket." He took it to the well.

Too soon for her to work out a solution to her problem, he returned.

"I'll take care of the mules," he said. Afterwards, he took the four children to his place to fix lunch. When the meal was ready, he left Billy, Trudy, Bailey, and Buddy for a few minutes while he went to fetch Zoe.

Walking along on the way back to his house, he gave her a little hug. Zoe thought he was ludicrous for trying too hard to grow their relationship. Yet, he was an uncommonly handsome man, who shared her interests and concerns. Why didn't he realize that his arm touching her provoked a sizzle? Her heart was cavorting like Bob Mule on a windy day. He was a dear friend and her husband's best friend. Too little time had passed since her husband's accidental death. He stirred inappropriate cravings within her. In addition to coping with her desire to snuggle next to him, she was frustrated by nesting instincts.

Samuel must have considered a romantic relationship between them a solution to several problems. With her husband's baby on the way and no money of her own, she willed herself not to feel anything for him, but her will was weak. She tried to back away. She couldn't avoid him; so she tried to stiffen when he came near.

After lunch, the Camerons went home for a nap. Zoe wanted to spend her relaxing time trying to visualize William's way of thinking. Over the years what had she seen him do that could serve as a clue?

In the uninhibited brain lull of rest, she remembered what she and William did the last morning they spent together. He realized she was still furious at him for not telling her where he hid his money, even though they had stopped arguing. Her anger because he'd slapped her created a barrier between them. No matter how mad she was, he refused to give her the information she needed. She supposed he thought he'd live forever.

She didn't like the way he made up with her. A few minutes before lunch that morning he came back from somewhere. What had he been doing? He wore fresh clothes, too clean for farm work. Taking her hand, he led her to the sofa in the parlor. If he had not hurt her by shutting her out, that morning would have been glorious. She cringed when she remembered going to the sofa with him. She found it revolting that her temper excited William.

After lunch he left again that day with a sack in his hands, and when he came home the fire. Some things she would never know. No opportunity to change him or herself existed, and she had no way to communicate.

Weeks after his death and the fire, she dozed on the hot breezeless porch. What, she wondered, did William tote with such care in that sack the day he died? He kept secrets, not just about money—other things.

As soon as naptime passed, the Bentons showed up at the cabin again. "Let's play ball." Samuel, in her opinion, worked at being a kid for the four children's sake. Since Sarah's death, he had never stopped trying to make everybody happy. William's death made him try harder than ever.

The ballgame was one Samuel had devised. To keep it fair, he explained that he would alternate the personnel of the two teams. As soon as the game settled to a smooth start, he walked back to the porch.

"Is your money in your house?" Zoe asked. "You have to be sure some lowlife won't steal it."

"I put it in the bank." He dipped a drink of water for himself from the bucket on the porch shelf. Wiping his mouth with the tail of his shirt, he was masculine and adult but childlike at the same time. She loved the new way he was combing his hair.

"We need to talk." He gazed at her.

"What is it?" She wondered whether his eyes had always been such a striking shade of light blue. As long as she was married to William, she never noticed Samuel's physical appearance. Besides, he looked like a different man now without the beard and long hair.

He leaned against a porch post, but it broke from the floor. Chuckling as he recovered from falling back, he drew one leg up onto the floor as he pivoted toward her. "One day soon I'll fix that post. In the meantime be careful."

Zoe watched the children. Trudy glanced back toward the porch too often to keep up with the ballgame. "Pay attention, Sis," Billy yelled.

Samuel began a speech. "When Sarah died, William told me that I would need to carry on. William was a wise man and a loyal friend."

"You've done a marvelous job. Lately I've thought about the way you've managed—a man with two new babies. You've been an inspiration."

"If you and William hadn't helped me, I would have been forced to give the twins up. What a sorrowful life that would have been."

"For you and them. We were just being neighborly."

253

"Do you remember? That's when I started raising beef cattle and selling timber. I didn't have time to farm row crops and take care of two babies without a mother."

"Yes, I remember. It's paid off for you."

"If you don't object, I can help you make your life easier by reorganizing your farm."

"That sounds good." She studied her sewing. "Do you miss Sarah?"

"You know I do. I wish she could see these precious children. I loved Sarah with all my heart." They stared at the ballgame. "And I loved William like a brother. You have been a sister to me."

She returned to her sewing.

"William would want us to carry on," he said.

"Uh huh."

"Will you marry me?"

"No, not for those reasons." Zoe didn't waste a second with her answer.

"I have more to say." Samuel ran his fingers through his hair. Moments passed while he watched the ballgame and she sewed.

He looked toward the field across the road. "I . . . I . . . uh . . . I love you, Zoe." He seemed embarrassed. With a tremor, he managed to say, "With passion."

She stayed busy at the machine. "Still not enough." Her voice was snippy, and her eyes focused on the fabric. Her chin jutted out in a hard line as she hung a hatpin from her lips. "I need time to heal."

"I can wait," he said.

"If in the distant future I decide to get married again, it will be more for love than anything else. A man is going to have to love me with all his heart. No man will take William Cameron's place, but whoever marries me will need to have a great big love for me. If you don't love me in a romantic way, don't expect me to marry you."

She knew life could be miserable even when two people loved each other without reserve. Samuel, or any other man, couldn't love her enough to cover all the hurt and sin that crept into a relationship. She had too many problems to win that kind of devotion. As she talked, she risked the danger that Samuel would realize her heart was thumping so fast she was short of breath. The idea of being his wife—she had to hide such feelings.

"I do love you enough." He looked away again.

"You don't sound as though you do." Except to brush her hair out of her face, she didn't stop sewing.

"Girl, you are giving me a report card on my marriage proposal."

"No, not at all." She laid the garment down and gazed at him. "It's just that we have such a good friendship that I don't want to ruin it. Samuel, you can't fake romance." While she presented this argument, her heart disagreed.

"I'm not faking, but I'll admit I was rushing," he said. "Like I told you, I'll wait."

"Thank you, Samuel." She would never marry a man for any reason but passionate feelings not only coming from her soul but from his also. Love for her children's future was not enough. Compassion was not enough. Neither was his desire to give her a place to live. Samuel was deceiving himself. He didn't feel desire for her, but she had trouble denying a feeling she had. Since she was in love with him, it would have been easy to accept his proposal.

"I didn't bring those vegetables and watermelons down here to interrupt your work. I'll take them to the Mercantile for you tomorrow morning."

"That's too much."

"Not for me. I'll move them to my place this evening."

She ran her hands over the fabric. "I'm carrying William's baby."

Samuel stood in silence as the color drained from his face. "I had no idea. I thought you were ill with some mysterious disease." More moments passed. "That doesn't change anything for me. I still feel the same." He stood and looked at her as though he intended to say something.

"Out with it, Samuel."

"You've been working harder than most men do," he said. "We need to take care of you and the baby."

"I can't worry about that. If this baby is meant to be, he or she will have to tough it out. As far as I'm concerned, I can't coddle myself. After Trudy was born, William and I lost five babies. I lounged all the time and let William pamper me. It didn't work, but this time things are different. This wee person has settled inside my belly with no desire so far to leave early."

"I've got to take better care of you."

"I'm fine. I'm asking one thing of you: don't tell anyone, especially the children." For the first time that day, she let him see her gaze at him. "I'm sorry, Samuel. I was thinking about me and what my children need while you stand there quivering."

"It's hard." His voice broke.

"Yes, proposing to me must be hard."

"My best friend's wife." Hands thrust into his pockets, he paced. "I can't help feeling a little guilty."

"You haven't done anything wrong," she said, but within her own heart, she knew how he felt.

"I know, but even though you don't choose to believe me, I have feelings for you. And now you tell me you're expecting William's baby. What I feel right now is the need to sweep you up and take all of you home."

"Thank you, but you need more than that, and so will I. It may seem best at this moment for the children, but what kind of life will it be with them as they realize they are in a home where the father has no loving feeling? What will they learn about real love as it should be?"

"I said I love you with passion. Sometimes I think you don't listen to me," he said.

"I'm sorry. That's all I can say. I don't want to use you."

"Am I that unattractive?" With a handkerchief from his pocket, he wiped copious sweat from his face. With his fingers he brushed through his hair.

She shuddered. "No, Samuel." Her voice grew soft as she shook her head. "You are a very attractive man. I—le t's drop this, okay?"

~Chapter Thirty-Four~

The following morning presented an ideal time for Zoe and the children to return to the crib. Samuel, miffed at her, wouldn't come around. Furthermore, he had a passel of vegetables to clean and take to the Mercantile. She had already rehearsed what she'd say if he caught them in the crib.

"We're looking for some of William's things." She could manage a general statement. The children wouldn't volunteer additional information. At that point she'd lock the door to the crib and walk away with a nonchalant attitude.

"We're going back to the crib," she said as they turned the cows into the north pasture.

"Great." Trudy slung her arm into the air with what seemed to be forced enthusiasm.

"Let's get to work, King," Billy said.

As soon as Zoe unlocked the door, they coaxed their dog to hop inside the crib. King slung stale hay and kicked up dust.

"Let's think a minute. William—Papa—had plenty of money he hid somewhere. It had to be in this crib. This is the only building he locked."

Trudy shook her head slightly and rolled her eyes upward.

Zoe said, "He never would tell me where he stashed it."

They propped themselves against the wagon parked in the shed in front of the crib while their faithful dog performed the task of scaring off the varmints.

"What if he didn't want you to know how much he had?"

"Sister, there you go talking crazy again."

259

"Let's not start that today." Zoe placed a firm hand on Billy's shoulder. "Trudy, if you know something or maybe you can think of something—what I'm saying is that you and your pa were close. Whatever you think, now's the time to come out with it."

"If we could find enough money to pay the bill at the Mercantile, it would be worth looking," Trudy said.

"Right, little darling."

"Mama, I don't know anything. Really." Trudy frowned and lowered her head. "This is probably nothing."

"Go ahead. What is it?" Zoe encouraged Trudy to talk while she silenced Billy with her palm pointed toward him.

"Sometimes when I'd come out of a stall after milking a cow, I'd see Papa walking out of here and locking the door. One time I walked over here and stuck my head in to look at the scales we used to weigh cotton. He had his coin purse in his hand, and he jumped."

"You startled him." Zoe sat in the doorway and stared into the distance. "Your papa didn't smoke, but he liked those little flat Prince Albert tins."

"Think hard, Mama," Billy said.

"Would you like for me to rub your shoulders?" Trudy asked.

"Not now. Thanks, though. Let's get busy." They looked everywhere but saw no evidence of Prince Albert cans. A pile of hay-covered junk filled the back left corner. Digging into it, they did nothing but stir more dust.

After what seemed an hour's work, Zoe said, "Time to get a drink of water."

They wasted no time going to the cabin and returning.

"I need to put some puzzle pieces together." Zoe threw some old sacks on the ground for her children to sit on. She sat in the doorway. They looked up at her like hungry baby birds.

"Three years ago those cans came on the market. Papa started collecting them. He'd pick them up on the side of the road and wash them out. Even asked people to save them for him."

"I remember," Billy said. "I wanted some Prince Albert cans to play with, but he told me they weren't toys."

"The cans would disappear. So would your papa. He always worked hard, and so did I. A couple of years ago, he made a mess washing the cans. I asked him, 'Will, what are you doing with all those cans?'"

Billy and Trudy leaned forward.

"He said . . . he said, 'Something good. You'll see.'" Silent tears flowed. "I get too emotional."

They sat until the shrill sounds of birds near the barnyard startled them. Zoe jumped up. So did the children. King barked. "That's it."

She rushed into the crib with the children and dog scampering behind her. She grabbed a crowbar. Concentrating the force of her muscles, she pried against a wallboard, but it didn't require considerable force. It popped off. Between the studs were braces that could serve as little shelves. On these, Prince Albert cans stood in neat rows like tin soldiers arranged by a child.

"There they are. King, guard the door." The cans were the perfect size to stack on the two by fours. She lowered her voice to a whisper. "Be quiet."

The first tin she popped open was full of gold coins. The three of them caught their breath. One after another, they opened tins of gold coins. She continued to remove boards and look behind them.

Trudy laced her fingers and squeezed her knuckles until they were white. With her head bowed, she whispered, "Thank you."

"Yes, thank you. Son, fetch some croker sacks."

He reached outside and picked up three sacks. With as little noise as possible, they slipped the tins into them. With Billy's help, Zoe replaced the board. Trudy arranged junk in front of it.

The sacks were so heavy they couldn't carry them.

"Get more sacks," Zoe said.

They placed manageable loads in a dozen sacks. Along the way they had to stop and rest. They dared not talk. Zoe felt a sharp pain across her lower back. In fast motion they made four trips from the crib to the house.

In the shack, they hung sheets over the kitchen windows. King, who usually lived outside, found himself stationed in the big front room. They latched the front door and closed the door to the kitchen. "This would be a horrible time for Samuel to show up," Zoe said.

They poured money in a massive pile onto the table to inspect it. Billy spoke in soft awe. "We're rich."

Zoe spoke softer than a whisper. "There may be more. We'll have to keep looking."

"Wow," Trudy whispered. There really was hidden money.

"I wonder where he hid it before he started using these little flat cans," Zoe said. They stacked similar coins in groups of ten.

"William was a generous provider. He believed we shouldn't waste. Someday he would have shared it with us. I'm sorry he never did. He could have enjoyed it."

"Like Mr. Sam," Billy said.

"Yes." Zoe felt her face redden in the hot kitchen. They continued to make stacks of gold coins. Most of them were identical. "One tenth. That means ten percent."

"The tithe," Trudy said.

"Papa may have already tithed it. We're tithing it anyway. God doesn't need this money, but we need to be blessed by giving it to him."

She counted out another ten percent.

"The savings," Billy said. They still spoke in hushed but excited tones.

Zoe pulled out more stacks. "Thirty percent."

Billy said, "I suppose we can buy school clothes and stuff like that. Mama, you need a new dress and shoes."

"Thanks, Son. First I have to go to Taylorsburg and pay Mr. Jake. The $25.00 balance I owe him seems like nothing now."

"After we hold out thirty percent to live on, that leaves fifty percent." Billy remembered.

"I think we know what we'll do with it," Zoe said.

"A new house." Trudy lowered her voice. "Everybody gets a room. We get a parlor with a piano in it. What do you want, Brother?"

"A Model T. Mama, you'll have to learn to drive. I think I can learn fast. You can drive too, Sis."

They placed the designated amounts of money in separate bags and hid them under the piles of clothes in the back room. After scrubbing their hands with lye soap, they pulled down the sheets and piled them in a corner.

"Let's keep this our secret until we find a safe place to store the money," Zoe said.

Brother nodded in agreement. "Like you always say, Mama, we need time to think."

They clasped hands and reached into hugs. "You're right," Zoe said. "In the meantime, I'm hungry. Are you two? We forgot to eat lunch."

~Chapter Thirty-Five~

"Try to act like nothing's changed, even though nothing will ever be the same," Zoe reminded her children as the Camerons waited on the porch Saturday morning.

"We can look at stuff though, can't we, Mama?" Trudy whispered.

"It's all right to look at things you like in the Mercantile, but we're not buying today. There'll be time to buy what we need when the money's in a secure place."

Samuel and the twins puttered into the yard. In a bright tone, Billy said, "Good morning."

"Good morning." Samuel blocked a wheel. "I'm surprised to see you all already out here. You in a hurry for some reason?"

"I have to take these dresses to Mrs. Bently." Zoe suppressed her smile as she gathered her things. Billy presented a sack of corn. Trudy eased a basket of wrapped eggs into the car.

"Come on in, King." With a proffered pone of fried cornbread, Zoe coaxed the dog to go inside the cabin.

"What are you doing?" Samuel demanded. "Now that you have a few nice things, aren't you afraid he'll tear something up? You never leave the dog inside."

She fastened the front door. In an offhanded way she said, "Oh, nothing. Sometimes we let King in. I thought he might enjoy being inside today. He's valuable to us. We wouldn't want to lose him." She paused for a breath. "J. V. Milford doesn't like King. I don't trust that man. There's nothing in this old house the dog can hurt. We put the mattresses up high."

She didn't lie, but she hated not telling all the truth to her best friend.

While the others browsed through the Mercantile, Zoe spoke in a half voice to Jake. "Could we go back to your desk a minute?"

"Sure." Jake led the way. "Have a seat."

She leaned across the desk and passed him a twenty-dollar gold piece. "We brought some more produce, and I brought the dresses. This money won't quite pay my balance off, but I'll pay the rest of it real soon. I'm sorry I've taken so long."

"Zoe, I'm not worried about it. You're probably overpaying me." Jake pulled his reading glasses from his pocket and opened the ledger to Zoe's page.

"Just credit my bill. I'll spend it soon."

He flashed a knowing smile. "Find a coin in some of William's things?"

Zoe bit her lip. "Yes."

Sunday the Camerons stood waiting in their best clothes. King barked from the inside while they loaded into the Model T.

As they often did, they sang on the way to church. The six of them harmonized well. When the offering plate went by, the twins gave coins saved from their tithe pile. Trudy and Billy each dropped twenty-dollar gold pieces into it. Zoe dropped in five coins. Samuel inspected the plate as it passed him. He exchanged confused looks with the wide-eyed twins.

"What's going on?" he asked Zoe as they walked toward his automobile after church.

"What do you mean?" Zoe shrugged. "Nothing."

"Something is."

"Let's go." Zoe dipped her head hoping not to seem impatient.

"The twins and I would like for you all to share lunch with us today. We got up early to cook."

"I'm sorry. I can't, but the children will be glad to eat with you."

"Was I too forward?"

"No, you weren't, but I have things I must do. We can visit soon."

"It's the Lord's day."

"The ox is in the ditch." And she needed to guard the gold.

Monday Zoe devised plans for the new week. Sitting on the front porch with Billy, and Trudy, she talked in hushed tones. "Don't let me upset you, but we must be cautious."

"Burglars." Billy folded his arms and jutted out his chin.

"We have to make a strategic decision."

"Yes, Mama." Trudy pursed her lips and tilted her head.

"Kids, we're facing a new dilemma. Either way we go there's danger."

"Either way we go angels are watching over us," Trudy said.

"Both of you are right. The gold has been safe in the crib all these years. Now here's the situation. We may find more. Isn't that an exciting problem?" Zoe laughed.

"Let's go get it." Billy started walking.

"Come back. Not so fast. If we leave this money here and take King with us, we won't be able to watch it. We can't be both places at once. I believe the angels will watch over us, but God expects us to use our common sense."

"So, you think we ought to put it in the bank before we go looking for more," he said.

"Probably."

"Is the bank safe?" Billy asked.

"You remember what happened last year. The president robbed the bank, but he went to jail. I think our bank is safer than ever now. Probably one of the reasons your papa was afraid to put his money in there was he didn't trust Johnson Daniels, the bank president. Papa was right, but we no longer have to worry."

"Mr. Sam put the dream bucket money in the bank," Trudy said. "Remember we can't tell Buddy we're going to put our money there. He'll tell everybody."

"They have places where people can lock up things in the safe. Nobody has to know what it is. We'll put it in our private compartment instead of depositing it."

"I guess that's all right." Billy pondered the situation. "We can make it look like some old junk in a sack."

Zoe pulled them into a huddle. "Here's one plan. We can work hard at our chores as usual, but we can take turns guarding the house. As soon as I can get this money put up in a secure place, we can look for more." She caught her breath from the excitement.

So did the children.

"No," Zoe said. "That's too dangerous. We have to stay together. We can leave King in the house and look one more time."

"Mama, can we do that?" Trudy couldn't contain her excitement.

"Yes. Remember though either way we have risks. I'm not trying to upset you two."

A few moments later when the Bentons approached, the Camerons jumped as though they were caught in forbidden behavior. Zoe looked down.

"Hi, Mr. Sam." Billy chirped.

"Is something wrong?"

"No." All three of them tried to sound innocent.

"We ain't played Pinkerton in a long time," Buddy said. "Y'all want to play?"

"Count me out. I'm too tired." Trudy propped her back against the wall.

"I'm sorry, Buddy. I don't have time to play," Billy said.

"All of you act like you're mad at us." Bailey extended her bottom lip.

"No. We ain't—aren't mad. Just busy. It's been so hot. We've been picking peas and pulling corn. The garden is getting away from us, and the chores come around twice a day. The corn will soon be too hard to use as table food. The okra's going to waste. We've got watermelons rotting in the field." Billy tried to explain. "As much as I love it, we can't keep up with all this farming."

Samuel stood facing Zoe. "Have you thought any more about what you want to do with the farm?"

"Yes," Zoe said. "We have to harvest the corn."

"I was talking about long-range plans," Samuel said, "like getting some beef cows."

"I suppose we could run them in with the milk cows. I've been thinking about what you said. Maybe a neighboring farmer would swap some of the milk cows for beef cows. That way we could keep up better if we didn't have so much milking."

"Good idea," Samuel said.

"As I told you, I need to walk the fences, but I don't have the time or strength to make the repairs. My cows don't leave the herd, but if I get some new ones they'll need better fences."

"Mr. Sam, would you like some fresh corn?" Billy asked.

"Sure."

"I'll be right back," Billy said. "Can Buddy go with me?"

"Yes," Samuel said. "Be careful."

"Me and Bailey—Bailey and I can go pick tomatoes, if that's all right," Trudy said.

"All four of you need to go together, please," Zoe said.

"It's obvious I have offended you," Samuel said as soon as the children walked away.

"You didn't. We're just busy. That's all. Too busy to argue, Samuel Benton."

"What can I do to help you?"

"I have some business at the bank. I don't want the twins to hear about it yet."

"You're not going to borrow against your place?"

Zoe toed the floor while Samuel paced. She emitted a nervous laugh. "No, I'm not going to do that."

"Are you sure?"

"I'm sure."

"I'll be happy to drive you to the bank. May I wait until day after tomorrow? I don't have time tomorrow."

"See? You have things to do too sometimes." She laughed.

"Okay, I'll come pick y'all up in two days." His face showed he was not amused. "Will ten o'clock be all right?"

"That's fine."

Billy and Buddy returned with the corn. A few minutes later, the girls returned with two baskets of ripe tomatoes.

As soon as the neighbors were out of sight, Zoe grabbed their sunhats. "All right. Let's go."

"I thought they'd never leave." Billy locked King inside the shack.

The children ran to the barn. When Zoe fell behind, they returned to walk with her, one on each side hand-in-hand.

"We'll keep him inside the house when we do the chores too," Zoe said. "We should have been doing that."

"What about snakes in the crib?" Billy asked.

"He's run them away by now, don't you think?" Zoe said.

"Yes, ma'am." Trudy agreed.

"We should take some corn to your Uncle Stuart and Aunt Melva."

"They've ignored us for weeks." Billy stated the obvious.

"We can't think about the way they've acted, but maybe we shouldn't call attention to ourselves right now. I know Stuart inherited the same amount your papa did. It appears they have put theirs away somewhere. I don't believe William told anybody about hiding his money in the barn."

"We got to be careful for lots of reasons." Trudy stuck her tongue out at Billy.

"Stop treating your brother that way." She would remember to pray with her children for William's brother and sister-in-law. "Promise me you'll always be kind to one another. Missy, you can start now."

In the crib they pried off more boards. They found another huge stash of faded red Prince Alberts standing as sentinels waiting for them.

"Woo-ee," Trudy whispered. They slapped hands and hugged.

Catching her breath, Zoe leaned against the wall.

"We'll never know if this is all," Billy said.

"Not until we tear the barn down piece by piece."

"You all right, Mama?"

Zoe sat in the doorway and fanned herself with her hat. "I'm fine. Just exhausted from having so much money."

Lord, don't let anyone pass our way.

"Come on, kiddos." When she stood the barnyard buildings rotated around her.

"We could hitch up old Bob and Molasses to the wagon," Trudy said.

"Too much trouble," Billy went to work arranging the sacks and hugging the extra ones.

Zoe in slow motion and the children moving faster lugged three bags of gold coins down the hill.

As they walked back up the hill, Billy said, "Mama, if you'll just walk with us, we'll tote it."

"All right. I'll watch to make sure no one is coming."

Trip after trip, they took their croker sacks of rattling cans.

In the shack Trudy and Billy repeated the process of covering the windows and fastening the doors while Zoe sat with her head on the table. When everything was secure, the three of them sat.

"Both of you will get to go to college." Zoe's wavy voice contained a note of victory.

They stacked the money with care.

"If we manage the farm well and budget the money, I should be able to provide you with all the things you'll need."

Trudy peeked out the windows. "Nobody's out there. King's guarding the house."

"The time has come for me to explain what's going on to Samuel. He's going to take me to the bank tomorrow."

271

"Tell him not to tell Buddy," Billy reminded her.

"Right. For the time being, we'll have to give the tithe a little at a time. People would get too curious if we showed up with too much money at once."

"Mr. Sam gave almost all their tithe at once," Trudy said.

"It didn't matter," Zoe said. "Everybody knew about their money."

With the gold coins placed out of sight, they locked King inside and went to the garden. Zoe cut the okra from the plants with a knife. At lightning speed Trudy and Billy harvested other vegetables.

As they walked, loaded with produce, back down the hill, J. V. Milford walked by on the way to his house on the west side of the farm. They seldom saw him, but they knew he passed by from time to time. Sometimes he went home on the road through the Cameron barnyard and down through their pasture. It was a shortcut for J. V. to his house. If King was nearby when J. V. walked through the property, the interaction was unpleasant. They always had to call the dog. He grumbled about King from time to time. Instead of trying to make friends, he protected himself with sticks and rocks.

"Howdy," J. V. said.

"Good morning, J. V." Zoe stood waiting for him to pass.

"Did your dog die?"

"No, he's fine." Zoe snapped.

"Where is he?"

"He's around and about. How are your folks?"

"Doing very well, thank you," J. V. said.

After he walked away, Trudy said, "Mama, Mr. J. V. frightened me."

"The way he asked questions—was that it?"

"That, plus the way he looked at everything," Trudy said.

"He hit King the other day." Billy sounded furious.

Later that afternoon Zoe and Trudy shelled peas while Billy sorted corn.

"Now we have the money to solve our problems. We have to think what to do. Money is nothing but an implement for us. What fixes things is the wise use of it," Zoe said.

"You have to find some men to build a house." Billy talked as he bagged corn. He needed to be careful because some of the ears were too mature for cooking and eating.

"Finding someone to build our house is a big problem." Zoe looked pleasant. "We're blessed."

"You'll need to fix the fences," he said. "I heard you talking about that."

"Right. The first thing is to find some workers to help harvest this big corn crop."

Before they went to bed, Zoe gave Billy and Trudy a memory verse: "(God's mercies) are new every morning: great is thy faithfulness." (Lamentations 3:23)

~Chapter Thirty-Six~

Zoe pointed her finger. "Remember, I have to tell Samuel, but we're not telling Bailey and Buddy."

Minutes after the Camerons finished their chores, Samuel, with a hurt puppy-dog expression, hopped out of his Model T and blocked the wheel. He kept his hat pulled down on his head. The corners of his eyes folded toward his mouth, which had turned-down corners.

"Come on," Billy said. "We'll do some Pinkerton work while Mama finishes getting ready."

"Oh, good." Buddy jumped. "Let me show you where the arrowheads are. What else are we looking for?"

"Footprints." Billy led the twins and Trudy away from the cabin.

"Samuel, please come inside a minute." Zoe motioned to him. "I need to talk to you."

He followed her. "Did you change your mind?"

"Yes, I decided to tell you." Zoe walked toward the rag piles in the back room. "I intended to tell you, but first I wanted to talk to the children. We have made a pact to keep this a secret. Please don't tell Bailey and Buddy. They may not understand why. I'm surprised you guessed."

"We don't seem to be talking about the same thing."

"Maybe you don't know then. Billy and Trudy and I, we have all the money we need."

"What?" Samuel's mouth flew open.

"We found enough gold coins in William's crib to weight you and me down . . ."

"Incredible." Samuel wiped his face with his handkerchief.

"... twice."

"I'm happy for you." His face glowing. He turned his head toward her and gazed intensely. Without drawing a breath, a loud "whoo-ee" came out of his mouth.

"Shh." She placed her hands on his shoulders. "I need you to help me take it to the bank."

"You know I will." He hugged her in a fraternal way

"Please help me tote the money to the auto. It's mostly twenty-dollar gold pieces." She rooted through the mound of donated clothing.

"That's quite a stash. You must have worried about keeping it here."

"For the children and me, it became an exercise in trusting the Lord to send his angels."

"When I took the bucket money to the bank, I put it in a locked safe. After Johnson Daniels robbed the bank, the employees and new officers have been much more careful. I trust them now."

"I do too."

"So that's what you want to do with your money?"

"Yes." She handed him croker sacks of money, some so heavy she almost fell over. They loaded William's gold into Samuel's Model T. Zoe caught her breath. "We'll give our tithe in increments. I hid a bag of money for that. I labeled all the bags with notes inside the tops of them. We triple bagged the coins so people couldn't see what was in them. I'm carrying around some money in my purse for us to operate on. If we're careful, people won't know what this is."

"I'll park next to the front bank windows and try to walk in with these like they aren't heavy." He grinned at her.

She carried the yellowed documents folded inside a pillowcase. "Important papers we found," she explained.

"Is there more money where you found this?"

"I don't know. We'll keep looking. J. V. came by. He seemed to be looking for something. He asked questions about King."

"We need to watch him."

"This money brings new problems."

"I can identify with that."

"God makes sure I talk to him."

"Now I understand some things."

As soon as they were loaded, he helped lock King inside. "Come on, kids. Miss Zoe needs to go to town. We'll have a little adventure too."

They pulled up to the Mercantile. Zoe took the children inside while Samuel stayed in the auto. "Mr. Jake, please serve these young people ice cream cones. Samuel and I will be back in a few minutes. I think—I know they can be ladies and gentlemen while they eat their ice cream here in the back of the store."

~

A few nights later, the roar of thunder announced a violent storm. Lightning struck near Zoe's favorite window in the big room. They closed all the windows and let King come inside. Rain poured through the roof leaks. Zoe, Billy and Trudy ran from one waterfall to another with buckets, old gallon cans, and cooking pots to catch the rain. The leaks destroyed the tents. With lightning speed, they moved their mattress beds to a dry place. Trudy moved her red dress to a safe spot. Zoe pulled the clothes from the hangers down and placed them on the kitchen table, which was dry. She threw a blanket over her sewing machine and rolled it to the kitchen, where there were fewer leaks. They shoved the piles of clothes out of the rain.

"It's never rained this hard since we moved here," Zoe said. "This seems to be a big storm."

"I'm glad this is happening," Trudy said.

"You're stupid." Billy stamped his foot at her but slid in the process.

"No, Billy, I ain't. I'm glad it's happening the way it is. What if we hadn't been home?"

"Thank you for reminding me, Trudy, who is in charge here," Zoe said.

~

The rain slacked.

Trudy used some old rags for a mop. She put them under her foot to drag them back and forth until her invention absorbed all the loose water. She bent down to feel the floor, it would have to do, she placed her mattress on the spot and respread her bedcovers. Mama mopped with the real mop.

"What's wrong with your back?" Trudy asked.

"Just a catch in it," Mama said.

Billy fixed his bed under the kitchen table. Mama placed her mattress on a dried place.

"I'm so tired," Trudy said.

"I know, Trude. Me too," Mama said. "We'll sleep well tonight even in the moisture."

Trudy hoped they would. It had been a long time since she'd dreamed about Papa. She didn't want to dream. Sleep took her away.

Soft flowers, all colors. The light made a rainbow. The music—she loved the music. Hymns, so pretty. Papa was . . . everything looked perfect . . . he was singing. She'd never heard Papa sing before, even though he was a deacon and he understood music.

"Listen, Trudy, I'm telling you myself." Papa was talking.

"I'm listening."

"Trude, I'm not coming back. I'm staying up here. Stop looking for me."

"Papa, I didn't know I was looking for you."

Mama had told her not to try to talk to Papa, but she couldn't control her dreams. Uninterrupted sleep filled the remainder of the night.

When she awakened in the morning, the fragrance of climbing roses on the side fence poured in through the windows of the shack.

Heavenly Father, tell Papa I love him, but please don't allow the dream senders to deliver any more dreams about him to me ever again. He is with you and that's all I want to know. Thanks in the name of Jesus. One more thing—I love you.

~

The sewing machine hummed as Zoe fed cloth under the presser foot. She would keep her promise to complete all the sewing projects she had started.

Her children could rest in the security that all their needs would be met. They would attend high school and college without having to think about where the next meal would come from. With Samuel helping her work through the challenges of management—he was such a dear friend—she would be able to solve all her problems. It would take time.

She spread a veneer of happiness over herself so the others wouldn't see the longing that ached within her. She was supposed to be happy, and she was thankful for the blessings. In addition to the solutions to all of her family's difficulties, she had a new freedom: she could give her heart permission to be in love with Samuel Benton. She ached to hold someone—a man such as Samuel. At the same time, he would no longer have to pretend he was in love with her just because she needed someone to protect her from all that had threatened to destroy her and her little family.

As before, romance didn't exist. She knew she couldn't let her heart act in a romantic way toward him. Nothing had changed but the reasons. She felt no resentment toward him, he had proposed to her simply to try to help her, he wouldn't ask her again, he was not in love with her. She would not marry a man because he felt sorry for her.

If, however, he could ever love her—she let such a remote possibility slide away.

~Chapter Thirty-Seven~

After milking and caring for the livestock, Trudy and Billy took a planned play day.

"I don't like to leave you." Trudy squeezed her mother's hand.

"I'll stay here. King and the angels will watch over me. You kids need to play sometimes. Otherwise, you'll forget how young you are."

"Mama, you don't have to sew every minute."

"Got to finish this. Obligated myself to do it. Then I promise I'll slow down sewing for other people."

"Come on, B. J." Trudy patted his back.

When Trudy and Billy rounded the Bentons' garage, Sam was standing on his porch. "It's good to see you neighbors coming over to spend the day. Seems like a while since you've come here."

"We've been busy," Trudy said.

"Let's go find some clues." Buddy pulled them into the yard. "Let's go, Billy, Trudy."

"I'll be there in a minute."

The others went to the far side of the fenced yard.

"Mr. Sam, we need to have a talk." She turned her earnest freckled face toward him.

"Sure."

"Are you and Mama still friends?"

"I suppose we'll always be friends." Mr. Sam rubbed the stubble on his face. He needed a shave and a haircut.

"I was wondering what if you asked her—" Trudy giggled.

"To marry me? I did. She said no."

"You still want to marry her, I hope." Her face felt hot.

"You bet, but I won't ask her again."

"Why not?"

"She'll turn me down. I don't want to make more hard feelings."

"You two would make a sweet couple. We could all be family."

"Convince your mama."

"Propose," Trudy said.

"I did but I didn't say it right."

"Do it again. Say it better."

"There's no use. I can't seem to get it right."

"Do you want to marry Mama or not?"

"I told you I do." He scratched the back of his neck.

"Wait a minute, Mr. Sam. I don't mean to be disrespectful, but I've got to know. Will you beat Mama?"

"Of course not."

"Will you hit her, even if she says something she shouldn't say?"

"No."

"I've got to have your promise. I can't stand to see my mama hurt."

"I promise you I'll never strike her no matter what."

"Okay, then. Let's go back to the business of how you're going to get Mama to marry you."

"Yes, ma'am." Mr. Sam smiled.

"Let's get serious. When you proposed to her, did you kneel on one knee?"

He shook his head. "I did not."

"One more question, Mr. Sam—maybe my new papa: Do you believe men should beat their wives?"

"No."

"Irregardless?"

"Regardless of everything. You already have my word on that one, Trude. We don't have to go over it again."

"I'm sorry. One more question. I know you want to help Mama and me and Billy Jack. What I've got my doubts about is if you'll protect her."

"Of course, I will."

"Please excuse me for being disrespectful. I want you to be my new papa, but before you take charge of me, I've got to clear up something." Trudy raised her voice. "I was so mad when you let that creep grab Mama in the calaboose."

"We all make mistakes," he said.

"Do you love my mama?"

"You know I do."

"Don't let anybody hurt her then. Keep her out of the calaboose. Keep her away from Jethro."

"You have my word. I promise to be more careful. I'll do my best to watch over her and the twins. You and Billy Jack will be as precious to me as my own. I want you to be my daughter and my son. I'll love you and protect all of us."

"In that case, we can move on. I'm a girl, and I know what you have to do. You offered her a diamond ring, I'm sure. Or maybe a ruby ring."

"No."

"Stay out here." She called, "Hey, Billy. Come here."

"What?"

"We've got a new case. We have to help Mr. Sam. He wants to marry Mama, but he didn't propose right."

"That's not a case." Billy shook his head as he walked toward her.

"Shut up. It most certainly is. We're investigating a crime."

Billy pondered the situation. "Oh, I know. Mama is being mean to Mr. Sam."

"I think that's it, but it's his fault," Trudy said.

"You're blaming him for what Mama is doing?"

"He broke the rules of engagement. No kneeling on one knee. No diamond ring. No mushy love."

Billy threw up his hands.

Mr. Sam mimicked him. "Women."

"Women," Billy echoed.

"To hear them tell it, men never do anything right." Mr. Sam laughed.

"Well, if you can't say your proposal right, you should write it down. That way you'll have evidence in case some of us Pinkertons accuse you of other crimes," Trudy said.

"Dear Zoe." Trudy started dictating.

"Wait a minute. Let me get a pencil and sheet of paper."

As soon as he returned, she resumed. "Dear Zoe, I owe you one diamond ring. Signed: Love, Mr. Sam."

He wrote it down and read it. "Dear Zoe, I owe you one diamond ring. Samuel."

"You left out the love."

He started erasing his name. "I'll fix it."

"No, no, no. That won't do. It looks like you just threw the love in. Rewrite it, please."

Buddy ran to get another sheet of paper. Samuel rewrote the letter. "I O U one diamond ring. Love, Samuel."

"What now?" Mr. Sam smiled. "If I hand this to her, I'll feel silly. I know. I could mail it."

Trudy placed her hands on her hips. "No, sir. That would take too long. Drop it into the dream bucket. We'll deliver it."

Bailey ran to get the bucket so Samuel could drop the note into it.

Trudy hesitated a second. "That ain't good enough. Write another note. Keep this one, but write another one. This time write some mushy stuff."

"It's worth a try." Mr. Sam went for more paper, returned, and sat to write.

The giggling children watched him.

He wadded the letter into a ball and threw it on the porch floor. He wrote and crumpled one attempt and another and another until he made a pile of paper balls

"You told us not to waste paper, Papa." Buddy couldn't stop giggling.

"I don't know what I'm supposed to say in this note."

"This is important," Trudy said. "Let's all write letters and put them in the bucket."

They did.

"Come on, Mr. Sam. You can do it."

He went inside and returned with his Bible. "Let me see. First Corinthians 13."He read then wrote, read again then wrote some more. Then he slipped the note into the bottom of the bucket.

Bailey presented a red ribbon from her hair bow collection. "We need a bow. Papa, help me please."

Mr. Sam adorned the bucket handle.

"What do you all think?" Bailey asked.

"Looks good." Trudy placed her hand on her chin to consider things. "This is an important job. We should dress up."

"The boys have to wear shoes," Bailey said.

"It's the middle of the week." Buddy stuck out his lip. "We ain't going to town, and we ain't headed for church."

"Wear shoes." Trudy spoke with force.

"It's summer." Buddy frowned.

"Come on, Sister. We've got to get some clothes out of the cabin. I'm not sure how we'll manage this."

"Come on, Buddy. Bath time." Mr. Sam said.

Trudy had to think of a way to make this part of the plan work. King would be guarding Mama. She'd have to think of something to say to explain why they were taking their dress clothes out of the cabin. Mama would know something was up. She'd have to think fast and tell Billy the plan. Or maybe he would have an idea.

"How're we going to get past Mama?" Billy asked.

"I don't know. You thought all this up anyway."

When Billy and Trudy appeared at the cabin, King didn't bark. "Mama must be outside somewhere," Trudy whispered. They were able to sneak inside and get their clothes.

"I bet she's in the garden," Trudy said. "She oughtn't go off and leave the place open."

"Shh," Billy said. 'We'll talk about it later."

Back at the Bentons' house, Buddy sat in the parlor. "I'm glad Mr. Sam has wet combed your hair." Trudy thought the boy looked good in his white shirt with Sunday trousers, shoes, and socks. Wearing her red dress with shoes and socks, Bailey entered the room and sat in a lady's pose.

"Billy, use Buddy's room," Mr. Sam said. "Trudy, get ready in Bailey's room."

Minutes later they appeared, and Mr. Sam checked them over. "You all look your best. I can't believe you're doing all this for me."

"For you and Mama," Trudy said. "Let's go."

"I was laying out my clothes and heating water so I can shave. It's going to take time. I haven't shaved since Saturday. Give me a few minutes before you leave." He went to the stove to get a kettle of hot water. Sitting in the parlor, they sang while they waited.

As soon as he finished shaving, the children headed over to the cabin. Along the way, they added a few flowers to the contents of the bucket. Buddy pulled one of his best arrowheads from his pocket to add to the arrangement. He found a smooth pink rock. A frog hopped from the side of the road. Buddy reached for it.

"No," Billy said.

Just before they arrived, King, evidently having taken a recent bath in the fishing hole, sprinted toward them. The dog jumped up on Buddy. Two big muddy paw prints decorated the boy's white shirt.

"Down, King."

When they reached the cabin, Mama sat shelling peas on the porch and stacking the hulls in a tub for the cows. They formed two lines with Billy and Trudy in the back. Bailey, holding the dream bucket, stood by Buddy.

Billy counted, "One two three."

"Let me call you sweetheart." They swayed with gestures.

Bailey, stepping forward, handed Miss Zoe the bucket, then returned to her place in the formation.

"What lovely flowers—violets, daisies, black-eyed Susans. Thank you. A neat rock. An arrowhead." Mama smiled.

"There's letters in the bucket too," Bailey said.

"Let's see." Mama pulled out the top paper. "Dear Miss Zoe, I dreamed I had a mommy and she looked just like you. Love, Bailey."

Trudy's eyes glistened. "Keep reading."

"U R the best in the world. I wish I had U 4 mine. (picture of heart) Buddy." Tears slid down Zoe's cheeks. "I'm sorry. Just can't help it."

"Next." Trudy motioned with her hand.

"Thank you for loving me, Trudy." Mama smiled at Trudy.

"Don't be mean to Mr. Sam. B. J." She looked at Billy.

"Was I mean to Samuel?" Mama asked.

Billy twisted his mouth into a grin and nodded.

She pulled out another one. "I O U one diamond ring. Love, Samuel." She spread the letter on top of the others. "How nice, but I don't know why he said that."

Buddy stood in front of the others. "Will you marry us?"

"There's one more letter." Trudy said.

Zoe dug a folded sheet of paper from the bottom of the bucket. "My darling Zoe, trying to say this to you, I get tangled up. So I'm writing you a letter."

She read softly. "Whether or not you love me—and I hope you do—I will never give up loving you. Helping you have whatever you need and providing for the children matters to me more than anything else in the world. Once again, I ask for your hand in marriage."

Her hand went to her throat. "I can't force you to love me. If you say no, I won't change. I'll just wait and hope. My love for you will never die. Your neighbor, Samuel."

Zoe ran inside. The children squeezed one another in a wait that seemed forever. She walked back onto the porch with a sheet of paper and a pencil.

As she wrote, she talked. "Dear Samuel, since you wrote me, I will respond in a letter." She flashed a smile. "YES. Love, Zoe." She dropped the letter into the bucket. The children started to leave. "Wait a minute. I'll go with you."

She rushed back into the cabin, and again they waited. Wearing a fresh dress with a floppy hat and her best shoes, she emerged, smelling sweet like rosewater, smiling, moving in a hurry.

"King, come with us." Billy called as he carried the bucket. They rushed to the Bentons' house.

~

Zoe spotted him. With open arms, Samuel, dressed in his best suit, stood in the road under the shade of a live oak. Prancing doves cooed with urgency on the telephone wires. She let go of the children and ran ahead. The guineas chattered at the excitement.

Grabbing her and lifting her off the ground, he smelled of spicy shaving lotion blended with his own uniqueness.

She held onto his firm body. Never before had she realized he had muscular shoulders. She stepped back. Standing there on her tiptoes, she looked at him as though she saw him for the first time. She noticed distinctive traits about him she had not given herself permission to observe. His way of grinning from the side of his mouth—had he always done that? A tiny dark mole near the end of his right eyebrow accentuated his eyes. Where had he hid that cowlick? He was wearing a starched and ironed white shirt with a tie in her honor. She allowed her hands to trail over his arms with a light touch, then tentatively studied his freshly shaven face, his earlobes, his hair.

He gave her a light kiss on her forehead.

She turned her face up to him to let him know she didn't care who saw.

He bent down to brush her lips.

The look they exchanged caused her to burn with loving feelings. The next kiss he gave her removed all her doubts. Finally she knew he really loved her as a man loved a woman.

Although it was the middle of the day, the rooster crowed. King wagged his tail as he barked his approval. The Bentons' bird dogs sidled up to her and whimpered.

Zoe stood holding Samuel's hands. He gazed at her with twinkling eyes.

"Mmm." She hummed with delight.

He winked at her and she blushed. "I can't believe this is happening," Samuel said. Again he took her into his arms. As he stood near her, he was all he had ever been—the good friend, the widower with needs, the helpful neighbor. Yet he was more—the man she loved. Her heart overflowed with new passion, too long repressed. She had not forgotten the old yearning for William—oh no, not at all. For Samuel she knew a fresh love, the love of a new moment that would last a lifetime. It felt right. Excitement ran wild within her, and she shivered.

"Zoe, my love," he whispered.

With all the emotion and commitment she had to give him that day, she loved Samuel as a man, hers. And she was his. She knew he felt the same with every tender touch of his hands on her face, every kiss they shared, every loving squeeze. His children were her children, and she knew hers would become his. Together they would grow into a unified family.

"Come here," he said. He pulled all of them into a circle.

~

289

The news spread throughout the Taylorsburg community like fire in a hayfield.

Jethro's mother visited the calaboose. "I thought you could get out of here on bail."

"No. Marshal Canterbury knows my intentions."

"What are you talking about?"

"I'm going to kill Elvin Trutledge. While he was in jail here with me, he tried to hurt Zoe. I'll murder him."

"Son, you talk crazy."

"I'm going to protect Zoe from Samuel and his bunch. I won't let them take advantage of her. I'm going to slaughter all three of the Bentons. Then she'll see the truth. She'll be my woman."

~Chapter Thirty-Eight~

Darkness fell before Sam noticed. Another day of helping his beloved and preparing for their marriage had soared by. It was time for him and the twins to exercise their bedtime ritual. He usually read to them a chapter of a children's classic. The current book was *Black Beauty: The Autobiography of a Horse*.

A chapter from the Bible followed. They were going through the book of Nehemiah. After prayers, he hugged each child, and they rushed off to bed. He cherished everything about them—the way they snuggled beside him while he read, the way they corrected him if he tried to skip a paragraph or verse, and the way they scampered around to do whatever he required of them.

As was his habit, Sam read a few more minutes. This evening it was the Brownings: "Grow old with me . . ."

As he had done since Sarah died, he journaled his thoughts. He wrote:

I haven't been happier in years. It's strange that I could have been so happy when my heart was torn with grief over the death of William Cameron. First, I felt guilty.

Every priceless moment of watching all four children grow, falling in love with Zoe and realizing how blessed I am to know she loves me, seeing her trust the Lord to help her overcome her adversity—it's all been a summer I hope I never forget. All six of us have grown.

Some moments have horrified me, the time Zoe and I shot the bear, the morning I realized Billy's shoes were too tight, the emotional struggles Trudy suffers as she comes of age and works through her grief.

What hurt the worst? It's difficult to say. I thought my heart would turn to stone when the dream bucket disappeared, but that was only a material loss. I shiver when I recall the day we almost lost Bailey. That was it. Nothing was more painful.

Zoe Cameron, soon to be Benton, is the strongest woman I have ever known. At the same time she is the most fragile. Fifty years from now, I suppose I will love her more, but I cannot imagine how I could. She fills my heart.

And I have one more blessing. Unbelievable. I'll have the privilege of helping Zoe take care of William's baby. I'm hoping for a boy. He'll be my son as if I had been his biological father. Or maybe we'll have a darling little girl.

I will never stop missing Sarah and William. I hope I would not have fallen in love with Zoe if William had lived. The prospect gives me a chill.

Little Buddy's impulsivity will be a challenge for me. Maybe he'll grow out of it. I must confess he inherited it from me.

I hope I've recorded all that happened correctly. Sometimes I've had to guess what people thought. I'll need to interview all of the ones who are available to clarify some issues. This journal has gaps in the narrative. Some of the story as I have seen it is too tender to ask sensitive souls. I've tried to imagine what was going on. Some people, such as Jacob MacGregor, have already supplied helpful information. My sweet Zoe has been sharing her thoughts. I now understand many of her character traits that had been problematic for me.

He turned down the wick of the coal oil lamp and went to check the children. First, he went to Buddy's room. The boy lay quietly with a peaceful look on his face.

Next, he went to Bailey's room. As soon as he finished, he would go out on the porch and call the dogs with his supersonic whistle. He'd reward each with a piece of rawhide. Then he'd go to bed.

The moonlight poured into the window as he looked at Bailey's bed. Empty. Back to the window: it was open.

Sam heard squirming in the corner. As his eyes adjusted, he realized she stood gagged and restrained. A man dressed in black held onto her. He had tied a black bandana over his mouth. "Okay, Benton. I gave you an opportunity. I explained to you that you would have to keep your hands off Zoe Cameron."

Sam inched closer. "Did I tell you to move toward me? Step back, Sam. Everything is going my way tonight. The dogs didn't bark when I came up. That's because I feed them every night when I pass through here to look in Zoe's window."

Sam backed away into a dark shadow and blew his supersonic whistle. Zeke and Spot came to him with whimpers. When he blew again, they bounded through the window. The man wearing the bandana let go of Bailey so he could protect his face from the attacking beasts. Zeke went for his throat; Spot grabbed his right arm.

Sam pulled his little girl into his arms and untied her. "Get another rope." He wasn't sure the rope Jethro had used would be long enough.

"Yes, Papa." She ran to find a rope in the kitchen pantry. As soon as she delivered it, she went to wake up Buddy.

"A monster broke into my room and tried to hurt me."

"Huh?"

"Come on. Papa and the dogs are getting the bad man." The twins trotted by to look through Bailey's doorway and back to the living room.

Bailey ran to the telephone. "Central, get Marshal Canterbury. Emergency."

She waited a few minutes. "Mr. Canterbury, this is Bailey Benton. Samuel Benton, my papa, is tying up a man that broke into my room. He tried to hurt me. Come quick."

~Chapter Thirty-Nine~

Jethro told his story to some of the others at Parchman so they'd know he was too tough to mess with:

"Do you actually expect me to answer that question, Your Honor?" I says to the judge. There I stand in the front of the dingy courtroom. Mama's worried because I'm thin. I look sunk-eyed. Folks stare at my clothes. I wear a white and smoky gray striped suit. Ugly. I ain't a prisoner yet. I've got my rights. All of them says I'm crazy, but I ain't. I make perfect sense.

"Go ahead," the judge says.

I take a deep breath as I commence pacing from one side of the silly room to the other. I pull a ball and chain. It don't slow me down none, but the noise is driving the jury crazy. "Judge Franks, why should I have to starve to death? Why should I work all the time and not have a decent place to live? Why can't I go where I want to? Why should I scrape for pennies? Why should I wear rags when other people has fine clothes? Ain't this America?"

The judge looks over his spectacles at me. I don't know why he calls himself having a gentle nature. Truth is he sends some fool to the slammer almost every time one of us comes before him, no matter what. He wants me to say something that will make the jury think I'm a beast. I'm trying to explain to him and them why it is necessary to kill three—no, four people. They stare at me like I'm some kind of a freak. If only they could see things my way.

"I'm as good a man as Jacob MacGregor. I've got just as much right to that mercantile store as he does."

At least I'll say this for the judge. He listens to me. I wish I could explain it better so he'd understand.

The judge asks, "Even though he inherited it from his uncle?"

"Circumstances like that don't have nothing to do with folks deserving things." Now I wave my hands to make my point. "The store should have gone to a man like me. The government should change these things. I'm too smart to spend my life pushing a broom."

"Jacob MacGregor is a good man, and he has a college degree."

"That don't make him no better than me." I am shouting. "When did I ever get a chance to go to college?" I look at the judge with a stare that ought to have scared the tarnation out of him.

"Continue," he says.

"Talking now about the cotton gin south of town. Why don't the government take it away from old man Grainger and give it to me? I could do a better job."

The judge makes me madder than a fighting jaybird. He's baiting me and don't think I've got sense to know what he's doing. He says, "You think you are entitled?"

My eyes cut him like Arkansas toothpicks. "I'm entitled to a good life. Men work their whole lives in cotton fields like slaves. Or coal mines. Or out on the range. What do they get? Nothing. I'm entitled to happiness and property. Ain't that what the Constitution says?"

Then he gets down to the meat of the matter. He asks me, "Do you think you have the right to take another person's life?"

"Certainly. Some have to die to protect the others." Those twelve old men sitting in the jury box stop paying attention to me. They get noisy.

"There are three people I'm looking after." Can't them idiots see I'm honest? "No one else counts. Let me loose, and I'll get rid of some of that trash what don't got no reason to live. I've got a kill list." The judge perched up there in that black house frock, he beat hard with that wood hammer. He looks like a simpleton. I keep on till all of them get riled up.

I walked many a night right by my darling's window. She sat on an old bucket and laid her head in the windowsill. I could have reached out and touched her. She was meant to be mine. I could have taken her. She is the most beautiful woman in the world. Other nights I'd go up to the window and look at them sleeping. They never saw me. Her dog don't bark at me.

"You won't believe this, but it's the honest truth. One night I was roaming around the barnyard looking for something I knew had to be there. I walked over toward the wagon. It was a moonlit night."

The judge took off his glasses and wiped his face with his handkerchief. "What were you looking for?"

"I'll get to that a little later on," I says.

"A man at least fifteen foot tall and dressed in sparkly white stood in front of me. Lightning sparks was shooting out of him. He had a round gold shield and the biggest sharpest sword I've ever seen. It was filed down on both sides. In a deep voice that sounded like he was talking through the creek, he said, 'Stay away from here.' I cleared out of there. I ran so fast I outran my shirt."

Nobody in the courtroom said nothing. They just looked at me.

"See, Your Honor? Don't you understand the injustice? Elvin Trutledge tried to choke Zoe to death. Samuel Benton flashed a knife in her face. All I could do was stand by and shout. I have every right to defend the ones I care about. Add to my need-to-be-killed list Elvin Trutledge. Too bad, Your Honor, I didn't always have a gun when I needed one."

"Back to what I was looking for, I seen Mr. William go into his crib and stay for a long time. He claimed he wasn't doing nothing, but I figured he was doing something. I needed the key to the crib. It ain't normal to lock a barnyard crib. After he died, I wanted to find what was in there."

It was time to bring this here to a halt.

"See it, Judge. Feel it. Hot bullets coming out of my gun. Hot blood gushing all over the ground." A hush falls over the room again.

The Judge he says, "Mr. McKenzie, tell us how you got out of the Taylorsburg jail."

"So, Your Honor, you want to know how I broke out. It was simple. That old tin calaboose is a joke. I just made a running start."

"A running start?" Judge Franks said.

I laughed but nary a person in that courthouse caught the joke. "I waited until it got dark and old man Canterbury left. He don't half do his job. Taylorsburg goes to sleep when the sun goes down, just like here in Ridley. They fold up the boardwalks. I just got in the front corner of my cell and ran to the backside near the corner where there weren't no studs. I worked myself up. After a manner of speaking, I pitched a wall-eyed fit. It took me seven times, and it left me sore. You see, I cut myself on the tin. Except for a few cuts, it was easy to pop open the wall.

"Judge, I heard them cotton rows up at Parchman farm is so long you can't see the end of them. Go ahead, Man. Send me up there. I've got the power. I'll break out in a few days, and when I do, there's going to be one more name on my kill list: yours. Judge Franks, I'll kill you."

The jury took seven minutes to reach a verdict on me. Three hours after I left the courtroom, two armed guards rode with me in a passenger car of a northbound train up here to Mississippi State Penitentiary. All my way up here I said whatever I felt like saying and let out what was in me.

~Chapter Forty~

Odors no longer made Zoe ill, but she had a heightened sense of smell. MacGregor's Mercantile with its air full of cinnamon, leather, coffee, and vanilla welcomed the Bentons and Camerons, who went on a shopping spree.

Geneva Bently took Zoe's arm. "Let me show you some of the new styles." They sat on a bench and shared a fashion magazine.

"I like that one."

"You'd look gorgeous in it. I'm sure you could take this picture and copy the dress." They studied it and some of the others, but they returned to Zoe's first choice. It was in two parts. The underneath dress was a semi-fitted white garment with a short train flowing behind.

"I'd make that dress cream colored," Zoe said.

Geneva laid a bolt of lightweight cream-colored satin onto the cutting table. "We also have this matching lace."

"Lovely."

"Notice there's a panel down the front of lace or designed fabric in the picture," Geneva said. "It's difficult to tell."

Trudy and Bailey stood by and smiled.

Samuel drifted over toward the ladies.

"Go away. It's a surprise." Zoe's eyes twinkled. "Take the girls with you."

"Oh, excuse me." Samuel broke into his boyish grin.

Geneva continued. "That square neckline would be flattering to you." The picture shows a full-length black coat in a slender line. The necklines match, and the coat has a band across the bust. It opens from top to bottom to reveal the panel.

"What could we use instead of black?"

"I think maybe a light color. Let's see what we have." Geneva pulled out a role of sheer fabric with abstract designs similar to the picture except it was two shades darker than the cream-colored fabric for the dress. "You could use either this or the lace for the front panel. Or you could make the coat out of satin covered with lace."

"This fabric would be perfect. Covering it all with lace would take a long time and add another layer of fabric. I'm hot natured these days."

"Sure."

"Geneva, I need to confide in you. Don't tell a soul. My kids don't know, and I want to be the first to tell them. I'll need the coat to cover my middle. I'm carrying William's baby."

Geneva Bently hugged Zoe.

"I know I have no right to have this wedding, especially in public."

"You look fine, Zoe."

"People will talk, but I don't care much."

"We'll have to find a hat."

"I thought I'd pin my hair up in the front and let it trail down in the back. I could design something from a piece of lace to match the panel."

"Sounds lovely. Caroline MacGregor would be a good person to help you with it."

"She could help me with my dress too. I'm sure she'd be glad to. Here he comes again." She stood and spread her hands to cover the cloth. "He's teasing me. Don't look, Samuel."

"Yes, ma'am." Samuel turned and fled.

~

The families returned to the shack.

"Zoe, you will not do any chores or pick any vegetables until you finish sewing that dress."

"Sounds like a holiday." Zoe laughed. "What about the corn?"

"I've already hired some help to harvest it."

"You make it all sound easy. What about the hay?"

"I'm having it cut on shares."

"The garden?"

"We'll manage it. Don't try to sneak to the barn and milk a cow or two. Just sew. I'll arrange for some helpers to take care of the chores."

"After the honeymoon, we'll rework our farms, I promise. I think we have everything out of that crib, but we'll tear down the barn one board at a time."

"The children and I will remove all the inside walls of the crib this week. In the meantime, Mrs. Cameron, may I fill my barn with some of your harvest?"

"Whatever you need to do will be fine."

He planted a smacky kiss on her lips, so loud the children heard it and snickered.

~

Two weeks later, five of them—all but Zoe—rode to the church together. Samuel sported a wide-brimmed black hat and a gray frock coat with gray pinstriped trousers. His flashy attire included a vest and a bow tie. The boys squirmed in their new matching gray suits.

After Zoe dressed at the MacGregors' house, she rode to church with Jake and Caroline. The little church, lighted with candles and decorated with ferns and satin bows, bulged with neighbors and friends. Caroline played "The Prince of Denmark's March" by Jeremiah Clarke on the manually pumped organ.

Reverend Black, Samuel, and his best man Jake waited for Zoe. Buddy brought the rings held in place with a stitch on a cream-colored satin pillow. Bailey carried the dream bucket decorated with ribbons. It was full of rose petals, which she scattered along the aisle. After Bailey took her position in the front of the church, Trudy, carrying a nosegay of mixed roses, walked from the back to join the wedding party. Both Bailey and Trudy had insisted on wearing their red dresses. Both had curls cascading from little lace headpieces tied on with ribbons. Trudy's hair, despite her efforts to wear bonnets and hats, lightened during the summer to a strawberry shade.

The friends, neighbors, and relatives stood when Zoe entered on Billy's arm. Except for Uncle Stuart and Aunt Melva, no one frowned. Senator Chad Clemons and his wife Loretta, who had traveled from Jackson, sat on a pew a few rows behind his daughter Caroline.

Zoe's wedding gown looked exactly as she and Geneva Bently had planned. A lace hat created by Caroline crowned her head. In her ungloved hands, she carried a bouquet of six roses of various colors and one unopened bud. On her left ring finger was a diamond and ruby engagement ring.

"Who gives this woman to be married to this man?" Reverend Black stood before the congregation.

Billy, Trudy, Bailey, and Buddy spoke in unison: "We do."

The reception was at the Benton home. Before Zoe and Samuel cut the cake, he raised a glass of punch. "If I could speak with one thousand tongues, I still could not begin to thank the Lord enough for allowing me to love you."

Zoe blushed as she raised her glass. "I love you too, Samuel." She lowered her voice. "I didn't know how much."

"Zoe, did I ever tell you how beautiful you are?"

The guests ate cake and drank punch.

~

Zoe unpinned her hair as she sat before the mirror at the dressing table. Samuel came and stood behind her. When she stood to face him, his fingertips trailed along her hands. With light caresses, he stroked her arms up to the soft flesh of her inner elbows. She sighed. Samuel took her wrists gently and pulled her into an urgent but lasting kiss. He held her in a close dance. "Never let me go, Samuel Benton."

~

The next day all the members of the new family dressed in their travel clothes. They stacked their suitcases on the porch. Zoe, Trudy, and Bailey had matching parasols and reticules. Samuel, Billy, and Buddy wore matching hats. Around their necks, they strapped binoculars.

"Don't worry about a thing. I've made sure it's all taken care of. We'd better hurry to catch the train," Samuel said.

"The milking. King. The feeding. The horses. The mules." Zoe went on.

"Everything."

"Spot and Zeke. The guineas. The chickens."

"All of it. Are you sure you're up to this trip?"

She laughed. "After all the rough wagon rides I've had this summer, riding in the train shouldn't be a problem. I don't even have to push the wagon out of the shed and help hitch up the mules on this trip. Come on. We're going. Besides, I don't care what anybody thinks about a woman in a delicate condition taking public transportation."

Mr. Jake loaded their six suitcases into his Model T to take to the depot. The family piled into Samuel's Model T. Mr. Jake would keep it for them behind the Mercantile.

"We're going to Niagara Falls for our honeymoon," Bailey said.

~Epilogue~

Jacob Cameron Benton, a handsome full-term boy with a lusty cry, found his way without difficulty to his earthly home.

The Covington Chronicles

Even though some of the same characters and places appear in the four books, the novels in this series are independent stories. Jacob MacGregor, the owner of MacGregor Mercantile, moves from center stage in the first book to a supporting role.

Book One
Secret Promise
A Village Love Story

Caroline has her dream fulfilled. In Taylorsburg, Mississippi, in 1907, there is a new school where she teaches lower elementary classes. As a young woman with a servant's heart, she seeks nothing for herself. She suffers a wound that refuses to heal. Believing that the damage she has endured from abuse has rendered her unlovable, she knows she will never marry or allow any man to fall in love with her.

Meanwhile, Jake MacGregor moves to Taylorsburg to take over his uncle's store. He is a desirable bachelor, the type many local young women have dreamed of. His brain tells him he needs the business of socially prominent women for his store to survive. His heart tells him that the lovely Caroline, who seems to be an outcast, is the most interesting woman he has ever met.

Social issues of racial discord, abuse, inadequate education, and prohibition dominate the scene of Mississippi in the early 1900's. In this setting, will Caroline have enough courage to embrace life? Will Jake overcome his anger at God for taking his parents and uncle from him in a tornado? How will he deal with having his plans dashed?

Come share the oppression of African Americans in impoverished Mississippi as a new century comes with hope to leave the bitter years of Reconstruction behind. Feel the pain of abuse and discrimination. Shop at the Mercantile and share supper at the Covington Hotel dining room.

Book Two

The Courtship

Of Miss Loretta Larson

Will a Woman in Her Thirties

Discover True Love?

The year is 1908. Loretta Larson has many blessings in her life. She is attractive and accomplished. She has so much money that her salary from teaching is not enough for her to notice. In her thirties she is living in the village of Taylorsburg, a south Mississippi railroad town. What she does not have is a man who loves her. She suffers in a damaging relationship with a cruel and dishonest banker. Will she ever find love?

An unusual woman for her time, she is an independent, strong-minded person, who has a cloud over her past, a quirky style in the present, and boundless hope for a joyful future.

She is the kind of woman who has compassion for the down and out with little regard for what others think of her. To live her life requires courage and ingenuity. She relies on the Lord to help her through her problems. Sometimes the help comes in unusual ways. For example, her cat Pinkie saves her from disaster.

The story contains fun-filled pranks, the joy of being alive, and outrage over social injustice. Come spend more time with Caroline, Jacob, and Chad. Return to the Covington Hotel and the Mercantile. Although *The Courtship of Miss Loretta Larson* is the second in the series, it is enjoyable reading and stands independent of *Secret Promise*.

Book Three
The Dream Bucket
A Young Girl Coming of Age
Her Mother Facing
Unspeakable Challenges

The year is 1909. A wife has no right to know specific details about her husband's finances. The man handles the money, but what is a woman to do if she loses him?

It is springtime in the Mississippi hill country. Ten-year-old Trudy Cameron, who adores her father William, hears him slap her mother for asking where he keeps his money. Two days later he dies in a fire that destroys their antebellum mansion. Her goal becomes taking care of Zoe, her mother while Zoe's goal is to take care of Billy, the twelve-year-old son, and Trudy. Destitute, the three family members move into a rat-infested, leaky shack.

Terror fills their lives. Zoe, a mixture of savage strength and feminine weakness, shoots a black bear and faints afterwards. Willing to risk her life, she defends her children with a long-bladed knife. When existence becomes as complicated as she can imagine, new problems arise.

Down the road Samuel Benton, a widower who was like a brother to William, cares for his six-year-old twins. While Samuel tries to help Zoe with her problems, he and his children face hardships that challenge them to maintain the wellbeing of their own family.

That summer is a time for learning to cope with grief—to grow in the realization of God's love. *The Dream Bucket* is third in the Covington Chronicles.

After sharing in the lives of Jake and Caroline, come spend some more time at MacGregor's Mercantile and the Covington Hotel. Even though *The Dream Bucket* is third in the series, it is an independent story.

The Dream Bucket placed second in the Texas Christian Writers Conference hosted by Inspirational Writers Alive in the book proposal category.

Book Four
Manuela Blayne
One Suffering for Another

A new day dawns for Trudy . . .

In the summer of 1910, Trudy Cameron witnesses the aftershock of an event that will disturb her the rest of her life

It is more than the consequences of the crime that concern her. Cruelty dominates the evolving social system of the South, the only home she knows.

Never will she comprehend all the hurt suffered by her friend Manuela Blayne, but Trudy wants to understand.

She witnesses firsthand what forgiveness can be. She observes hardships she has never imagined.

In a world that denies mercy to her friend, Will Trudy's faith shrink or blossom? She is always honest with herself about her emotions.

On a happier note, Trudy wonders whether she is too young to fall in love. Trudy tells her story in first person.

Come spend some time with the Bentons and Camerons. Delight in the parenting skills of Samuel Benton, as he tries to distract Trudy from her anguish over Manuela Blayne.

Have a dish of ice cream in the Covington and float on a watermelon in the swim hole at Hot Coffee. Witness the mischief Trudy dares not tell.

Acknowledgements

In the early 1900's farmers possessed the treasures that mattered most—a sense of humor, love for one another, respect for the land, and reliance on the Lord to see them through any situation. I'd like to acknowledge the sturdy kind of people our ancestors were as we look back at their lives and the way they dealt with whatever joys or adversities came their way.

I hope that readers grasp the joy of the characters in *The Dream Bucket*. As always, it is a great honor to have each of you read something I've written.

The ideas for this book began before I wrote the two that preceded it in the series. In fact the book started forming in my mind when I was a teenager. The list of all who helped me with it would be as long as the book, and then I'd have the nagging fear that I'd forgotten several people.

Professional writing groups with members who have critiqued it include Panhandle Professional Writers of Amarillo, Inspirational Writers Alive of Texas (both the local Amarillo group and the statewide organization), and American Christian Fiction Writers (the local Shreveport chapter and the critique loop). Several writers have encouraged me.

Thanks to Greg Austin, who has been a writing mentor; Kathy McKinsey, who proofread it; and Rosie Buhrer, who helped publish the book in Kindle format.

We always judge a book by its cover, don't we? The unique and haunting cover of *The Dream Bucket* was designed by John Cooke. In all ways John has supported this project.

When I began writing *The Dream Bucket*, Ruth Ishee, my sister, listened to the entire book over the phone. Even though the book is not biographical, she knew intuitively what was supposed to happen next and interrupted my reading when I omitted something that needed to be included in the story. The book is dedicated to her.

My nephew Jameson Gregg, who has been selected as Georgia Author of the Year for his comic and satirical novel, *Luck Be a Chicken,* has been both a constant source of inspiration and advice.

Christie Underwood, my daughter, who is all the daughter a mother could ever hope for, has listened to me talk about this project every step of the way. She never hesitates to tell me what she thinks, and she's always right.

I'm grateful to Amazon.com for making the Kindle experience a reality to Kindle Scout for featuring *The Dream Bucket* in a thirty-day campaign. During those thirty days, you, my friends, kept it in the "hot and trending" list on the Kindle Scout website. The outpouring of enthusiasm from Facebook friends amazed me.

Clay Lomakayu narrated *The Dream Bucket,* and it is available on Amazon.com, Audible.com, and I-Tunes. His deep, expressive voice lifts *The Dream Bucket* off the page. Thanks to Clay for the incredible performance.

Jessie Boyett, owner and manager of the Bernice Banner, Bernice, LA, deserves my appreciation for nudging me to print this book.

To all who read The Dream Bucket—

Fill and empty and refill your own bucket of dreams. Always dream big.

Mary Lou Cheatham

About the Author

Mary Lou Cheatham began her life on a Mississippi farm north of Hot Coffee. Her family spent their winter evenings playing games, reading, and conversing by the fireplace. Mary's parents, two of the world's greatest storytellers, bequeathed a legacy of yarn spinning to their children and grandchildren.

She lives in Shreveport, Louisiana, and is the mother of one daughter, who lives in Texas. She has had careers as a teacher and registered nurse. Mary enjoys writing inspirational historical novels and story cookbooks.

A member of Panhandle Professional Writers, Grave Expectations, and American Christian Fiction Writers, she has served as a judge in the ACFW Carol Awards Contest. Three of her novels—*The Courtship of Miss Loretta Larson*, *The Dream Bucket*, and *Abi of Cyrene*—have won awards.

Photo by April Hendrick

53723828R00190

Made in the USA
Lexington, KY
16 July 2016